The Lost Ranger
An Alex Rogers Adventure
Book 1

By CW Lamb

I would like to dedicate this book to the AL:ICE readers that supported and defended my style of storytelling.

Edited By: Patrick LoBrutto

Cover Design: www.art4artists.com.au

Copyright © 2016 by CW Lamb   www.cw-lamb.com

All rights reserved. No part of this publication may be reproduced, distributed, or transmitted in any form or by any means, including photocopying, recording, or other electronic or mechanical methods, without the prior written permission of the Author, except in the case of brief quotations embodied in critical reviews and certain other noncommercial uses permitted by copyright law.

First Edition

14 13 12 11 10 9 8 7 6 5 4

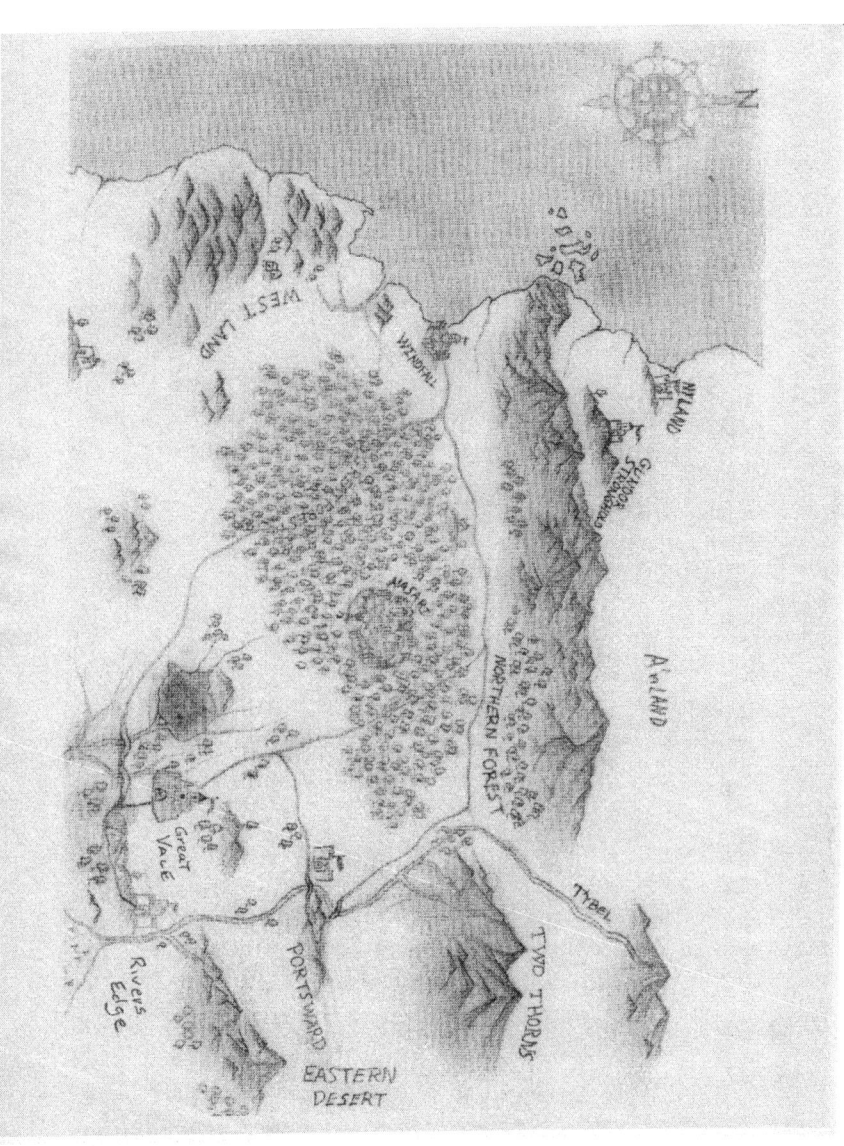

Chapter 1

The increasing vibrations of something pounding the ground woke Alex from a dead sleep. His head hurt and his body ached as if he had been sleeping on rocks. As the pounding increased, he opened his eyes and found he was lying on the ground, just inside a line of trees. Beyond the trees, he could see a dirt road and several horses as they went past at a full gallop.

Sitting up, he looked around with a feeling of total disorientation. He had been sleeping on a rough hewn, multicolor blanket. For a cover, he was under a brown cloak that had a fur inner liner. On one side of this bedroll was a fire pit, between him and the road, with ashes still smoldering. On his other side was a large black horse generally ignoring his presence.

Looking around, he saw a number of items nearby. A dark, silver trimmed saddle, with large leather pouches that resembled saddlebags, sat between him and the horse. There was a bow with a full quiver, and a hand-and-a-half sword in its sheath on the other side near the fire.

All this gear lay nearby, supposedly his, though none was familiar to him. Even the saddle and bags looked nothing like the western gear he was comfortable with, but all were similar enough to be recognizable.

Looking around further, he realized his dog, Kinsey, was nowhere to be found. As he was preparing to shout for her, Alex heard a woman scream a short distance away. Without thinking, he pushed off the cloak and grabbed the sheathed sword. In a practiced move, he slung its long belt over one shoulder so it rode diagonally across his back. He then reached for the bow and quiver, and dashed in the direction the horses had just gone, toward the scream.

Slipping in between the trees, he turned down the dirt road at a dead run. Heavy forest on both sides of the road blocked most sounds but those ahead of him. In a few moments, he could hear the clang of metal on metal and men shouting. He rounded a bend in the road just in time to see several men fighting. With swords flying, it looked like a scene from a Robin Hood movie. Everyone was in tunics and chain mail, long swords flailing. They were apparently from two different groups as some tunics were in red with gold trim while others were mostly blue.

To the right side of the road was an ornate enclosed coach, its horse team cut loose and nowhere in sight. Alex could see where the harnesses had been cut free, the coach stranded along the side of the road. Standing next to the coach was a young woman in an exquisite, full-length dress, her long brown hair nearly to her waist.

From the look on her face, she was very distressed and most likely the screamer that Alex heard earlier. Between her and the fighting was another woman, in full body armor, polished and shiny, with her red hair pulled back away from her face. Her sword was drawn, and she was holding it out in front of her in a defensive stance. She had her other arm out as if to shield the first woman from harm.

All around the fighting were the bodies of men from both sides, laying on the ground, either already dead or dying. There was blood everywhere; causing those still battling to slip in the mud it created. The men fought with care or risked slipping …and a fall could prove fatal.

"Where the hell am I? And where's Kinsey?" Alex asked himself, shaking his head at the scene before him.

"Yesterday we were hiking in Washington State…this isn't the Cascade Mountains."

Alex shook his head, he couldn't try to figure that out now. His attention was drawn back as the four men in the same medieval type red uniform skewered the remaining two blue soldiers, taking advantage of the unequal numbers. From their actions and location, Alex assumed the blue had been defending the women by the coach. From the reaction of the two women, the anguish clear on their faces, he assumed they knew the dying men.

On the far side of all the fighting sat three men on horseback, watching. Two looked like dandies, the men dressed in fanciful attire, also trimmed in red. They did not appear to be wearing chainmail and their clothing was not suited for battle. The third man was dressed like the men in red on the ground. He held a crossbow across his lap, pointed at no one in general.

Alex was sure he must be delusional at this point. He figured he was really laying at the bottom of a hole somewhere in the Washington forest. He was sure if it. This all looked like something out of one of the fantasy novels he liked to read, although the blood and gore was far too realistic for his tastes.

The four soldiers started to approach the women, swords menacing. Without thinking about it, Alex shouted, "Hey, back off!"

With that shout, all eyes turned to Alex. One of the men on horseback shouted something Alex didn't understand, but his gestures clearly indicated he wanted Alex to butt out.

Alex wasn't sure what to do next as this whole situation seemed completely unreal to him. Everyone seemed to pause for a moment, and then the same dandy on horseback issued another command, this time to the rider with the crossbow.

In one swift move, the rider lifted the crossbow and fired it at Alex. Without mentally acknowledging it, Alex had nocked an arrow in his bow earlier, while watching the fighting. Smoothly sidestepping the crossbow bolt, he raised the bow and let fly in return. In a flash, the arrow hit the rider in the left eye, the shaft appearing at the back of his head as he fell from the horse.

With that, the dandy shouted again, and the four swordsmen in red turned to Alex. He quickly released two more shafts in rapid succession, dropping two men, as the others closed on him. He then dropped the bow in his left hand and with his right hand drew the sword from its sheath across his back. Then in his left, he drew a fighting dagger from his belt he hadn't even realized he carried.

Alex was moving like a man possessed; he had no idea at all what he was doing. It could be called muscle memory, except he had never practiced the moves he was now performing with proficient skill. He knew, from his reading, that he was using what was called the Florentine Technique for sword fighting. The disconcerting thing was he had never, in his life, done it.

He slipped to one side, engaging the closer swordsman, deflecting his attack with the sword while slashing at him with the dagger. As the man retreated, Alex continued the spin, catching the second attacker off guard and driving the dagger into his exposed shoulder.

Alex withdrew just in time to avoid the renewed attack from the first man, parrying the swing with his own sword and then driving the dagger into the man's exposed middle. It was then that Alex noticed both men had chainmail under their tunics, but the dagger was slicing through it as if it were mere cloth.

Pushing off to break away from the man as he was falling, Alex caught a glimpse of the wounded swordsman driving toward him with raised sword, too close for Alex to block in time.

Suddenly, a black mass of fur and teeth leaped passed Alex, grabbing on to the swordsman's arm and wrenching him to the ground. A second snap at his throat had blood spouting everywhere. As Alex recovered, he braced and backed away to address the large black wolf that turned to face him.

As its face looked up to meet his, its tail started wagging. Looking into its eyes, Alex couldn't believe what he saw.

"Kinsey?"

Kinsey came up to Alex, tail flying in both directions and licking the offered hand.

As Alex was patting her head, the redheaded woman in armor shouted something at him, and pointed up the trail. At the same moment, the other woman darted forward, checking the fallen in blue. Alex turned to see the two dandies riding away at a hurried pace. The redhead shouted again, pointing at Alex's bow, and then the riders, while stepping forward to cover the other woman with her sword.

"What?" Alex asked, shrugging his shoulders at her.

She again pointed at the riders more insistently, repeating whatever she had said before.

Not waiting to interpret further, he dropped the sword and then picked up his bow. As he stepped forward, he pulled an arrow out of one of the fallen men in red and drew back on the bow. Again, with a skill he didn't understand, he waited and then let the shaft fly. All three watched as the shaft and rider converged, the arrow striking the rider in the right shoulder. It was a solid hit, but without enough force to displace the rider from his saddle. It had hit the man who had been shouting orders earlier.

Turning to the women, he watched as the one in armor started to raise her sword, apparently to confront him. Before she could advance, the other snapped at her, pointing to Alex and then all the dead.

With that, she lowered the blade, but did not sheath it.

At this point Alex was completely confused and wanted to puke. He had just killed five men and his fifty-pound dog had become a two hundred pound wolf. Everyone was speaking a language he didn't understand and so far none had understood a word he said in reply.

Returning to pick up his sword, he re-sheathed it. While he stood petting Kinsey, he watched as the woman in the dress checked the rest of the fallen blue soldiers, sadly shaking her head. Alex interpreted that to mean all had perished. After checking the fallen, she walked over to the redhead and said something that seemed to set off an argument. The one in the dress kept pointing up the road, in the direction that the two dandies had ran off. The one in armor kept pointing back at the men on the ground.

Finally, the one in armor went over to the bodies in the red uniform that had attacked Alex, cutting the small leather pouches off their belts. After she had all eight of the swordsman and the crossbowman's, she went over to the other woman and started emptying each of them, one by one.

With each one she emptied, Alex could see a mixture of what appeared to be gold, silver and copper or bronze coins. She would point to the gold coins and then say something to the woman in the dress. The best Alex could interpret from her actions was as if she was saying, "See!" with every gold coin.

It appeared each man possessed two shiny new gold coins, the balance being a mixture of several dull silver and bronze coins. There were never more than two golds, except for the crossbowman, who had three.

It seemed clear to Alex that someone had paid off the men to attack these women. The woman in the dress nodded and pointed back down the road in the direction Alex had come. Again, the redhead shook her head no, while pointing to the fallen in red.

Finally, the one in the dress pointed into the woods to Alex's right. The two talked further until the one in armor seemed to agree, reluctantly. She then she scooped all the coins into one bag, handing them to the woman in the dress.

During this entire exchange, Alex had been scratching Kinsey between the ears and wondering when he was going to wake from whatever coma he must be in. He laughed to himself, as at least his delusions included pretty women.

While the woman in armor kept a wary eye, the one in the dress approached Alex. Extending the bag with all the coins, she spoke while looking at Kinsey nervously. Alex couldn't understand a word; he had heard French, Spanish, German, Italian and several Eastern European languages and none sounded like this.

"Look, I have no idea what you are saying," Alex replied while accepting the bag.

She looked to be in her mid-twenties, the other in armor appearing to be about the same age. However, while this one was no more than 5' 5", the one in armor had to be 5' 10" at a minimum. Both women just stared at him for a moment, and then the one in the dress said, "Abrianna," pointing at herself. She then said, "Cassie," pointing at the redhead.

"Cassandra!" said the other in sharp reply.

"Alex," he replied, getting the gist of the exchange, and then said, "Kinsey," pointing to the wolf.

Abrianna looked nervously at Kinsey for a minute and then repeated, "Alex, Kinsey, Cassie, Abrianna," and then pointed to the woods behind her.

"Cassandra!" the one in armor repeated again, though Alex could see she had started gathering horses and other items. He understood they were asking him to go with them.

"One moment, stay here," he said while pointing to both the women and then to the ground. He then turned and at a trot and with Kinsey close behind him, returned to the spot where he had awoken earlier. The big black horse and all the gear still sat where he had left it. At least his delusions were consistent.

He began saddling the horse as best he could. He eventually figured out how the cinch worked and attached the bedroll and bags to the back. Leading the horse back out onto the road, he found the women still waiting where he had left them.

They had been very busy; all of the men in blue had been pulled to the side of the road, and lay in a row near the coach. Each had a cloth covering the body, although for most it only covered their faces. All the soldiers in red lay where they had fallen.

The women had also prepared two horses for riding, and a third burdened with supplies and gear from the coach. Two of the horses had the red and gold trimmed saddle blanket of the men Alex killed. None of the three horses seemed all that happy with Kinsey, but Alex's mount appeared ambivalent to her presence.

Alex also noticed Abrianna had changed out of her dress and into a more functional riding outfit. With no idea what was going on or where he was going, Alex and Kinsey followed as the two women led them off the road and into the woods.

Chapter 2

Alex was completely lost. While he usually knew exactly where he was at all times, he wasn't even sure what country he was in, never mind the state. He had seen a map the women had and did not recognize a single feature. As for the marks that must have represented words, they were completely unintelligible to him.

As they traveled through the forest, the trees seemed spaced to allow easy passage, and he marveled at the quiet. The day was not too hot, and the shade provided by the trees was interlaced with beams of sunlight. If he had to guess, he would say it was close to noon local time, unsure of where that actually was.

He also wasn't sure what the deal was between these two women, but if they didn't stop bickering, he was going to scream. Since leaving the dirt road and the scene of the fight, they seemed to disagree at every turn. Several times, they stopped and hovered over the map, each pointing out differing routes marked there. They would then debate for a period and finally mount up and head off.

He was still in a bit of shock over the whole battle thing. He couldn't explain his new fighting skills or the spectacular shots with the bow. The bow itself was nothing like he had ever seen. It was shaped like a typical recurve bow, but with what looked like a black lacquer finish. The grip was of some kind of black leather and was very firm and comfortable in his hand.

The sword and dagger grips were made of the same material. The blade of the dagger had the appearance of Damascus steel and was sharp enough to shave the hair off his arm. The sword blade was of the same metal, but it had etchings the entire length in some scribble Alex couldn't make out. It looked like writing, but was like nothing he had ever seen before, and not the same as on the map Abrianna carried.

He also noted his clothing was not even close to the t-shirt, jeans and hiking shoes he had started the day with. His shirt was now a long sleeved pullover made of a light brown, almost tan, cotton like material. It was soft and seemed to breathe well in the warm midday air, though a very tight weave and fairly form fitting. His pants were of a heavier weave and more of a dark green. His hiking shoes had been replaced with leather pull on boots, but with a soft sole, more like moccasins. The fur-lined cloak he had awoken in was rolled up and tied behind the saddle, with his bedroll.

With several hours of riding behind them, the woman in armor stopped and, after a short conversation with Abrianna, dismounted. Alex remembered her distaste for being called Cassie, so he refrained from calling her that. Abrianna had done so several times during the ride, without correction. He decided it must just be him she objected to using the name, rather than a general dislike of the familiar usage.

It was getting late in the day, so following the others lead, he dismounted and started pulling his gear off his mount. Not the most experienced of riders, Alex was pleased at how accommodating his horse had been. There was an unknown familiarity there, as if it were an old friend, but one he didn't remember.

During the entire operation, Cassandra kept one eye on Alex. It appeared Abrianna didn't participate in these types of chores as she surveyed the area and pointed to various spots while speaking to Cassandra. At one point, she used Alex's name and indicated he should gather wood. He assumed she wanted a fire as she dropped two pieces of wood in a small depression and then pointed around her at more.

Doing as he was told, Alex first hobbled his horse, turning it free to graze and then started collecting wood. Happy for the familiar task, he first started piling it near the depression. When he finally gathered enough, he started picking and choosing the right pieces to kindle a fire.

Glancing up, he noticed the two women watching him with curiosity. Once he had everything set up, he riffled through his bags looking for something with which to start the fire. Since there was a fire pit smoldering where he woke, he assumed he had something. He shifted through his bags, but there wasn't anything resembling a flint and steel or any other fire making tools, much less matches or a lighter.

Grabbing a strip of leather to use as a string, he picked through the wood he had gathered until he had the pieces he needed for a fire drill. He could hear the women whispering as he pulled his dagger out to shape the pieces he required. With Kinsey watching disinterestedly, he began assembling the bow. He looped the string around the shaft, and working the bow back and forth, he began rotating the shaft. The rotation created friction on the base, where Alex had placed some wood shavings. After a few minutes, he had a glowing ember that he could drop on the tinder.

Blowing gently, it burst into flames, igniting the smaller kindling. Looking up, Alex noted the women looked more confused now than before he started. It was as if they had never seen someone make fire by hand before.

By now, Cassandra had spread out two bedrolls on one side of the fire, while indicating Alex should find a spot on the far side, away from them. He had noticed Abrianna had smiled several times during the day, but Alex couldn't recall a single grin from Cassandra.

Alex believed her sour mood was due, in part at least, to all the movement in her armor. Up to this point, all the activities she had performed were done standing. However, as they were getting ready to prepare a meal, she was not going to be able to move well in the suit. She had removed a few pieces herself, but while never having worn one himself, Alex was sure you needed help to get completely out of armor. Why she wouldn't ask Abrianna to help was odd.

He watched her struggle to bend and crouch for a few minutes before he finally stood up and said, "Cassandra."

As she turned to him, he slowly approached. He could see her tense as he reached out, knocking his hand away as he reached for the straps that held the breastplate in place.

With Abrianna watching them both, he reached out more firmly this time, grabbing the plate at her neck with one hand, while pulling on the leather strap with the other, releasing the top strap. Raising her arm, he got the ones on the side, allowing her to open the front and back like a clamshell.

His mission completed, he stepped back and returned to his place on the far side of the fire. Cassandra stood watching him for a moment before sliding the plate mail off and then removing the rest of her armor herself. Once free of its restrictions, she started gathering supplies for a meal.

With that settled, Alex started rooting through his own bags, looking to see what food his hallucination had provided him with. He found a large wrapped object in one of the bags. Opening the waxlike paper, he found a bone, about a foot long, with pieces of meat partially dried on it.

He looked over to see Kinsey eyeing him intently, so he tossed the bone to her. She caught it easily and then lay back down, happily chewing away. Alex found several more similarly wrapped items in his bags, but as he was preparing to offer some to the women, Cassandra stepped over. She handed Alex a skewer with a large piece of raw meat on the end. In her other hand, was a fist sized round of bread.

"Thanks," he said.

She acknowledged the comment, obviously not understanding the words. She then returned to her side of the fire where Abrianna was already roasting her piece over the fire. Amongst the many items Alex had found when he packed up after the fight was a large water skin. He had been drinking from it all day and poured some water in a depression in the rock for Kinsey before drinking himself.

The women had a similar one, although Cassandra was pouring what looked like wine from theirs into cups. She would first fill Abrianna's cup and then pour a smaller amount for herself. At one point, Abrianna made some comment to the redhead, indicating Alex as she was pouring. She hesitated for a moment and then made a move to get up. Assuming she was headed over to offer some of their drink, Alex held up one hand, halting her in mid motion. He then held up his water bag and dipped his head slightly, trying to display a "Thanks anyway" message. With whatever coma he was hallucinating in, even imaginary wine was not appealing at the moment.

The offer made, Cassandra sat with a short comment to Abrianna, who nodded in return. For the next half hour, they ate silently. Every so often, Kinsey would lift her head at some noise, only to settle down a minute later. In dog form, Alex had seen the same movements many times, as she guarded her home.

As he ate, Alex subtly appraised the two women in his delusion. Abrianna had a head of light brown hair, long, but very well groomed considering the circumstances. From her fine attire and delicate build and manner, he suspected she was some sort of aristocracy. She was very pretty, with her facial features soft and fine. She was kind to both he and Cassandra, although she tended to let "Cassie" perform the lion's share of the heavy lifting.

Cassie, on the other hand, was far from delicate, though still quite feminine. While her undergarments for her armor were almost as fine as Abrianna's, she was, well, just bigger. At least five to six inches taller than Abrianna, she was not out of proportion in any way. She was still a few inches shorter than Alex, but from the little exposed skin he could see, she was in very good shape.

Her skin was fairer than Abrianna's, who seemed a little tanner. With her light red hair, he took her to have an Irish heritage, supposing there was such a thing here in his delusion. Her hair was almost as long as Abrianna's, but she tied it in the back. Her face was very pretty as well, but she had more of that healthy, athletic, girl next-door look going for her.

He tried not to be too obvious, but he noticed he was getting just as much scrutiny from them. They would pass quiet comments back and forth as they ate, Abrianna doing her best not to make a mess of her meal.

Once everyone had finished, Alex noted a subtle but pointed exchange between the two women. Cassandra was not happy with something Abrianna had said. She had been eyeing Alex's dagger throughout the meal, as he had been using it to eat with. He cut both his and Kinsey pieces from the roasting meat strip with it. He had cleaned it earlier before eating and she had taken serious note of it then. Its sharpness was a marvel, slicing through the chain mail as easily as it sliced the meat off the skewer.

Taking the blade carefully, he presented the hilt to Cassandra, offering her a chance for a close look. She paused at first and then came around to accept the offering. Returning to her seat, she inspected it closely, and then presented it to Abrianna, saying something that drew a nod of agreement.

Carefully returning the dagger, hilt first, she returned to her seat and then, while Alex re-sheathed it, she and Abrianna began discussing something in earnest. This went on for several minutes before Cassandra finally threw her hands in the air, a clear sign of surrender. As Alex watched, both women moved around the fire and over to his side. Cassie was clearly on edge, so Alex made sure to keep both hands in his lap and away from the hilt of his dagger; his sword lay next to his bedroll.

Reaching down, Abrianna took Alex by the hand and led him to one side of the opening near the fire pit. With Abrianna leading the way, they both stopped, and then she turned to face him, taking his other hand in hers. Then Abrianna began speaking something, starting in almost a whisper. To Alex, it sounded like something between a chant and a rap.

Unexpectedly, as Alex watched her, Abrianna began to glow. Still holding his hands, he felt a tingling coming up his arms from her hands, her light green glow gaining intensity. As the intensity grew uncomfortable, there was suddenly a giant ball of white light exploding between the two of them, throwing all three to the ground in different directions. The last thing Alex felt was hitting the ground before he blacked out.

----*----

As he came to, Alex Rogers hoped he was free of his delusion and back in Washington. He remembered that day so clearly. He'd placed his backpack with all their supplies in the Jeep, and with Kinsey in the passenger seat, they headed out I-90 and then into the mountains.

Following a map segment he found in a book, he jumped off the nearest exit close to his destination and then headed back into the mountains. At this point, the roads were all dirt and very poorly maintained. The forest service considered them firebreaks, not roads. They had been driving for a good two hours to reach this deep into the forest.

He finally had to pull the Jeep off the narrow road and into a small opening in the trees. He climbed out with Kinsey at his heels, pulling the backpack out, and locking the Jeep. Shouldering his backpack, Alex checked his map and the GPS.

Alex prided himself on his sense of direction. Once oriented to his surroundings, he rarely ever needed the GPS or map. He would imprint his location in his head and constantly check his internal position against the features he had identified against the map. He boasted on more than one occasion that he was never lost.

While you couldn't call the route he followed a path, there was a natural spacing between the trees, allowing his and Kinsey's passage. The undergrowth was much heavier on either side of him and she would occasionally disappear into the foliage, only to reappear a few seconds later.

With such heavy growth in the area leaving no landmarks visible, Alex would stop every so often just to check his progress. When the trees above opened up sufficiently to give the GPS some visible sky, he would pause to get a reading. Without visible landmarks, and traveling an unmarked trail, distances were deceiving.

He took a break as he caught enough sky to get a good reading. They had walked about two miles, so Alex took the opportunity to give Kinsey some water. As it was midsummer, the temperature was in the 80's even here in the woods. Leaning his backpack against a tree, he pulled out a water bottle and filled a folding cloth dog bowl for her.

Suddenly, Alex heard a loud cracking, and the ground gave way beneath his feet. Before he knew it, both he and Kinsey was falling and then everything went black.

Alex was now having a "déjà vu" moment as he lay on the ground. His eyes were still closed and his head hurt. His ears were ringing, but through the ringing, he could hear someone talking…and knew he most certainly was not back in Washington.

"Brie, are you alright? I told you not to mess with that Ranger!"

Opening his eyes, Alex could see Cassandra hovering over Abrianna. At that moment, Kinsey came over and started licking Alex in the face.

"Yes, yes. Kinsey, I am ok!"

Turning back to the women, he saw them both staring at him now.

"Why didn't you tell me you had magic?" Abrianna snapped as Cassandra helped her to her feet.

"I have no idea what you are talking about," Alex snapped back. "And why can I understand you now?"

"That was a learning spell I was attempting. It was working fine until you released that defensive response."

"Look, I don't have any idea what the hell you are talking about. I am not magic, I don't believe in magic and I don't even have any idea where the hell I am."

Cassandra helped Abrianna back to her seat by the fire and then supplied a cup, filled from the wine skin. Alex did the same, moving to his side of the fire. As he drank from his own water skin, Kinsey settled next to him, intent on not letting him get too far from her protection.

After she drank the cup dry, Abrianna looked at Alex for a moment and then asked, "What did you see when I was performing the spell?"

Confused by the question, Alex considered it and then replied, "Well, once you started to speak, I saw you glow. As you continued, I felt my arms start to tingle. As the tingling increased to an uncomfortable level, that is when the explosion happened. I blacked out when I hit the ground."

"What color was I?" Abrianna asked.

"Color?" Alex asked, now completely confused.

"When you saw me glowing, what color was I?" She asked again, obviously irritated at having to repeat herself.

"Green, medium to light green," Alex replied after a few seconds of consideration.

"Only someone with magical abilities can see the colors of another," she stated flatly, as if to prove a point.

"And your light, what color was that?" she then asked more cautiously this time.

"It's not my light, but if you mean the exploding energy ball, it was white. Pure bright white."

At that, he saw both Abrianna and Cassandra go pale.

"What?" Alex asked.

"Are you sure about the color?" Cassandra asked pointedly.

"Could you be mistaken?" Abrianna asked more delicately.

"No, I am absolutely positive. It was bright white," Alex replied, a little irritated himself at this point.

Abrianna sighed, and then said, "Every magical being, male or female, has a color to their power. Mine is a green tint while my father is more of a light blue. My mother was not magical, nor is Cassie and many others."

"Was not?" Alex asked.

"My mother passed away when I was little. Cassie and her mother came to live with me after her father died. Her mother is my father's sister, and while we are cousins, we were raised like sisters."

Continuing, she said, "No one knows how many magical people there are in the realms; many keep it secret as they are feared by most non-magical commoners and royalty alike."

By this point Alex had mostly recovered, although he did not believe a word she was saying. He did feel as if someone had electrocuted him and drained his energy.

"You can tell the power of someone by how dark or light their color is. Most can hide their natural aura, as apparently you can, but once they perform magic, their color shows through."

"Ok," Alex replied, humoring his delusion, "so if I'm white, I have no color. What does that mean?"

Abrianna sighed again before answering, "The closer to white your color is, the more powerful you are. Light blue is stronger than dark blue, but white is the strongest of all."

"Thankfully, there hasn't been a white wizard in over two hundred years, until now," Cassandra added with a foreboding tone.

Chapter 3

The following morning, Alex woke with a headache and in a bad mood. After the discussion about magic and white wizards last night, both women refused to believe Alex when he proclaimed a lack of abilities. His inability to convince them otherwise frustrated him. Having decided this wasn't a delusion, he was still no closer to understanding where he was or how to get back home.

Home…only days before, Alex Rogers had been at his desk in a cubicle farm that stretched the length of half a football field. He was positive of the distance, since he had played in high school and sprinted the length too many times not to remember it well. He sorely missed those days, now eight years ago, as the most exciting years of his not overly extensive or thrilling life. At six foot three, and 220 pounds, he had played tight end and loved every moment of it.

Alex sighed, and thought about how unexciting his life had been.

Graduating from high school early, he had gone into college on an academic rather than sports scholarship, studying engineering. Originally interested in civil engineering, the lack of potential employment in that field after graduation had encouraged him to transfer to mechanical engineering. The change had cost him an additional year of study, but in the end, it landed him a job right out of college.

The not so humorous part of that good fortune was the firm that had hired him immediately assigned him to work with the understaffed civil engineering department. Thus began his career as an engineering generalist.

It turned out Alex had an aptitude for just about any kind of technical engineering. He worked with the Civil, Mechanical, Electrical, and Architectural groups at the firm, rotating in an ongoing basis. He even assisted in the overworked and understaffed IT department. He had a knack for seeing into the future and predicting trouble. Many a colleague had praised him, suggesting he was capable of working magic.

On the private side of his life though, if it were not for his outdoor interests, he would have had no personal life at all. Relocated from Southern California to Seattle, he was a stranger in town with no friends.

While he spent his weekdays and some weekends working in the city, he spent his rare free time all over the wilderness of the Cascade Mountains. He hiked, fished, and generally explored the woods, backpacking and camping whenever possible. For a change of scenery, he also ventured on to the more arid eastern parts of Washington state.

An avid reader growing up and in college, he imagined himself a sword-wielding woodsman, wandering the wilds and looking for adventure. He had managed to squeeze in several fencing classes in college, thus fueling his delusions of mastery with a blade.

Now, as ridiculous as this all might have seemed to some, Alex saw it as his sanity check. The reality of daily life was more than enough grounding. This was checking out of reality, plain and simple. While he never carried a sword into the woods, his bowie knife and bow were regular companions. On more than one occasion, he had scored with the bow, the rabbit providing dinner for him and his dog, Kinsey, his regular companion.

In college, he had never really connected with anyone, although he was told he was not unattractive to the female eye. He had enjoyed the company of more than one girlfriend over the years, but none had lasted.

On the shelf over his desk were several well-worn paperbacks. As he was a huge reader, he had several favorite genres, but his go to stories were all Science Fiction and Fantasy. They were mainly lunchtime entertainment, although several made the trip home and back.

One book in particular inspired the outing that landed him in this delusion, or whatever it was he was living in at the moment; he'd been in search of an abandoned mining settlement he had found on some old maps, hand drawn notes on a section of a USGS survey map. He actually needed to do a little research to locate the right area, as they were only partials of a larger map.

The area on the map was notorious for lost hikers, due to the number of abandoned mines at the location. Alex had read of a few cases where they suspected sinkholes had appeared on trails, due to cave in's from the mines below. He imagined hikers swallowed completely as they stepped onto what appeared to be solid ground. His only confusion was why it never happened to groups, only single hikers. Not even small parties of two or three. It seemed so fascinating at the time. At the present moment, he wished he'd found some other way to amuse himself.

Speaking of "the present moment" Alex felt that things were looking up…a little, anyway. On the plus side, now that he could speak to them, he learned about Cassandra's interest in the weapons Alex had in his possession. Apparently, the bow, dagger, and sword were all of Elven make, or so she claimed. She informed him that they all held magical powers and were quite valuable. The only way to acquire such weapons was as a gift or in battle. The latter was never a good bet though, since the weapons might not accept you as the new owner. It appears that they had a will of their own.

If they did not accept you, all the magical abilities would be nullified and they would be no better than a non-magical one. Since she had seen Alex slice through chain mail and send arrows on impossible flights, she assured him they must have been gifts. As he had no recollection of their delivery, he could hardly argue the point.

The fact that they believed there were such things as Elves was also not lost on Alex either. While he had a strong desire to grill the two on what other fictional races they believed in, he let it slide for now.

Discussing things he would never see was a waste of time and seemed to irritate the two women.

The women however, had pressed him on his memories prior to their meeting and displayed clear disbelief at his descriptions of cars and planes. They challenged him on how he could not believe in magic, yet have vehicles that moved without horses or flew through the air.

They were less mystified in his description of Kinsey prior to her current appearance, as transformation was a well-known magic. Kinsey just sat watching them, not overly concerned about anything at that point.

As that line of questioning was going nowhere, Alex asked Abrianna about the battle he stumbled upon that had brought them all together.

"I was on my way to Windfall, on behalf of my father, when we were attacked on the road. The soldiers were from Windfall and apparently all paid off," she replied.

"Why were you going there in the first place if they were just going to attack you?" Alex asked, thinking it an obvious question.

"We are not at odds with Windfall. My mission was only to meet the Crown Prince and discuss a joining of our two houses. His father is quite ill and as the new monarch, we wanted to establish new relations with the son. My father rules the lands in the south and those in Windfall rule in the west. A union would strengthen both our holdings. We are a huge agricultural kingdom while they hold the largest ports on the west coast. We could reach overseas markets through those ports, while they would reap huge shipping profits."

"So, you are a princess going to discuss joining of your houses?"

Abrianna blushed at the comment before replying.

"Yes, my father had suggested I might find the prince to my liking. As such, he sent me on this errand as his envoy. It allowed me an opportunity to meet the man before any formal proposal might be offered. Should I find him unappealing, father said I should defer making any commitments and he would find other avenues."

"Then why the attack? Who were those men?" Alex asked.

"I don't know. That's why we are in the woods at the moment, avoiding the roads," Abrianna replied.

"We are in the woods because I talked you out of continuing up the road!" Cassandra asserted.

"I still think we could have just turned around then and headed straight home," Abrianna countered.

"With Windfall soldiers at the inn and the border? If they are in league with the others, we would not last the day," Cassie replied.

Alex recalled the exchange before they left the coach. He now understood the why, but not the where. "So where are we headed?"

"We are headed east, to the river T'ybel, where we can secure passage south. Since you failed to kill the two riders, they will have reported our survival to whoever is behind the attack," Cassandra stated.

Alex took offense to her comment and her tone. As he had dispatched five of the seven, wounding the sixth, he was not feeling much in the way of gratitude in saving their lives. Abrianna must have sensed his irritation as she called a halt to the conversation for the night and they had all settled down to sleep.

Now, they put together a meager breakfast from their supplies, Kinsey appearing from the woods with what looked like a fair sized rabbit. Neither woman paid her more than cursory attention as she proceeded to devour her prize. Apparently, the behavior was not unusual in their experiences.

After eating, Alex and Cassandra began preparing the horses, while Abrianna hovered over the map. Alex stopped by to check it over himself, surprised that he could now read the scribbles that had previously been illegible. Abrianna pointed out their location, her home, named Great Vale, and her previous destination, labeled Windfall, all marked on the map. He assumed A'nland across the top indicated the name of the region.

Giving it more than the cursory glance he had previously, the map itself wasn't as crude as he had originally thought. While nothing close to the USGS maps he had used in the past, it did have some geographic detail as well as reasonable representations of the roads throughout the region.

He could see the bend in the road where he had intervened in the attack. He could also see the river marked T'ybel, that was their intended destination, and a city on its banks referenced as Portsward. If he judged the distances correctly, they were still several days' travel away from that community.

Returning to his previous activities, he asked Cassie to hand him some of their gear to load on the packhorse. She stopped for a moment, picked up the item in question, and then stepped up, getting well into Alex's personal space.

"Only Abrianna calls me that!" she snapped at him, shoving the bundle into his arms.

Nodding in understanding, Alex continued what he was doing while she turned abruptly and headed off.

With everything loaded up, both Cassandra and Alex gathered on either side of Abrianna, as she continued to survey the map.

"What's the problem?" Alex asked, as the women seemed concerned.

"We are heading to Portsward," Abrianna explained, "but the most direct route takes us here," she said while pointing to a dark spot on the map, in the middle of the large forest they were traveling in. There were some icons on the location that looked like ruins.

"What are these?" Alex asked, pointing to the icons.

"There was once a city here," Abrianna replied.

"Before my father's time it was a major power in the area. Its influence ran far west, beyond what is now Windfall's kingdom, and north to the Northern Mountains. It also went south into my homeland."

"What happened?" Alex asked.

"As they grew in power, their greed began to consume them. They drew on dark magic to increase their influence over their neighbors, until all the lands combined and attacked, besieging them. In the end, the dark magicians were defeated, but their deaths released a contamination that consumed the city and surrounding woods."

Alex listened intently, thinking this all made a great story. However, beyond a few spooky trees and building ruins, he didn't understand their concerns.

Apparently it was plain on his face as Cassandra added, "The residual dark magic is a magnet to creatures of evil. Orcs, trolls, goblins, and their like are all in residence here," she finished while pointing at the spot on the map.

"However, by passing through here," Abrianna stated while indicating the spot on the map, "we cut a day, maybe two, off our journey home. It's possible to make this distance in one day if we move quickly."

"Ok by me," Alex replied, still convinced they were scared of nonexistent creatures.

"This is not your decision, Ranger!" Cassandra snapped.

"That's the second time I have heard you call me that, what is it?" Alex replied.

"Are you not a forest Ranger?" Cassandra asked.

"What is that exactly?"

From their look, Alex assumed they thought he had lost his mind.

"You keep watch over the countryside and are widely feared for your combat skills. Normal non-magical commoners consider you a wizard of the black arts, but all educated people know that the Rangers of the Ranger's Guild do not associate with black magic. Most Rangers have some basic magical abilities, but not all. You are sworn to protect nature and slay foul creatures," Cassandra finished.

"Wow, that's a hell of a gig, but who pays the bills?"

Confused at first, Abrianna replied, "All are honor bound to provide for the Rangers. When not in the wilderness, living off the land, they are to receive room and board at no cost. In larger communities, there will be a Guild house to provide for you. The coins I gave you yesterday from the road are yours by right, hard fought. Any weapons or supplies are as well though you appeared to require neither."

"Why do they need money then?" Alex asked.

"Rangers sometimes leave small sums as gratitude for the hospitality provided. You can also use the coins to replace lost or damaged weapons or equipment, although again, all yours are like new and the best available. That shirt you wear would cost six to eight golds alone."

Alex looked down at his shirt, seeing nothing out of the ordinary about it. As he watched, Cassandra quickly drew her dagger, and before he could react, stabbed his arm. To his amazement, it didn't penetrate. It hurt a little, but never pierced the material or more importantly his arm. He also suspected Cassandra enjoyed her little demonstration a bit too much, but the point was well taken.

"This tunic I wear under my armor is of a similar make, allowing for protection where the plate gaps. Both yours and mine are of Elven manufacture," Cassandra stated while indicating the shirt she had on.

"And I take it eight golds is a lot of money?" Alex asked.

"Those solders you killed will make no more than one gold a month. Some will only see seven or eight silvers for their pay. For each to possess two to three golds indicated a recent payment for special services," Abrianna added.

Alex couldn't stop himself, being drawn into the fantasy of it all, "So I saw gold, silver and bronze or copper coins?"

"Yes," Abrianna replied, "each gold is worth ten silvers, and each silver is worth twenty-five coppers."

Knowing the cost of things was best compared to food and lodging, he asked, "So the average meal and room costs?"

Both women looked a bit confused at first, before Cassandra replied, "An evening meal and room for the night is three coppers. Five, if it includes a bath and breakfast the next morning."

Doing the math, five coppers a day for thirty days in a month required six silvers a month just to live. Abrianna could see Alex considering the information. She added, "Most soldiers will receive some consideration for sleeping, if they choose the barracks over an inn. Usually a large portion of their wages goes to drink and comfort women."

The last made Alex laugh, as he was sure there were more colorful names for whatever served as a brothel.

"So I have to ask," Alex said, drawing from his fantasy reading, "where are these Elves that make all this stuff and why are they selling it? Don't Elves avoid humans as a whole?"

Again, some of Alex's references seemed to confuse the women. After a moment, Abrianna replied, "Yes, as a rule, Elves avoid human contact. However, they are a race of nature worshipers and trade openly with the Rangers and other groups like the Druids who honor and protect nature. Your weapons and clothing likely came directly from them in a trade. Others, like Cassandra, have items that are hundreds of years old, passed down as family heirlooms or purchased at great expense."

"As to their location," Cassandra offered, "their cities are hidden. Only a very special few have ever been invited in. The Elves come out when they choose and disappear when their business is completed."

Focusing back on the issue at hand, Alex turned to Cassandra and said, "Ok, so if it's not my decision, what would you ladies like to do today?"

After a lengthy discussion, Abrianna and Cassandra decided to wait another day before deciding on the run through the dead city. As they were positive any move south would be met with discovery, the options were only north and then east, or just straight east. Both required one more days travel east. Windfall was well known for their border patrols, so the entire southern route was not a possibility.

----*----

Alex was astride his large black mare, leading the packhorse and following the two women as they headed further into the woods. Kinsey was following along beside Alex's horse, quietly trotting at her own comfortable pace. From his position, he could hear the two still bickering about the best path to follow.

Earlier, after Alex deferred to the women on their next course of action, they had haggled back and forth on the decision. Abrianna had suggested they make a beeline for the river, bisecting the dark woods and making the best possible time for their return trip home. She was concerned about her father's worry over her disappearance, as her lack of appearance in Windfall must have surely been reported by now.

Her additional concern was for her father. The evil that spawned the attack on her caravan might in turn, attack her father next. She wanted to warn him as soon as possible.

Cassandra, on the other hand, was more concerned about Abrianna's current security and was not in the least interested in the dark woods and the city inside beyond a talking point. While Abrianna listed Alex and Kinsey as able bodyguards, she countered with his lack of understanding on who, or even where he was. As for the wolf, she listed her as protection only for Alex to this point.

By mid-day, they passed through the ruins of a small village. There were two structures of stone, one with a tree growing in the middle of its walls. Both women took it as a good sign that they were on the right path. Abrianna explained to Alex that all roads contained traveler's inns, spaced one day's ride apart. This inn serviced the road to the dead city and as such was abandoned long ago. It did, however, enforce the notion that they were now a day's ride from the dead city.

By nightfall, Cassandra stopped the three riders in a small meadow, with a stream and soft grasses for bedding. Alex had a fire going before either of the women realized what happened. Cassandra had been watering the horses while Abrianna was arraigning the bedding for the two.

This time, Alex offered up the meat he had, while Cassandra produced more bread from her saddlebag. She also provided cheese, slicing wedges for Abrianna while permitting Alex to cut his own. The three ate in silence, the decision of tomorrow's route hanging over them.

Unlike the previous evening, there was no discussion; they all retired early.

The following morning, all rose with the sun and quickly packed. Cassandra and Abrianna started off arguing straight away on the direction they should take. They ate as they rode, the only silence provided as they chewed. The argument continued after mounting and heading east on the barely recognizable trail.

In the end, Abrianna won her over, or wore Cassandra down, depending on your opinion. Now moving at a fair clip, the group headed right into the center of the dark woods and straight to the ruins of the dead city at its heart.

As they moved along, Alex had to admit it was getting pretty creepy. He was sure it was just his imagination, but the woods seemed to be getting darker. He looked up to see the sunlight at the treetops as it struggled to reach the forest floor. The trees took on a look of misshapen, twisted trunks, rather than the long and straight versions he had seen earlier.

Shaking off the negative thoughts, he surveyed the two women in the lead. Both were constantly scanning the woods on both sides of the rough path they followed, quiet now and listening intently at the sounds around them. Every now and then Kinsey would let loose a low growl, obviously not pleased with some whiff of scent she had caught.

After a few hours of this, the trail suddenly halted abruptly at a high stone wall. The stone was gray with age, but solid and the wall was a good twenty feet tall. The trail they had been following split in either direction, paralleling the wall.

After his earlier rebuke for proposing a direction, Alex patiently waited for the two women to decide their next move. He caught several glances in his direction from both women as they argued. Alex detected that both were apparently now open for additional input.

Working his way forward to get parallel with the two astride their mounts, he looked both ways. Neither direction seemed to give them the access to the city they were looking for. Earlier, they had determined they needed to pass through the center of the city itself, to avoid the delay of going around the great wall. The idea was to clear the city and the dark woods on the far side before nightfall.

With no clear option, Alex called Kinsey up to the front.

"Ok Kinsey, which way?"

Kinsey looked up at Alex and stared.

"Which way, honey?" Alex asked as he pointed first to the right, and then to the left.

Both women watched as Alex talked to the wolf, their expression conveying their doubts to his sanity. Kinsey first sniffed one direction and then the other. Finally, she turned back to Alex's left and gave a bark, more wolf than dog like.

"There you have it," Alex stated as he followed her off to the left, the women dropping in behind him. Continuing along the wall, Alex began to question why this path was even here. If the city was abandoned as Abrianna claimed, then the forest should have grown right up to the outer wall of the city. However, as he inspected the ground below the horses' hooves, this had the look of a well-traveled pathway.

Soon enough, the trail led them to stone pavers and a gate in the wall. This was the opening into the city that they had been seeking. While the great wooden doors were long gone, with their remnants in plies nearby, the structures inside were all standing. There were stone structures everywhere though all in various stages of ruin. As the group turned the corner into the city, Alex turned back and smiled at both of the women, smug in his decision to let Kinsey choose.

Their expressions changed before his very eyes, the smiles fading from their faces. Turning to follow their gaze, he was appalled to see ten or twelve of the ugliest creatures he had ever seen in his life, and they were all armed.

"Orcs," stated Cassandra as Alex turned back to her, watching her hand as it went to her sword hilt.

"Ok, now I'm a believer," was all Alex could say as he turned back to survey the group standing menacingly in their path.

Chapter 4

Alex slowly climbed down off his horse while Kinsey stood next to him and gave a low growl of displeasure.

"You are not welcome here, Ranger," one of orcs bellowed, startling Alex, as he hadn't expected them to be able to speak.

"The others can stay though," another commented in an unappealing tone.

Alex did note several of the orcs eyeing the large black wolf by his side with unease. Not sure what else to do, he stated, "We just want to pass. Step aside and I won't feed you to Kinsey," while pointing to her.

At that, Kinsey paused mid growl and looked up at Alex as if to say, "I'm not putting that in my mouth," before returning her attention to the orcs.

While trying to decide his next move, Alex heard over his shoulder, "Out of our way, orcs! You dare to delay Princess Abrianna."

Alex was sure Cassie had not meant to aggravate the situation. However, the declaration that there was royalty in their midst did little to disperse the orcs. In fact, the mention of the princess seemed to increase their interest in the three travelers.

"I've never tasted princess before," one commented, while several others smacked their lips in support of the statement.

Alex was starting to stress. He had no idea how to deal with these things and while they didn't care for Kinsey in wolf form, they weren't backing off either. Instinctively, he drew his sword, which seemed to aggravate the orcs even more. Their posture changed from one of a casual bully to a serious combatant.

As several of the group started to fan out, three in the center formed up to challenge Alex directly. Menacing the orcs with his sword held out in front of him, he found himself wishing for a gun. He mentally envisioned spraying a line of gunfire, cutting the orcs down where they stood.

Suddenly, Alex felt a tingling down the arm holding the sword. From the tip of the sword, a line of white flame erupted, vaporizing first one, and then another of the orcs facing him. As he swept the blade to his right, it continued to decimate the targets it touched.

Reaching the last of the orcs to his right, it stopped as suddenly as it started. Quickly turning to his left, he held out the sword as he had done before, the four remaining orcs preparing to flee. Nothing happened.

He shook the blade in his hand. "Come on already."

Again, nothing came forth.

The four orcs first looked at one another and then charged, swinging their weapons wildly. Stepping into the first attacker, Alex drew his dagger and blocked the swing of the orc's blade with his own while driving the dagger into its neck. He was rewarded with a fountain of blood that was far more black than red.

Spinning away to his right, he was just in time to block a swing from a double bitted axe with his sword. As a third blade appeared, headed straight for his neck, a fourth blade diverted it from its target. Cassie had jumped from her saddle, sword in hand, and interceded just in time to save Alex's neck.

Alex drove his knee into the abdomen of the orc, causing it to double over. Driving his dagger into its back, he turned to see Cassie as she was being pressed by the other two orcs. Taking his dagger by the blade, he threw it with enough force to bury it hilt deep into one of the orc's ears.

Having only one opponent to deal with, Cassie slipped passed the orc's guard and took its head off cleanly. It rolled away as she stepped back, more of the black blood spraying forth. She then turned to Alex and as he stepped forward, he collapsed, falling face forward on the road.

----*----

Alex could feel Kinsey's tongue on his face, rapidly licking away, before he opened his eyes. His head was pounding, and he was beginning to think this pattern was becoming far too frequent. Opening his eyes, he discovered he had been rolled onto his back, with Abrianna kneeling next to him. She had his water bag in her hands and was attempting to get him to drink, while Kinsey was on the other side, giving kisses.

Gently pushing Kinsey aside, and taking the offered water, Alex could make out Cassie standing to one side, surveying their surroundings. Every now and then, she would look down at him, concern on her face. Once she saw his eyes upon her, she quickly looked away, becoming overly attentive to her guard duty.

"How do you feel?" Abrianna asked softly.

"Like my head is splitting," Alex replied, while trying to sit up.

"Give it a moment," Abrianna replied, pushing him back down, "you can't use that much magic without penalty. Here, drink," she added while giving him more from the water bag.

Finally acquiescing to the concept of magic itself, Alex assumed the magic he had just wielded generated from the sword. Cassie had said the weapons were magic. If Abrianna presumed he had something to do with the fire from the blade, she was very mistaken. He had no idea how to produce such an effect. If he had been magic, he would have mowed them down with an AK-47, burning ammo on full auto.

Eventually Abrianna let him sit up. As he surveyed the area around them, he saw dead orcs mixed in with ash piles, the remnants of several of the orcs he had fried, in all directions; the smell of burnt flesh was overpowering. He could also tell that Cassie was getting impatient with their delay.

Alex couldn't blame her, as they had just entered the walls of the city and already had to fight. Getting up slowly, and checking his balance, he found he was stable enough. He stooped to retrieve the sword and dagger he had dropped and sheathed both after cleaning the blades on the nearest orc. He turned to find everyone's eyes upon him, Kinsey included.

"I'm fine," he stated, "let's get moving before anything else turns up."

Out of the corner of his eye, he noticed that both women watched him mount his horse before doing the same.

"I assume there is a gate similar to this one on the far side of the city?" Alex asked Abrianna, as he started farther into the city. Unasked, Cassie had assumed the responsibility for the packhorse and trailed the two.

"Yes, all the ancient cities had two main gates, which were positioned following the major trade routes, though they did have many smaller gates as well. For this area, it would be an east/west route, trade goods coming to and from the coast in the west to the river in the east for movement north or south on the river," Abrianna replied.

"In this case, I know there are smaller gates for north/south travel as well."

"Wouldn't it be shorter to take the south gate and head straight home?" Alex asked, recalling the map he had seen earlier.

"Shorter, yes but not faster, or safer. Using the river T'ybel will cut a day out of the trip even though it's a longer distance traveled. Once we reach Rivers Edge, I can send word to my father. And this way we avoid any Windfall patrols at the border," Abrianna replied.

Alex remembered seeing a town on the map south of Portsward, also on the river. Labeled Rivers Edge, he assumed it was in her father's kingdom and connected to whatever communications system they used. That was how she intended on cutting a day out of their need to contact the king.

"This road should take us straight through the city center and out the other side. Unfortunately, I have no idea how far that is," Abrianna added while riding next to Alex.

As they rode along, Alex could feel his strength returning. With Kinsey near his foot opposite Abrianna's horse, they all traveled in silence. Every now and then, Alex swore he caught movement on one side or the other of the roadway, both populated with abandoned structures in various states of ruin.

On both sides of their route, Alex could see one and two story structures, mostly of either rock or stone. Almost all were missing the wooden parts of their original construction, although every now and then one retained its wooden roof or balcony. Alex had to wonder what kind of wood would withstand the ages.

Unable to contain himself any longer, Alex asked, "Ok, so what makes you think I was responsible for the magic? Cassie said the sword has Elf magic, why wasn't it the source?"

As Abrianna paused a moment before replying, Alex noted that Cassie didn't correct his accidental use of her more familiar name.

"First of all, the magic of the sword doesn't do what you just did. It's magic makes it strong, light, and sharp. It is magical, not a magic wielder. You gathered and focused free energy, pulling it in from all around you, channeling it through your body and eventually through the sword. The magic of the sword did lend assistance to your efforts, increasing its intensity. It was miraculous! I have only seen its equal once, and that was when several mages combined their efforts to carve an opening in a solid stone wall."

"Mages?" Alex asked.

"A mage is a practitioner of magic. They are able to interact with the forces of magic, the energy I described earlier. Only humans or Elves have the potential to become mages. I am a mage, but my art lies in healing. I channel the energy I manipulate into curing illness, though I can perform other spells, like the learning spell I used on you," Abrianna finished.

"Ok, so stupid question. You talked about a white wizard earlier and now we are talking mages, aren't they all the same thing?" he asked.

Cassie, who had been listening to the exchange, scoffed and rolled her eyes. Apparently, her tolerance of Alex had its limits.

Abrianna gave her a dirty look before answering, "No it's not a stupid question for someone who has no knowledge of magic. A mage is a magic user. They use their abilities as a stonemason or a tinker might. They are better paid than the other trades, but they are in fact tradesmen."

"A wizard studies magic. They are practitioners at the highest level, unlike the mages, and they pursue the more..." she paused as she searched for the right description, "extreme examples of the art."

At this point Cassie interjected, "What you just did was wizard level magic. Wizards are used in battle for the very reason you demonstrated. They can kill large groups with great effectiveness."

As she completed her statement, she looked hard at Alex. He interpreted her stare as containing a hint of both fear and admiration.

"You keep saying I did it, but I can say for a fact, burning down those orcs was the farthest thing from my mind."

"What were you thinking at the time?" Abrianna asked patiently.

Pausing to gather his thoughts, Alex replied, "Well, I was wishing I had an AK-47, a machine gun." He could see the confusion on her face so he added, "It's a weapon from my world where small metal slugs fly from it at such speed it would cut through the orcs, killing them where they stood."

Abrianna laughed at that, "And you don't see how that equates to the flame from your sword? Are these metal objects hot like fire?"

Alex nodded, as he had to admit they were. Although he had never been shot, the traditional description of hot burning lead was well known.

"Your mental image was translated into action here," Abrianna stated in a matter-of-fact tone. "A wizard makes a mental image of what he wants, and channels free energy into action or form."

"Form?" Alex asked.

"Yes, matter and energy are intertwined. Pure energy has very little matter, and solid, inanimate matter like a stone, has very little energy. Living beings are a balance of both. Mages and wizards manipulate matter and energy to restructure their form. Adding energy to matter or drawing out energy changes the balance and allows for manipulation."

As Alex considered her explanation, he continued to survey their surroundings. A definite movement had drawn his attention to one of the abandoned buildings. To his right were several structures set back from the roadway they traveled. At one time, he was sure they must have been shops or commercial businesses. It was funny how his construction and architecture background translated into that level of understanding here.

He stopped his horse, watching, but he saw no further indication of activity. He was sure someone or something was shadowing their progress. In due time, they proceeded into a large open square which must have been the city center. There were large multistory buildings on all four sides, and a huge fountain, long since gone dry and crumbling. At one point, the fountain must have held a statue at its top, but the feet were all that remained.

The buildings surrounding the square had the look of public structures to Alex. Several of the buildings sported great columns that made them reminiscent of Roman or Greek structures. All were made of stone that might have been light and grand looking in the distant past. Now they were dull and dark gray, both age and decay taking their toll.

Looking down, Alex could see where the paving stones of the roadway gave way to the broad flat rectangles of the city square. He had to admire the precision with which slab after slab lay in perfect rows. On the far side of the square, opposite their position, he saw the opening amid the buildings where a road left the square. He was sure that represented the roadway out and presumed it would lead to the far gate.

Once they were well into the city square proper, Alex could see that the fountain wasn't completely dry after all, as its base still held about a foot of water. It looked clean and clear, but so far, Alex hadn't seen anything that was as it appeared.

Reining up at its edge, he asked his companions, "Do you think it's safe for the horses?"

As he watched, Abrianna climbed down off her horse and stood next to the fountain. Kneeling, she leaned over the edge. Extending one hand out over the water, she sat in that position with her eyes closed.

"What's she doing?" Alex whispered to Cassie.

"Shhhh!" Cassie replied sternly.

After a moment, Abrianna stood up and said, "I was sensing the energy levels in the water. As I explained before, you can alter the matter and energy balance to change the nature of things. Poisoned or foul water has a very different energy matter balance than fresh water. This is OK."

Climbing down himself, with Cassie following suit, they led all four horses to the fountain's edge. Kinsey drank her fill next to the horses while Alex turned to examine the buildings at the mouth of the road that was their destination. In comparison to the way they had just come, the buildings were closer to the road and several stories tall. If he were going to jump someone, that would be the exact spot where he would do it.

"Stay here," he told them as he walked towards the opening, drawing his sword. Before he had proceeded half the distance, he felt Kinsey at his side. As they continued together across the square, Alex scanned the buildings on both sides of the opening. He was checking for any indication there might be a threat inside.

Kinsey gave a low growl, but didn't seem to focus on one side or the other. The pair stepped into the gap between the buildings, in the center of the roadway. Alex could see that the roadway opened up once you passed out of the city square and continued straight for quite a distance. He couldn't make out any gate or even the city wall at the far end, though he was sure at least the wall was there somewhere.

The roadway into the square was quite wide, easily spacious enough for two cars to pass. He laughed to himself at the comparison, as here it would be two carriages. This road was no exception; it was the buildings so close on either side of the road that had given it the appearance of being smaller. While his sense of unease wasn't going away, he still couldn't find anything amiss.

Alex first went over to one of the buildings, and then the other, peering through the open windows.

These were at street level, with their coverings long gone. Giving his eyes time to adjust to the dark, he still saw nothing of concern. Turning, he stepped away from the building and stepped back into the middle of the street, while shrugging his shoulders to the women.

It was then that Alex was knocked violently to the ground by something that dropped on him from above. Instinctively, he rolled to one side as he drove up with his sword from his prone position. Having no real target, he was still rewarded when the blade bit just under the chin and into the skull of...well, something he had never seen before.

With no time to evaluate his kill, he continued to roll to one side as three more of the things headed toward him with swords and axes of their own. The closest of them suddenly sprouted an arrow from its chest, courtesy of Cassandra using Alex's bow. Alex sidestepped the thing with the arrow in its chest as he engaged the next closest antagonist. It was then he realized it had no eyes.

The thing swung its axe wildly, but with enough skill that Alex had to parry several passes of the double bitted axe blades. Out of the corner of his eye, he caught Kinsey with the final creature. The two squared off until another of Cassie's arrows ended the confrontation.

At this point, Alex drew his dagger and again, using the Florentine Technique of dual weapon fighting, deftly deflected the axe swing while driving the dagger into its face. It would have been right where the eye was if it had any.

Pausing to catch his breath, Alex declared, "What the hell is that?" while pointing at one of the dead with his blade.

"That is a Gorm Orc," Abrianna answered as she and Cassie led the four horses to Alex and Kinsey.

"There must still be catacombs under the city. They hate living above ground," she finished.

As he inspected the dead, he noted they were stout, thick, and heavily muscled. He was already aching from the blow to the back. Fortunately, the one who had dropped on him hadn't been pointing his weapon at Alex's exposed head. The Gorm Orc had gray, scaly skin and while its face was humanoid, there were no eyes where you would expect them.

"Then why are they here?" Alex asked while taking a drink for the waterskin Abrianna offered him.

"They come out to raid," Cassie replied, "They take slaves or generally plunder, and then return below. Both must be sparse lately; they must be getting desperate."

Cassie handed him his bow and said, "This is very nice, but I can tell it prefers you."

Setting the bow aside, he motioned for Kinsey to come to him.

"I am really starting to hate this place," Alex stated as he took another drink and then offered Kinsey some. She took the water from his cupped palm and then sat while the others prepared to leave.

Chapter 5

The group only paused long enough to get their things together and then headed down the roadway Alex had just cleared of Gorm Orcs. As they rode, Abrianna informed Alex that it was not unusual for Gorm Orcs to travel above ground in small groups of only four or five. She said their big worry was underground, where there might be hundreds of them.

He was starting to think his education on mythical creatures would consist of those he managed to kill. It was now well past noon and Alex was starting to worry they might not get out of the city before dark. From what Abrianna described, the really nasty creatures came out then. Rolling everything that had happened so far through his mind, Alex was still stuck on one point.

"Hey Abrianna," Alex asked, "Why can I fight so well?"

Cassie shook her head. "You call that good?"

Abrianna gave Cassie another dirty look before answering.

"You have never trained with a blade or bow."

"Well, not really, I mean I did some fencing in college. And I have used the bow quite a bit, but have no real training with one."

She reflected on that and then replied, "So you have familiarity, just not expertise?"

"I guess that's a good description."

With a laugh, she said, "That's the simplest of magic. You are already knowledgeable, you just needed precision. Combat skills are a combination of education and repetition. You came here with the knowledge. Somehow you were gifted with great expertise."

Cassie scoffed at Abrianna's compliment, but withheld comment after another dark look.

"So the million dollar question is who did that?" Alex asked.

He could see she was confused at the reference, but before he could explain, she replied, "That I do not know, but I do know someone who might have the answer."

At that, Cassie offered, "Your father?"

"Yes," Abrianna answered, "he knows far more of the magical arts than I. His talents are far broader."

Alex was just about to ask more about her father when they turned a corner in the roadway and arrived at the far gate. This one had also lost its doors, so it was actually nothing more than an opening in the wall.

"We still need to be out of the dark woods before nightfall or we all die," Cassie announced as they passed through the opening and into the woods beyond.

"Is she always so cheery?" Alex asked Abrianna, as they both watched Cassie take the lead, her horse quickening into a trot.

----*----

It had been several hours since they passed through the far gate. From his earlier review of the map Abrianna carried, Alex was positive they had cleared the edge of the dark woods by now. Even though the sun was setting, Cassie didn't seem to be slowing in her quest to make the city walls nothing but a distant memory.

"Hey!" Alex hollered in an attempt to get her attention.

As she turned, he asked, "Don't we need to think about stopping for the night?"

He had done a fair bit of hiking and camping, he was no novice. He knew that wandering around in the woods after dark was a good way to get injured. She slowed at the question and started to look around on both sides of the path as if looking for something.

It was another good ten minutes of riding before she finally said, "There," while pointing to a small clearing to their left.

Slowing to a stop, they dismounted and walked the four horses into the clearing Cassie indicated. There was a small stream parallel to the trail, on the far side of the clearing, so they led the horses there to water them. While the horses were drinking, both Alex and Cassie started pulling their gear off the horses, while Abrianna collected wood for the fire.

By the time he and Cassie settled the horses in for the night, Abrianna had a sizable collection of wood. She had outlined a fire pit with stones cleared from the surrounding area.

Alex set about getting his bedding on one side of the fire pit. Once he was organized, he started to pull his fire making kit out. It was the same kit he had assembled the first day here.

"What are you doing?" Abrianna asked, as she watched him move over to the pit and kneel to begin the fire making ritual.

"Starting the fire," Alex replied, confused at the question.

"Not that way," she said, as she stepped up next to him.

While he watched, she stared in concentration at the wood in the pit before him. Within seconds, the pile burst into flames.

Not willing to abandon his fire tools just yet, Alex turned and replaced them in the saddlebags. "Do you want me to show you how?" Abrianna asked after he returned.

"If you don't mind?" Alex replied while stealing a sideways glance at Cassie. She had been ignoring the two, focusing on her own activities, until Abrianna made her offer. Now she was standing a few feet away, completely absorbed in their exchange.

With that, Abrianna picked up a stick and waved Alex over to her side.

"Take this," she said, handing him the stick.

"Now hold it out in front of you," she said while motioning for Alex to hold the stick out away from him and over the fire.

Alex did as instructed, and she continued, "Ok, now in this case, we are adding energy to matter. I want you to visualize the loose energy streams flowing into the stick while imagining it burning."

He dropped his hand holding the stick, turned and said, "Do what?"

"Remember, I explained a good part of magic is adding or drawing energy from matter. That energy is either locked in the matter or is free floating, like sunlight or the flames of the fire," she said as she pointed to the flames before them.

"You need to create a mental visualization of what that looks like to you, before you can manipulate it. For me, I think of wisps of smoke that I draw to or from the object." She motioned for Alex to continue the exercise.

Alex turned back to the fire pit, holding the stick out. He imagined rays of sunlight streaming into the stick, igniting it into flame. Suddenly it burst into ash and crumbled from his fingers.

Alex heard Cassie laugh. Abrianna ignored the outburst and said, "Excellent! Now you just need to temper your manipulations. What did you envision?"

Alex dusted the ash from his hand before stooping to grab another stick. "I was thinking about sunbeams."

"Ah, so here is the next piece of the process. The visualization also affects the intensity. As you discovered with the orcs, your visualization of what you called an A 47 manifested into an intense energy discharge. For more subtle work, your visualizations must be delicate," Abrianna explained.

Alex skipped correcting her on the AK-47 reference and lifted the second stick as before. This time he imagined a small swirling cloud of smoke, just at the top of the stick. Within a second, the end burst into flame.

"Perfect!" Abrianna said, complimenting his success.

He dropped the burning branch into the fire, smiling. He felt like a six-year-old receiving praise for his first A on a spelling test. He caught the look on Cassie's face before she returned to her duties. That look, a cross between worry and fear, bothered him.

----*----

Alex woke the next morning before the others, or so he thought. They had spent most of the previous evening eating and in small talk. Abrianna and Alex had discussed more aspects of magic while Cassie sat quietly listening. She either had nothing to offer on the subject or simply chose not to share.

He had been tempted to ask Cassie outright about her apparent distress, but feared it might be some kind of insult. As she had never exhibited the slightest magical ability, it might be like asking someone who was tone deaf to a sing-along.

Rising from his bedroll, he could see Abrianna was still fast asleep. However, Cassie was nowhere to be found. In a panic, he drew his sword, spinning in place as he did so. He stood silently, listening for any indication of foul play. After a moment of complete silence, he realized he was over reacting and sheathed his sword while grabbing the shirt he had discarded at bedtime.

Alex realized he should have little concern for Cassie's ability to take care of herself. She was, after all, a native. Taking his dagger, but leaving the sword, he headed past the horses. He wandered over to the stream while Kinsey drifted off on her own mission. He hadn't bathed in several days now, and he was not overly pleased at the results.

Walking through the trees to the stream, he reached down and touched the water. Alex shook his hand dry, deciding it was going to be a chilly bath. He headed upstream into the more wooded area, in an attempt to try to find a more discreet location to clean up. He followed the stream bank until he turned a corner where the trees had grown so thick they blocked the view upstream.

There, in the center of a pool where the stream had widened, stood Cassie, not more than 10 feet away. She had her back to Alex in a little more than waist deep water. He couldn't help but admire her finely toned body, her well-proportioned figure.

From the clothing spread out drying on the bushes, he assumed she was completely naked. It looked as if she had just finished rinsing out her hair as she was wringing it out in front of her. With her hair normally tied back or tucked away, Alex was surprised to see it was actually quite long and very red. He watched as she tied it in a loose knot at the top of her head, still facing away from him.

The whole image was incredibly alluring, and Alex was seeing her in a completely different light. He found his attraction to her a bit disconcerting as he tried back slowly away without being discovered.

"For a Ranger, you sure make a lot of noise," she said without turning.

"I'm sorry, I didn't know you were here," he replied.

"I didn't mean to disturb you."

"Yet you're still here." She replied, as she dropped to submerge her torso before turning. Facing him now, only her head and shoulders were exposed above the water.

Alex stumbled a bit, taken in by her beauty. With her hair drawn back, her face glistened from the water still dripping off her cheeks; she was stunning. He didn't have a good reply, other than the obvious, so he changed the subject.

"Why are you afraid of me?"

Cassie started to rise as if to challenge the question, then settled back in the water.

"Because you are dangerous and don't even know it. Every time a great wizard appears, people start dying," she said in a matter-of-fact tone.

"I'm no great wizard, and all I want is to go home!" Alex replied in return.

"I wish I could send you," she answered sourly.

"Unfortunately that is not in my power. In case you haven't already figured it out, I am not a mage. While Abrianna received abilities from our ancestors, I have no ability to perform magic as she. I inherited other....traits."

"You have very impressive fighting skills."

"Yes, I have trained my entire life to perfect them. Yet you appeared with equal or better abilities without a day's practice," she snapped.

Alex could see he was not making points with her. He was, however, arriving at the root of Cassie's attitude regarding him.

"Ok, so I get it, I'm the trust fund kid," he replied.

"I have no idea what that means, but if I had any good sense, I would have run you through the day we met you," she snapped back.

"Why would you do that?" Alex asked, irritated at her comment. He had definitely saved their lives that day.

"That fire trick you learned in a few minutes. That takes good magicians months of practice to master. You did it on your second try!"

"So?" Alex answered.

"When I was growing up, I learned about all the great wizards of the past. In every single case, death and destruction followed in their wake, despite all the grand descriptions of their achievements. Not all were evil; many were good and honorable men and women. That still didn't prevent the rest of the world from burning."

"I don't see how this all applies to me."

"You have great power, Abrianna says so. You don't know how to use it now, but in time you will master it and then the world will burn again," she said sadly.

Alex stood there for a second and then started to turn away before Cassandra spoke again.

"Those history lessons I mentioned, I always asked my tutors why someone didn't just kill the wizard before the destruction started. If someone had just slit their throat before their powers grew, so many lives would be saved."

Turning back to her, he waded out into the pool. Standing no more than a foot away, he drew his dagger and extended it to her. "Then why don't you?"

She stared at him for a moment before rising out of the water and standing to face him, the water running down the length of her torso.

"Because I like you."

Cassandra then turned her back to him and waded to the edge of the pool where her clothes hung. As she dressed, Alex headed to the other side of the pool and began to undress. As Cassie left, he began to do his own laundry and bathe.

----*----

By the time Alex returned to the camp, Cassie had packed up most of her and Abrianna's gear. Alex's was left untouched, but that was normal. Kinsey had returned with a fresh kill and proceeded to devour it while Alex packed, and then all three ate their breakfast in silence.

Abrianna swapped several glances between Alex and Cassie during their meal. While she seemed to sense the dynamics between the two had changed, she chose not to ask directly about what had happened. With the camp struck and breakfast completed, Alex finally asked, "Where to now?"

"There is a small town a few hours east of here where we can resupply. It was a major stop on the travel route before the city fell to darkness. It is now no more than a few buildings, but it still services travelers," Abrianna explained.

Cassie had not uttered a word since the stream encounter, so Alex decided that he would take her lead and leave her alone for now. They all saddled up and Alex called to Kinsey as they started back out onto the trail they had been following the prior day.

Cassie took the lead as before, but started at a more reduced pace. She maintained enough distance between herself and the rest to prevent any idle chatter though. Abrianna finally gave Alex a questioning look, tipping her head towards Cassie in an inquiring fashion. Alex decided to play dumb and shrugged. The look on Abrianna's face told Alex she didn't believe him but she pressed no further as they all continued in silence.

Chapter 6

It was close to noon when the three riders reached the outskirts of the community Abrianna had described that morning. In Alex's opinion, calling this place a town was way too generous. It was located in the woods, rather than at its outskirts, and the trail they followed went right down its center. It appeared to be the only visible roadway through town, making avoiding it all but impossible.

Upon closer inspection, Alex could make out the ruins of abandoned structures mixed in the trees. Apparently, as the town had shrunk considerably, the woods had reclaimed the unused structures. The trees now bordered the trail, leaving just enough space to permit travelers to pass.

From this village, he got a better idea of what the ruins on the other side of the dead city had once looked like. In this town, the number of serviceable buildings lining either side of the roadway was no more than three or four per side. Most were constructed of wood, though one two story building was rock masonry on the first floor with a wooden second story. From the sign out front, Alex assumed it was the local pub and boarding house.

The dozen or so people moving about the street paid the three riders little mind, although all eyed Kinsey with apprehension. Once passed the group, most seemed focused on their own business. Cassie reined up in front of a one story wooden structure with various tables in front. Most of the tables were stacked with vegetables, fruits or other perishables. There were crates and sacks that Alex assumed held staples.

All three dismounted and Cassie turned to Alex and held out her hand, "I need some of those coppers and silvers Abrianna gave you. In a town like this, golds would draw undue attention."

Alex handed her the entire leather sack that Abrianna had given him the first day they met. The three moved to one side, away from prying eyes, before she opened it. As he watched, she sorted through the coins, separating out several silvers and even more coppers before handing the bag back to him.

"Why don't you two water the horses while I do a little resupplying," Cassie stated, pointing to a large round stone structure on the far side of the pub. There already were several horses there, all unattended.

With that, Cassie headed into the building while Alex and Abrianna led the four horses and Kinsey over to the watering trough. As they walked along, Abrianna finally spoke up, "So do you want to tell me what happened this morning?"

They led the horses passed the pub and over to the trough. Once there, they turned all four loose to drink. Alex could see a road intersecting the one they traveled. It seemed to be heading north and south, explaining why this place still existed. He doubted the road west they had just traveled got much use.

Alex pondered how to answer the question before finally just deciding to come clean, "I accidently interrupted Cassie while bathing in the stream. I tried to back away, but she apparently heard me coming. I hope I didn't upset her."

Abrianna got a funny expression on her face that seemed a cross between irritation and humor.

She reflected on the information before asking, "Did she say anything to you?"

"I asked her why she feared me. Cassie explained that she thinks I have great magic, and great magic brings great devastation," Alex answered without going into more detail.

Abrianna nodded at the statement, and then asked in surprise, "She said you could call her Cassie?"

"Ah, no, that I only said to you," Alex replied with a grin, and then added, "but I think we've made progress. She said she wouldn't kill me because she liked me."

Abrianna stopped at that, her face serious, "She said she wouldn't kill you because she likes you?"

"I was handing her a dagger to slit my throat at the time, but yes, she did," he answered.

It was then that Cassie walked up with two large sacks slung over one shoulder. She headed right to the packhorse and started stowing her purchases in the various bags slung over its back.

"I was able to get us enough food for seven days, though we shouldn't need near that much. We need to go back for the additional bedding and other cooking supplies," she said over her shoulder. She turned to face them after she was done, only to find a very upset Abrianna confronting her.

"Cassie how could you?" she nearly shouted.

Cassie initially stumbled, struggling with a response before blurting, "Well I didn't drown him!"

Alex was confused at the exchange. They were in waist deep water, so of course she couldn't drown him.

"Because you like him?" Abrianna countered.

At that, Cassie's face turned as red as her hair, "Yes, I like him!" she replied before storming off to get the remainder of her purchases.

"Am I missing something here," Alex said.

"We were in waist deep water."

Abrianna gave a deep sigh before answering, "It's true Cassie doesn't have magical abilities like you or I, but she does have magic. She is part Water Nymph."

Abrianna continued after Alex displayed he had no idea what that meant.

"Long ago, one of our ancestors was seduced by a Water Nymph. They frequently mate with humans and if the offspring are more human than Nymph, they are drowned. In rare cases like ours, they return the baby to the father. While I inherited the ability to do magic anywhere, her magic comes from being in water. While on dry land, she appears entirely human, but in the water, she exudes a sexual aura that human men cannot resist. She intended to lure you to that pool to kill you. She fears your power will bring destruction to us all."

"Ok," Alex replied, while trying to take it all in. Once again, his learning was coming at the near cost of his life.

"Why did she change her mind?" he asked.

Again, Abrianna sighed, "Water Nymphs are generally not dangerous unless you threaten their water source. Many men think them a good omen, as they are a bit promiscuous. However, they can be very dangerous if provoked, and are well known to have jealous tendencies. Once they decide they like something or someone, they can become quite possessive. You have seen how she treats me."

Alex had always assumed Cassie's attitude around Abrianna had more to do with the cousin/princess bodyguard thing. He now realized it had its roots in something else entirely.

At this point, an irritated Cassie reappeared, pushing her way between the two rather than stepping around them. She began tying down the new bedding and other supplies between the four horses. Alex noticed that part of the new acquisitions were intended for his use as well. The way she was tugging and pulling on the various ties securing the new loads, Alex could tell she was also very angry.

"Let's eat," she said as she finished and headed into the pub, pushing her way between the two a second time.

After she passed, Abrianna whispered to Alex as they followed, "I wouldn't give 2 Indian Head pennies for anything she has to say until she calms down."

Alex laughed, but then stopped and took Abrianna's arm, "Where did you get that saying from?"

She looked at him for a moment as if trying to recall, then said, "My father. He says it all the time. Why?"

Before he could reply, Cassie shouted impatiently from the doorway, "Are you two coming?"

"I'll explain later," Alex replied, as they followed Cassie inside.

Stopping at the door, Alex asked Abrianna, "What about Kinsey?"

At that point, Kinsey was standing at Alex's side, looking up.

"It is not uncommon for Rangers to travel with animals. So long as she is well behaved, no one will challenge you," Abrianna said, reaching over to scratch Kinsey between the ears. She received a tail wag in reply.

"I'm more concerned about Cassie misbehaving," Alex replied with a smile.

Entering the pub, it took a moment for Alex's eyes to adjust to the darkened room. He immediately identified Cassie sitting to their left at a small square table, with her back to the wall. He also noted every eye in the room focused on Kinsey.

"Come," Alex said to her as he followed Abrianna to the table. He laughed to himself as he noted the look of disapproval on several faces, but not one person voiced objection. Once seated to Cassie's right, he had Kinsey lay down next to him while Abrianna sat across the table from him.

They sat there in silence for a few minutes before the server made his way to their table. As they waited, Alex surveyed the room. By now, most of the other occupants had gone back to eating, talking, or whatever else they had been doing.

As the man approached their table, he slid to Abrianna's side, putting as much distance between Kinsey and himself as possible. Alex looked the man over, noting that aprons apparently were the norm in this world as in his for serving staff.

"Ranger eats for free. What can I get you?" he asked while looking the two women over. Alex was a bit surprised that there was no discussion of menu options.

"Bread fresh?" Cassie asked.

"Dark and white, baked this morning. A copper for two," the man replied.

"Have some from yesterday for half price."

"Give us two fresh dark now and wrap up eight more to take with us," she directed.

"And to eat now?" He asked.

"I'll take the strips," Cassie stated.

"Stew please," Abrianna said.

At that, everyone looked at Alex, who had no idea what to do.

"Ranger?" the man asked.

"Strips for him as well," Cassie said sharply after waiting a moment.

"A bone for the wolf?" Alex asked.

"Sorry, Ranger, stew bones gonna be a copper," he said hesitantly.

Cassie drew a silver out of a pocket in her belt and said, "Give us three. Two for the trip," She finished while looking at Abrianna.

"Water, ale, or wine," the man asked while snatching up the silver.

"Pitcher of water, and a bowl for Kinsey," Cassie answered, pointing to the wolf where she lay next to Alex.

"You can keep the rest if the service is good."

The man broke out in a broad grin.

"Yes Ma'am!" he replied as he rushed off to fill their order.

Alex did a little math in his head. While he was supposed to eat free, he would have paid anyway on principle. That silver was worth 25 coppers. From what Abrianna told him, each meal should be about two or three coppers, five for the bread and the three for Kinsey's bones. That made a total of 17 coppers at most to pay the bill, so the man had just made a tidy tip if she was satisfied.

The three sat in an awkward silence for a few minutes before Alex finally asked, "Ok, so how did you know what to order?"

Abrianna replied, "Every travel stop provides a standard fare. A local meat, seasoned, roasted, and cut in strips. They will also provide a stew with the same meat, but cubed and cooked with vegetables and tubers, either potato or yam."

Not to be left out, Cassie added, "If there is anything else available they will mention it when they come to the table. Sometimes you will get local specialties. Fish is more common near the coast and rivers."

Just then, the man returned with a clay jug and three wooden cups. He had been balancing a wooden bowl with a bone in it on top of the jug. Again, giving Kinsey a wide berth, he set everything on the table closest to Abrianna and then made a hasty retreat.

Alex took the bone and handed it to an excited Kinsey while he watched Abrianna take the pitcher in both hands. As he had seen her do before, she was silently mouthing a spell, her eyes closed.

"Checking for poison?" Alex asked, more in jest than serious.

"Removing impurities and chilling it," Abrianna replied after a moment, her eyes still closed.

Opening her eyes, she smiled and then took the bowl, pouring until it was about two thirds full. Passing the bowl to Alex, she then filled the three cups before setting the pitcher in the center of the table. Alex smiled at the consideration she was giving Kinsey over their own needs. He placed the bowl next to Kinsey, making sure neither she nor the waiter would spill its contents on the wooden floor.

Abrianna opened the conversation, pandering to Cassandra in an attempt to lighten her mood. They discussed the route to the river, which was their intended destination for the boat ride home. Alex kept silent, letting Abrianna work her magic on her cousin's mood.

In due time, the waiter reappeared, distributing wooden plates and bowls with stew, meat and bread for the three. Although he provided Abrianna a wooden spoon for her stew, Alex noted neither he nor Cassie was offered a fork or knife. He paused, watching the other two begin eating.

Cassie grabbed one of the two loaves and broke it into thirds. She distributed the portions by dropping one on Alex's plate and handing Abrianna hers. She then produced her dagger and began cutting her meat strips into smaller pieces and then skewering them to eat.

"Ah, my dagger has Orc and Gorm Orc on it. Not sure I want it in my mouth," Alex stated hesitantly.

"By all the gods!" Cassie swore while producing one of the many smaller throwing knifes from her belt and handing it to Alex.

"Thanks," he replied a bit sheepishly. He noted Abrianna, smiling broadly as she set her cup down. Apparently, the gesture spoke volumes to her.

From that point, they ate in silence with the only interruption being the waiter returning to fill their water pitcher and deliver the wrapped bread and bones as requested. As they finished their meal, Alex noted four men enter through the front doorway. All were dressed in the same red tunics as the men he had killed protecting Cassie and Abrianna.

One of the four grabbed the waiter as he passed and asked something in a hushed tone. The waiter shrugged, shaking his head no and then hurried off. The four men stood, surveying the room and all its occupants before selecting a table near the entrance.

Alex watched them out of the corner of his eye, trying not to draw attention to himself. As he did so, he observed them whispering to one another. The one Alex took to be the leader apparently asked one of the others for something. The man searched a leather bag he carried and produced a folded parchment which he handed to the leader.

After spending a few minutes reading and then rereading it, he turned again to review all the occupants in the room. When they came in there had been several tables between the four and Alex and his companions. From their current seats, they now had a clear view of Kinsey and the three.

"We may have a problem," Alex said, without taking his eye off the four men.

"Yes, I saw," replied Cassie, her hand slowly moving to the hilt of the sword she had removed so she could sit.

Abrianna collected the bread and bones, all in preparation of a hasty retreat. As the three watched, the leader scanned the room until he settled on their table. Going back to the document he held, he said something, and all four rose. Alex subtly grabbed the edge of their table and rocked it to see if it was fixed to the floor, finding it was not. Turning to Cassie, Alex started a discussion on the quality of the food as the four approached their table.

"You own that horse out front with the Windfall blanket?" the leader asked in a loud voice.

Alex noted they had migrated to the side away from Kinsey, who had growled in disapproval.

"Several," Alex replied, before either of the women could respond.

"Not your business, Ranger," one of the four blurted.

"I'm afraid it is, as neither of these ladies owns a horse. Since that was your question, you must be addressing me," he stated while turning to his right to face the four better.

That took the leader off guard for a moment, then he replied, "We are here on King's business and you all will come with us!"

"What king?" Alex replied as he stood, indicating Cassie and Abrianna remain seated and silent.

That really threw the leader for a loop. It was as if he had never been questioned before.

"Why, his Royal Highness of Windfall," he replied with far too much pomp.

Turning to Cassie and Abrianna, Alex shouted, "This is Windfall? You lied to me."

With the last, he leaned forward as if to pound the table, but instead grabbed the far edge in front of Cassie and pulled hard. The table came flying out squarely into the bunched four, driving them back. Two of the four tripped over other seated occupants, taking them all to the floor in a tangle.

At that, Cassie stood, sword in hand, as Alex drew his own in time to engage the leader's lunge. Cassie stepped in behind them to engage the only other standing antagonist, running him through the neck before he even drew his sword.

Unfortunately, that placed her behind the man battling Alex. With blades locked, a hard shove from Alex sent the man and Cassie tumbling to the floor. By this time, one of the others had recovered his footing and took a swing with his sword at Alex, only to find Kinsey attached to his sword arm. As she bit down, a terrible crunching sound indicated a broken bone.

Alex turned to find the fourth man standing over Cassie, preparing to strike at the prone figure. Alex drew the small throwing knife Cassie had lent him earlier with his left hand. He had tucked it away in his belt subconsciously when the four stood from their table. He quickly released it, driving it cleanly across the short distance into the man's exposed throat.

As Cassie rolled away to Alex's left, the leader rolled to Alex's right and regained his feet in time to take Alex's blade through his chest. The man's chainmail was no deterrent to the thrust. The leader fell to the floor, sliding off Alex's blade, dead.

By now, Cassie had regained her feet and all three surveyed the damage. Abrianna had watched the entire exchange from the wall near Cassie's original seat. At this point, the other patrons had either departed or stood at the far end of the room with the waiter.

Kinsey was still standing over the only surviving soldier, growling any time he made the slightest attempt to move. He was cradling a broken arm, bleeding where Kinsey's teeth had broken the skin.

"Get our things," Alex instructed the others while searching the dead leader for the parchment he had seen him studying. Then, grabbing the wounded man by the collar and pulling him to his feet, he headed out. With Kinsey in the lead, they all walked to the door. Before exiting, Alex stopped and turned, looking for the waiter.

Pulling a coin out of his pouch, he tossed it to the man, "Sorry for the mess. Oh, and we were never here."

He thought the man was going to faint when he realized it was a gold.

"Yes, Ranger," was all he could manage in reply.

As they headed outside, Alex noted Cassie had retrieved her knife from the man's throat.

Pulling up at the stone watering trough, he jerked the wounded man around so he could sit on its edge.

"Sit!"

"Nicely handled," Abrianna stated as she stood next to Alex while he opened the paper.

"I've just about had it with people or things trying to kill me," he replied, glancing at Cassie before returning his attention to the paper in his hand.

"So what does it say?" Abrianna asked, while Cassie stood next to the wounded man, her unsheathed blade still in hand.

"Apparently, you are now a wanted woman. You attempted to kill the royal prince, drove a shaft right through his shoulder from behind." He handed her the document with descriptions of all four of them, Kinsey included.

Chapter 7

While Cassie and Abrianna read the parchment, Alex packed the bread and bones away. Kinsey had parked herself next to the wounded soldier, appearing to be none too pleased at his survival.

"That was Crown Prince Renfeld?" Abrianna finally said, apparently shocked at his involvement in the attack.

"Guess he wasn't too keen on being your husband," Alex said in a disinterested tone.

"He didn't know about that, remember. I was simply going as my father's representative," she snapped.

Alex stopped for a moment and then asked, "Abrianna, who would inherit if your father had no heirs?"

Abrianna looked up from reading the paper for the 10th time, "Well, several people could make a valid claim, Cassie included."

Alex gave Cassie a knowing look before the redhead replied, "Don't even think it!"

With a laugh, he asked, "Seriously, would Windfall have any direct claim to those lands?"

Abrianna thought about the question before replying, "Not directly. However, with Cassie and me both assassinated, there would be none in line to rally the army to oppose their invasion if my father was gone. They could take Great Vale and assume the throne before any resistance could be mounted."

"Well then, my guess is the crown prince of Windfall wants to expand his kingdom," Alex replied, while moving up next to the wounded man.

"So tell me my friend, how many of you are there out looking for us?" Alex asked while resting his hand on the man's broken arm. The wince he received in return ensured he had the man's entire attention.

"Patrols have been dispatched to every community between here and the river. They were also sent south to all checkpoints to block passage across the border," he replied.

"Your orders?" he asked the man, his hand still in place on his arm.

The man hesitated for a moment, but he started as soon as Alex's fingers flexed on his arm, "We are to capture you alive if possible, but if not, return with your heads."

At that, Alex removed his hand and turned to the women, "I guess we better stock up, food sources are going to be in short supply in the future. I'll deal with this one."

Both Cassie and Abrianna stared at Alex as if they were seeing him for the very first time.

"You can be a hard man," Cassie said as she turned and headed back to the dry goods store for more shopping.

"Now that she's gone, can you heal him and wipe his memory?" Alex asked Abrianna quietly.

At that, Abrianna laughed and said, "Not quite as ruthless as you appear. Yes, I can do as you ask, but the locals will still know what happened."

Reaching into his pouch, he pulled out a few more golds. Holding them up, he said, "I can work a little memory magic of my own. I will guarantee they only remember a Ranger killed those three over drinks and stun spelled this one. Will you be ok while I…?" he asked while pointing at the pub.

"With Kinsey here, yes," she replied with a smile.

Alex went into the pub, where he found several people busy cleaning up the mess and dragging the three dead bodies out the back of the building. Without indicating he noticed anything, he noted the pile of items stripped from bodies before removal in the back of the room.

With the distribution of coin and a few practiced statements, he left the locals to their business. He was just in time to catch Cassie returning with her latest load. The wounded man was now sitting in the dirt, his back to the watering trough, and arm apparently on the mend. He looked to be sleeping peacefully.

"All ready?" Alex asked.

"When he wakes, he won't remember a thing except a Ranger killing the others in a fight over drink," Abrianna responded.

Cassie glanced at Alex with a look of confusion. He figured she had expected him to dispatch the man out of hand.

"Waste not, want not," he said while pulling their horses around to stow the latest supplies. For the first time, Alex caught the subtle indications of a smile on Cassie's face.

Once everything was properly stowed, the three mounted and with Kinsey falling in next to Alex, headed east. Cassie started in the lead as before, only this time she didn't put the distance between her and the rest that she had previously. Abrianna caught Alex's eye, and with a bob of her head, indicated he should catch up with her.

Spurring his mount forward, he slowly drew abreast of Cassie. She turned her head to acknowledge his presence without speaking and then went back to focusing on the trail ahead. In due course, she finally spoke to him.

"Thank you for saving my life," she said curtly.

"Good thing you didn't kill me after all," he replied with a smile.

At that, she turned to face him, "I didn't want to, you know. I was only thinking of the people that are likely to die in your future."

Upon reflection, Alex couldn't argue with her. He hadn't been here for more than a few days and already nine men and a greater number of mythical creatures had perished by his hand. While an argument could be made that it was all in self-defense, he didn't see that Cassie would care.

Not sure what to say at that point, he decided to change the subject, "So, Water Nymph, huh?"

Cassie seemed to stiffen at the question, and then Alex could see her relax as she replied, "Yeah, growing up I was always drawn to the water. It wasn't until I was about 13 that the reason became apparent. Brie and I were swimming in the small river near Great Vale, when we noticed the local boys lining the bank, watching us. From then on, my mother would never let me near water in public. That is also when I began serious combat training."

"That gives a whole new meaning to having to beat them off with a stick," Alex replied with a laugh. Cassie gave him a look of confusion.

"It's a saying where I come from. Means you were so pretty you had to beat them off with a stick," he explained. "It's a compliment."

That actually produced a smile from Cassie.

"So how does it work, the nymph magic?" Alex asked.

Cassie paused for a moment, and then replied, "When I am in water, it's like this whole other part of me comes alive. It enhances all my senses, magnifying my sight, smell, and hearing. My skin seems to tingle all over. I know everything in the water for miles around me."

"So that's how you heard me coming," Alex asked.

Cassie actually laughed, blushing slightly. "That was unfair of me. I knew where you were the minute you touched the water in the stream. As opposed to nymphs who are tied to one place, any water I occupy becomes an extension of my being."

"And your control over men?" Alex asked.

That drew an even deeper blush.

"Yes, while I'm in the water I have the ability to influence men. I can make them do just about anything I want, but its effect dissipates once I leave the water."

"Then why am I still so attracted to you?" Alex said to himself. He couldn't shake the memory of Cassie standing waist deep in the stream.

Turning to look back, he caught a glimpse of Abrianna, a smile spread wide across her face.

As they rode along, Alex continued to chat with Cassie, mostly talking about what lay ahead. They would need to camp at least one more night, and then the trip south would be one more day by water. Their conversation continued along those lines for quite a while.

----*----

Abrianna rode in silence, watching her two companions talk casually with one another. To anyone less familiar with the parties involved, they would see nothing particularly special about the exchange. To Abrianna though, it was nothing less than miraculous.

She had known Cassie her entire life, and not once had she ever seen her interact with a member of the opposite sex as she did with Alex. While it was common knowledge that nymphs had the ability to attract men, a lesser-known fact was they could push men away with equal efficiency.

Once Cassie's true nature had revealed itself, she had watched her reject every suitor that attempted to woo her. She had taken up every masculine endeavor she could convince her uncle, the king, to allow. With those skills, she had challenged and beat into submission every nobleman foolish enough to cross swords with her.

Now Abrianna was watching her openly flirt with this lost Ranger. She was actually acting like a lady... well as much of a lady as Cassie could muster. Abrianna could tell by their relaxed posture and mannerisms that the two were enjoying each other's company.

Perhaps the attraction was the fact that Alex saved their lives on several occasions, or that he possessed great magical powers. Either way, he had brought down the walls and reached a part of Cassie that hadn't been seen since childhood.

Abrianna's fear was that her father would find a way to send the Ranger away, and Cassie's happiness with him.

----*----

The three found a nice meadow just before sunset, and decided to stop for the day. By now, they all had the drill down, and were able to put their campsite in order quickly. Alex took all the horses to the stream for watering after removing their loads and saddles.

Upon his return, he noted three bedrolls laid out, his just slightly farther to one side, but decidedly not opposite the other two. Alex caught Abrianna's eye, nodding towards the bedding. She pointed to Cassie with a smile.

Abrianna had worked her magic as well; the fire was already burning with a pile of wood stacked neatly nearby. Cassie was rummaging through the supply bags, withdrawing various items acquired earlier that day. As he and Abrianna watched, Cassie assembled and prepared a meal.

When all was ready, Cassie produced one of the bones purchased from the pub earlier that day and tossed it to Kinsey before passing out everyone else's meal. As he was eating the meat, roasted over the campfire, something occurred to Alex.

"Hey, again this may sound stupid, but what keeps the meat from spoiling?"

"Magic!" Cassie offered with a bit of a giggle.

Even Abrianna turned to look at Cassie after the reply. Suppressing a giggle of her own at Cassie's outburst, Abrianna replied, "Most successful shopkeepers have a little magical ability or have access to a mage. They add a small amount of energy into the meat to extend its spoilage limits. It rarely adds more than a day or two, but in most cases that's plenty."

The three continued to chat while they ate, Cassie flirting during the entire time. Finally, Abrianna asked her to go check on the horses while she and Alex cleaned up. Once she was out of earshot, Abrianna pulled Alex to one side. In whispered tones, she began explaining Cassie's outbursts.

"Alex, remember how I mentioned that nymphs can be somewhat promiscuous? Well, it happens when they take a fancy to someone. It appears Cassie has taken more than a passing interest in you."

After taking a deep breath, Alex confessed, "I can't say I don't feel the same way. After you explained her, well, magic, I thought it was just that. However, she said earlier today that it should wear off shortly after leaving the water. It's not wearing off."

Alex was surprised to see the smile on Abrianna's face.

"That's a relief. I was afraid that you didn't share her interest, with all the comments of returning home."

At that, Alex winced. "Yeah, that's a problem."

Abrianna interrupted him before he could say any more, "Well, not one that will be solved soon. I need to tell you this before she returns.

Cassie has always kept men at arm's length. Should she develop feelings for one, well, she gets silly. Normally I would rejoice at her interest in you, but we are still far from home and we need her sharp and focused. Whatever happens, do not let her seduce you. If that happens…"

Abrianna was cut short with Cassie's return. She embraced Abrianna with a hug and then turned to Alex. The two stood no more than inches apart, locked in a gaze. As Alex reached for Cassie, Abrianna announced, "Ok, time for bed."

Abrianna grabbed Cassie's arm and spun her around to face her.

"Come on honey, time for bed," Abrianna repeated, leading her to the bedroll farthest from Alex's.

He watched Abrianna lead her away, receiving a look of disappointment from Cassie and a sharp glare from Abrianna at his clear failure of control.

Once everyone had settled in, Alex found himself bedded down on the far side from Cassie. Both Abrianna and Kinsey had put themselves between the couple.

----*----

The next morning Alex woke to find Cassie's hand covering his mouth. She was holding a finger to her lips, indicating he should be quiet and then pointed to Abrianna, still sound asleep nearby. Kinsey however was wide-awake, and while unmoving, was keeping her keen eyes directed at the two.

Rising as quietly as he could, he pulled his boots on and followed Cassie, with Kinsey following him. Alex could see she was heading to the stream. He hoped it was so the sound of the moving water would cover their conversation. Upon reaching their destination, Cassie first slipped off her boots and then her pants, leaving her tunic in place. It was off white and somewhat big on her. The shirt reminded Alex of a long sleeved mini-dress, as it stopped mid-thigh.

As she started to wade out into the stream, Alex started to feel like he had made a mistake in following her. Before he could say anything, Cassie turned and held out her arms, beckoning him to join her.

At first, he resisted, and then it was as if he were seeing her for the first time.

He could see her glow, in a turquoise blue aura, similar to the tropical waters of the Caribbean. Her amazing green eyes and red hair highlighted a cherub face, alluring in its beauty. He took one step, and then another, not bothering to remove his boots or pants. Soon he found himself standing knee deep in the stream, face to face with Cassie.

As he started to lean in for a kiss, Kinsey let go with a snarl and growl that caused them both to turn around and look.

"Well, well, what do we have here?"

On the bank behind them was a raggedy group of five men, all well armed. One had a frightened

Abrianna in his grasp, a knife to her throat. With the spell broken, Alex suddenly realized neither had brought a weapon. As he turned to face the group, still in the stream next to Cassie, she took his hand in hers.

"So you all wouldn't be the three that the Windfall patrols are looking for, are you?" Asked the same man who spoke initially.

"I wouldn't know," Alex replied.

"They said finding a Ranger and two women traveling with a black wolf would earn us ten golds a head," the man replied, "wolf included." Kinsey replied with another snarl, her teeth bared.

"I think you have the wrong people, I would suggest you retreat while you still can," Alex stated, with a bravado he didn't feel.

"Don't see that you are in any position to give orders here, Ranger. I think we need to search you all for weapons, starting with these two beauties," the man pointed to Cassie and Abrianna with his sword.

"And then let the soldiers decide."

The crude reference to molesting the women gave Alex an idea. He whispered to Cassie, "Charm them."

From the corner of his eye, he could see her shaking her head no. "I've never….."

Alex realized that Cassie had never used her talents on any man before him. It made him feel dirty to ask her, but he didn't see any other option.

"Cassie, just entrance them, I'll take care of the rest," he said, trying to reassure her. "They will hurt Brie."

She shook her head no again and then stopped. Alex felt her squeeze his hand tightly and then let go. He turned his head slightly toward her as she began to glow as before.

"Look away!" she mouthed as she returned her focus on the five intruders.

Alex did as instructed. He watched as the five stared at first in curiosity, and then in awe.

"Tell them to drop their weapons," Alex whispered, trying not to break her concentration.

Taking the lead from Alex, she had them all disarm, releasing Abrianna in the process. She made them all sit while Alex tied each one to a nearby stand of trees. Abrianna gathered all the abandoned weapons and tossed them in the stream, far from the bound men.

Alex was very careful to avoid looking at Cassie during the entire time. Finally, once he was sure all were secure, he declared, "We are good, Cassie."

Looking up from the kneeling position he was in, while checking the last of the bonds, he was gifted with a last look of her fading magic. It took a minute for him to shake it off before he could get up and approach her.

Cassie was back on the bank, pulling her pants on when he reached out to help.

"Get away from me!" she snapped, grabbing her boots, and stomping back to their camp in bare feet.

Alex watched her leave and then turned to Abrianna.

"Are you ok?"

"Well, I woke up with a knife at my throat, my protectors nowhere to be found. Then a band of outlaws, who apparently intended to assault us and turn us in for bounty, dragged me here. Other than that, I'm just great," she replied, obviously not happy with Alex, Kinsey, or Cassie.

"Ah, ok. Can you tell me why Cassie is now pissed at me?" he asked, hoping a subject change would help.

"If pissed means angry, no, but I suggest we pack up and leave this place before her charm spell wears off," she replied, turning and heading back to camp herself.

With that, Alex followed Abrianna back to camp, where they found Cassandra furiously packing up all their gear, except for anything involving Alex. The two joined in, and in a very short time, all were in the saddle and headed east. Alex could just make out the yelling in the distance, from the men they left tied to the trees.

He again found himself responsible for the packhorse and trailing the two women at a good distance. At this point, both seemed incredibly angry with him.

"Had to come to an exotic, magical land just to piss off the local women because there obviously weren't enough to piss off at home," he mumbled to himself as he rode along with Kinsey happily trotting just ahead.

Chapter 8

They rode for several hours in silence, only stopping long enough to rest the horses and eat a much delayed breakfast. While Abrianna seemed to be cooling off from the morning's fiasco, Cassandra wouldn't talk to either of them. With Abrianna, she was at least civil; with Alex, however, she was outright hostile, rebuffing any attempt he made to assist or console her.

When they stopped to fill their water skins, he was about to attempt connecting with Cassie again, but caught Abrianna waving him off. Cassie was headed to a nearby spring, with everyone but Alex's water skin in hand. Once she disappeared into the trees, Abrianna motioned him over.

"Leave her be for now. I have never seen her this angry," she said quietly.

"What did I do?" Alex asked. He was confused at what he possibly could have done to put her in such a state.

"Honestly, I have no idea. I have never seen her like this," Abrianna replied, shaking her head.

----*----

Cassie walked straight for the spring. The water nymph in her gave her the natural ability to locate water with ease.

This spring was very old and surrounded by large flat stones. The clear cool water tugged at Cassie's soul, but something deep inside told her this was not hers. She was welcome to take her fill, but then she must leave.

After filling the water skins, she removed her boots and put her feet in the cool water. As she sat there brooding, a vision of loveliness appeared before her.

She was fair skinned and blonde, her long hair falling both in front and behind her to her waist. Her gown was white and gauzy, still dry though she had just emerged from the pool. Cassie knew water nymphs could displace water when they wished.

"What's wrong, Sister?" The nymph asked.

"I'm not your sister," Cassie snapped in return, looking down at her feet in the pool.

"You may hide your true nature from others, but you cannot from me," she replied lightly, not put off in the least by Cassie's rudeness.

"I have spent my entire life suppressing that part of me. I get around men I like and I become stupid, flirty and want to do things….well, I won't say what things."

The nymph laughed, "I know what things. Since you have tried to hide from yourself, you have never learned to control those urges. It takes practice. Then again, with some men, why even try?"

"How does one practice being in love?" Cassie asked, in a quiet tone, surprised to hear the words pass her lips.

"Oh," the nymph replied, "with the human man dressed like a Ranger? You know he is quite powerful, magically speaking."

"Yes, I should have drowned him," she replied in a depressed voice.

Again, the nymph laughed, "You might have tried, but he is touched by Elf magic." She became serious and said, "I fear he is here to help restore the Balance. If that is true, you are all in a lot of trouble."

"What balance?" Cassie asked.

"I cannot say any more on the subject. The Elves are quite secretive on such things and do not take kindly to those that gossip about their business. Sister, take my advice and embrace your true nature with this man while you are able. If he is what I think he is, you may not live long enough to find another." With that the nymph slid slowly back into the pool and disappeared from sight.

Cassie considered the nymph's advice as she gathered her things.

----*----

Alex and Abrianna had been sitting mostly in silence, waiting for Cassie to return. He had been tempted to take his water skin to the spring as Cassie had left it purposely behind. However, Abrianna stopped him, suggesting Cassie just might need some alone time at the spring. Water was her medium and it might help calm her.

They both turned at the sound of Cassie's return. She walked up to them, took one of the skins, and shoved it at Alex.

"For you," was all she said as she continued on to the horses.

"I see that as a huge improvement," Abrianna said with a broad smile. They mounted up and returned to the trail, heading east. While Alex was again in the rear with the packhorse in tow, he could tell the mood of the women was significantly lighter than before. They rode in silence for the first half hour before Cassie finally spoke to Abrianna.

"I suggest we avoid Portsward if at all possible. Those bandits we left tied to the trees had mentioned the soldiers looking for us."

Abrianna considered her statement, and then replied, "We might cut south some then. There are several smaller settlements along the banks of the river there. We may find passage on a river barge or fishing boat."

Alex was in earshot of the entire exchange, even though he hadn't been included in the conversation. He noted they were traveling much closer to him than earlier; Cassie even glanced back from time to time, as if to check on him. He would smile, acknowledging her, but she would simply return her attention to the trail ahead.

He considered it progress that she wasn't scowling at him, but he was still clueless at the severe attitude change. As he rode along, Kinsey trotted at his side now, never wandering too far from him or the trail. He was happy having at least one female in his life content with his company.

They traveled the entire day at a steady pace. With the risk of discovery hanging over their heads, it made good sense to get to the river as quickly as possible. On two occasions, they had to duck into the woods as travelers passed by, headed west. Fortunately, both groups seemed to be ignorant of the noise they were making, as even Alex detected their coming long before they were seen.

As dusk approached, they cleared the heavily wooded forest and emerged onto rolling green hills dotted with occasional stands of trees. In the distance, to his left, Alex saw what he suspected was Portsward. He could see a substantial number of buildings, and in the waning sunlight, he could make out several lighted windows. Combined with all the chimney smoke, it appeared to be a thriving community.

On the far side of town, he could just make out the docks with ships of various sizes anchored in the river. The river T'ybel itself was as big as any Alex had seen. He had been to both the Mississippi and Missouri Rivers and this one was equal to either.

As he continued to scan right, he made out several smaller collections of buildings well outside of town. The docks were smaller and there were far fewer ships moored nearby. These had that look of less affluent, lower income locations. Beyond that was barren riverbank for as far south as he could see.

Cassie and Abrianna had pulled up, surveying the scene before them, allowing Alex to come abreast of them.

"Portsward," Abrianna said, indicating the large community and confirming Alex's assumption.

"I don't have to point out the soldiers at the checkpoint," Alex said flatly.

He had noticed in his earlier appraisal that the road they traveled eventually led straight into the center of town. That same roadway had soldiers parked just outside of town checking everyone who passed by. The telltale behavior was they only molested travelers heading into Portsward.

"Luckily, we aren't going there," Abrianna replied, "After dark, we will head to those buildings south of town. That's where the fishermen come in. Portsward pushed them out of town long ago to reduce the smell."

Alex could see several vessels that had the look of working boats, not intended for passenger usage.

"I seriously doubt there are no soldiers about," Alex commented while pointing at the docks.

"Cassie and I will go in and secure passage. Two women are far less obvious than a Ranger and his wolf," she replied.

"Besides, you have no idea what you are doing," Cassie said, finally breaking her silence with him.

Both Abrianna and Alex turned to look at her. The fact that she had said what should have been a scathing insult, with a caring and concerned tone, had taken them both by surprise.

"We will talk later," she said to Alex, before turning back to Abrianna "Let's get moving."

By now, the sun was setting, and the roadway was getting hard to follow. They had to pick their way carefully across open country to ensure they didn't run afoul of any holes or crevasses. Thankfully, the buildings they were heading to were well lit and off the main trail leading to Portsward proper.

By the time they reached the edge of the southernmost group of buildings, it had been dark for quite a while. Huddled in an alley, they could hear the sounds from a nearby pub.

"Normally I would say we cut the packhorse loose at this point, but it may help pay our passage," Abrianna said while holding her hand out to Alex. After a second, he realized she wanted his coin bag. Handing it over, he commented, "I'm not sure I like the idea of you two wandering the docks at night. Where I come from it's not the safest place."

"Oh, it's not safe here either," Cassie replied, while handing Alex the reins of their horses. With a smile, she turned and followed in Abrianna's wake.

Alex looked down at Kinsey, who was sitting calmly watching him, and waiting. After what seemed far too long, both women came back with a third person.

"Alex, this is Captain Hagen. She has a cargo boat for hire," Abrianna said.

Captain Hagen's eyes however, never left the black wolf at Alex's side.

Glancing back at Alex, she asked, "You a Ranger?"

Catching the subtle nod from Cassie, Alex replied, "Yes."

At that, she seemed somewhat satisfied, "You keep that wolf in line, or it's swimming home."

Alex reached down to scratch between Kinsey's ears in a show of control. With that, Cassie went over to the packhorse and removed several items, including her armor, before saying, "Here's your horse. I'd advise burning the saddle blanket."

Captain Hagen came around and took the reins from Cassie, inspecting the horse. After a few minutes, she said, "We leave in one hour. Have your horses and any other supplies at the dock before then."

They watched as the captain led the horse off into the darkness.

"Horses?" Alex asked.

"Yes, once we get to Rivers Edge, it is still more than a day's ride to Great Vale. Don't worry, her vessel is quite large and can accommodate our mounts and equipment," Abrianna said.

Alex turned to watch Cassie stow all that she had removed from the packhorse between the remaining three mounts. While he wouldn't call her manner warm, she was at least far less hostile to him. In short order, she had everything ready to go. They led their horses around back behind the buildings and well into the darkness.

Following Abrianna south, they rounded the last of the buildings in the row and turned left to the river. They stopped right before the building gave way to the wharf that granted access to the various piers extending out into the water.

Peering around the corner, Alex was surprised to see the ships nosed into the wharf. The bows were squared to allow loading ramps to be dropped in place permitting easy on and off access of cargo. Two ships down from where they stood was Captain Hagen, directing her crew in preparations for departure. Unfortunately, just beyond her were two Windfall soldiers, slowly patrolling the length of the wharf.

Turning to the women, Alex said, "Well, I can kill them." He was gratified to see both shake their heads no.

"I suggest we try going one at a time. Perhaps they won't pay undue attention to single passengers," Abrianna replied.

"And Kinsey?" Alex asked, "They are not going to miss a two hundred pound black wolf?"

Abrianna thought for a minute and said, "Will she come with me?"

Alex had to think for a minute but replied, "I think so."

Abrianna smiled. "Ok, I'll go first then as this will only last a short time."

Reaching down to place both hands on the wolf, Abrianna closed her eyes and began whispering something Alex couldn't hear. After a few seconds, he could see Kinsey's coat start to change. It lightened up until it was almost white and her fur looked longer. Alex wasn't sure what she was supposed to be, but she looked nothing like a black wolf.

"Many of the aristocracy prefer exotic pets. Sometimes they will have a mage alter an animal to appear unusual, making a one of a kind creation," Abrianna replied, responding to the unasked question.

"Won't someone question aristocracy traveling on a river barge?" Alex asked.

Smiling again, Abrianna replied, "The ne'er do well imitate the aristocracy."

With that, she took the reins of Alex's black mare and called Kinsey to follow. Kinsey looked at Alex, who pointed to Abrianna and said, "Go with Abrianna."

She looked at Abrianna and then back to Alex before trotting off behind the woman.

Alex and Cassie watched from the shadows as Abrianna led the horse and Kinsey up to Captain Hagen. The combination of black horse and white wolf certainly did look trendy and upscale.

They exchanged a few words, followed by the captain instructing a crewmember to assist in loading the horse. With Kinsey close behind, Abrianna boarded using the ramp on the bow, leaving the captain alone on the wharf once more.

The two soldiers had paid no attention to the exchange as they had intercepted a larger party headed to an adjacent barge.

"Ok, your turn," Alex said to Cassie.

They had agreed it might be best for Cassie to take the two horses at once, leaving Alex free to intercede should things go badly. They had also taken the precaution of flipping the saddle blankets upside down, hiding the Windfall colors. They weren't suitable to ride that way, but for this, it was fine.

They both stepped back from the corner while Cassie gathered the reins in her hand. As she turned to go, she stopped and faced Alex. No more than inches apart, she stared into his eyes, pausing as if to say something. Impulsively she gave him a quick kiss and then hurried off around the corner.

That was absolutely the last thing Alex expected, so he was slow to respond. She was gone before he could say a word, and with bow in hand, he moved to the corner to cover her. As he watched, she casually led the horses to Captain Hagen's loading ramp. Again, he watched as the two exchanged a few words and she repeated the orders to assist in loading the animals.

As Cassie boarded the horses, Alex could see Abrianna and Kinsey on the deck above, watching.

By now, the soldiers had satisfied themselves that the people they were interrogating were not those whom they were seeking. One of them had noticed Cassie loading the horses and as Alex watched, they went to the captain.

After a brisk exchange of words, the pair engaged in an intense argument with Captain Hagen. Unstringing his bow, Alex stepped out of the shadows using his bow like a walking stick. He casually wandered down the wharf, evaluating the situation.

"Problem gentleman?" he asked as he reached the three.

"Not your business, Ranger," one of the two soldiers snapped.

Undaunted by the remark, Alex continued while handing the captain his bow and then placing a hand on each soldier's shoulders, "You know, I had a fellow say that very thing to me the other day. I had to explain to him as well that he was very much mistaken."

Suddenly both soldiers started hopping around as if they were on fire. They began beating their hands all over their bodies and then ran off down the wharf and into the darkness. The sound of splashing could be detected after a moment.

Alex looked at Captain Hagen and said, "About time we departed, isn't it?"

Chapter 9

The next morning Alex found himself alone on deck, watching the riverbank go by as they traveled downstream. In the daylight, he could see more details about the craft they traveled in. The bow was squared off at the top but became more rounded as it tapered and approached the waterline.

There was a large central mast with a square sail, currently stowed, allowing them to go with the wind when possible. The stern was similar to the bow, he presumed to allow them to go stern in for cargo transfer if desired.

At about 120 feet long and 30 feet wide, it had a main deck for some cargo, an enclosed galley, and crew's quarters with an upper deck containing passenger staterooms. Below decks was 100% cargo space, with accommodations for the horses. Both the bow and stern had open areas where the upper deck stopped short.

Alex laughed to himself. Calling the passenger rooms' staterooms was a great exaggeration. His room was a double bunk on one wall, with a small sink and storage space for luggage, which in his case were his saddlebags. There were common heads, or bathrooms, at both ends of a long central hallway. Abrianna and Cassie shared the cabin across from his.

Once they departed Portsward last night without further incident, the two women had retreated to their room. Kinsey and Alex were left to wander the deck, exploring the ship, before retiring to their own quarters.

That morning Kinsey had shown no indications of rising, once Alex was up, so he left her in the room while he further investigated the ship. As he debated raiding the galley, Cassie appeared from the passage and headed toward him.

"Good morning," Alex said, greeting her with a smile.

"Good morning to you," she replied, with more enthusiasm than he had seen from her in days.

"I love being on the water," she added, as if to explain her good mood.

Leaning on the rail next to Alex, and looking out on the riverbank, Cassie asked with a bit of a giggle,

"So what did you do to those soldiers last night?"

Alex laughed before replying, "I used the trick Abrianna taught me and added a little energy to their chainmail."

Laughing now, Cassie replied, "Alex, that's amazing. That is not junior level magic. It could have backfired on you."

"Yeah, but I was running out of ideas that didn't involve death."

Without looking at him, Cassie said, "I'm sorry I was so angry with you. There is so much I need to explain. And so much I don't understand myself."

Alex wasn't sure what to say, so as they stood leaning on the rail, shoulder to shoulder, he took her hand in his.

----*----

Abrianna was in her cabin assessing everything she had learned last night. She and Cassie had been up late, and Cassie had let the dam burst. She now understood her cousin's outburst and anger, not at Alex, but at what he represented. For Cassie to find love, she was going to have to address all that she had been suppressing her entire life.

What Abrianna was concerned about was what the nymph had revealed to Cassie at the spring; Alex was somehow involved with an Elf plot to restore the balance. What balance, which Elves?

Like all other creatures, the Elves were a multifaceted race. There were Dark Elves that shunned most of the peace loving species. Then there were the Wood and Aquatic Elves, which were most commonly involved in the interspecies activities creating stability in the realms.

It explained the weapons Alex was provided upon his arrival, but not the intent. It was also the last part of Cassie's tale that had her most concerned. She said the nymph at the spring didn't believe they would survive Alex's interaction. What was it the nymph had said to Cassie? "If he is what I think he is, you may not live long enough to find another."

That morning she had told Cassie to go to Alex and make up with him. She had told her honestly that she thought he was a good man and worth her trust. Privately she questioned if being a good man was going to be enough to save them from whatever was coming.

----*----

Alex and Cassie met Abrianna in the galley, the latter waving them in from the passenger deck above the main deck. She had thoughtfully checked in on Kinsey before heading down from the passenger quarters and released her from the confines of their room. Alex would have normally left the door ajar, however on a moving vessel that was unwise.

The galley was clean and neat if spartan in appearance. The rectangular tables and benches were in orderly rows and all were fixed to the deck. The three selected a table and slid onto their benches, starting at one end or the other. Kinsey elected to lay under the table rather than in the aisle between the benches.

Alex was surprised to learn there was a galley steward to serve them, rather than a serve yourself arrangement. The steward had delivered some sort of fruit juice when Alex caught the smirk on Abrianna's face. Cassie had elected to sit next to Alex, rather than with her, across from him, as had been more the norm.

Looking around the galley, Alex had concluded that they must be the only paying passengers on the ship. The few tables currently occupied beyond their own had the look of crew. His attention was brought back to the table when Cassie tapped his hand.

"Hey, are you listening?" she asked in a playful tone.

"Huh, no, I'm sorry. Hey, are we the only passengers on this boat?" He asked.

"Yes, Captain Hagen said this was normally a cargo run. Trade goods brought in from Windfall in the west and from Two Thorns in the eastern mountains are shipped south. They make a couple of stops along the way before the final landing at Rivers Edge. There they unload and on the return run they bring grain and produce from Great Vale to those same markets," replied Abrianna.

"Sorry, so what were you saying?" Alex asked Cassie, with a smile.

"Brie and I were talking last night, and we think you should apprentice with her father. He is the most accomplished wizard in all of A'nland and can teach you more control." Cassie was far more pleasant than the day before.

Alex noted that the statement included no mention of helping him return home. As he was in limbo on the subject, with the focus of his desire seated next to him, he remained mute on the issue.

"That assumes your father is even interested in taking on an apprentice."

"The only person he dotes on as much as his daughter, is his niece," Abrianna stated with a smile.

The implications of the statement were clear to Alex, but before he could say any more, the steward returned with four plates full of food. He placed one plate in front of each of the three people and slid the fourth under the table near Kinsey. Alex had noted the final plate held twice as much food as the others.

"I told them that if Kinsey was fed well, she was less likely to eat anyone," Abrianna said with a huge smile.

That brought a laugh from everyone at the table. Alex still had a vision of the little fifty-pound dog that wandered the wilderness with him. The thought of her devouring anyone was laughable.

Looking down at his plate, he swore it looked like egg battered bread similar to French Toast with a slice of meat on the side. He cut a piece off the bread and found it sweetened with honey. The meat was the seasoned strips he had experienced in the pub. "What is this?"

"Oh, I'm sorry, but the food on these ships is fairly simple. This bread is likely yesterdays or maybe even the day before, soaked in an egg batter to soften it up; at home, we call it French Toast. They added honey to this batch to sweeten it some. The meat you've had before. Most times you have to rough it on these cargo transports," Abrianna explained.

Two things stuck with Alex. The first was she had assumed he was complaining when in fact he loved French Toast and had eaten far more simple fare. The second was that was at least the second time she had used an idiom Alex recognized from his own world. The likelihood that Indian Head penny or French Toast had occurred independently in both places was remote. Someone in Abrianna's home had exposure to Alex's world.

"Oh, I'm not complaining, it's just that this is like breakfast at home," he replied with a smile.

At that, he got a look from both women. It was something like a cross between empathy, and pity for having grown up poor. He did not intend to correct their impressions of his background.

They ate their fill, chatting casually. For the first time since they had met, they were in no rush to do anything and no one was trying to kill them. By the time everyone was finished, a distinct bump reverberated throughout the ship.

Returning to the main deck with Kinsey following behind, they discovered the ship had docked. They had arrived at the first of several stops along their route to Rivers Edge where the group would disembark. With the ship nosed in as it had been in Portsward, the dockworkers dropped a ramp and the crew opened the cargo access.

Alex led everyone up to the passenger deck where they could see the entire operation without interfering with the crew. As they watched, a wooden dock crane lifted several crates from within the ship's hold.

Either the worker underestimated the weight of the crates, or was inexperienced, but he dropped the crates violently on the dock. Upon impact, the bottom wooden box came apart, spilling its contents. Alex could clearly identify swords and various knives dumped all over the wharf.

"That must be from Two Thorns," Cassie commented.

Turning to look at her, Alex asked, "What makes you think that?"

"Two Thorns is surrounded by mines. The smiths there are renowned for their metal working skills. They are also in the center of the Mountain Dwarves' domain. There are rumors that much of what they claim to make is actually bartered from the Dwarves," Abrianna offered. "Their swords are prized by armies all over the realms. Most palace guards are armed with Two Thorns blades when Elven are unavailable."

"Abrianna is far more educated on the politics and economics of the area," Cassie replied with a smile.

"I am more versed in the usage of their products."

It made Alex smile to see this part of Cassie. Compared to their first few days together, she was far more lighthearted and playful. She wasn't even in the water, and she was enchanting him. They watched as the dockworkers on the wharf scrambled to collect all the loose items.

"So we are transporting weapons?" Alex asked.

Abrianna thought for a moment and then replied, "Now that you mention it that is a large shipment for this region. That was three crates, enough blades for 100 men per crate."

"Are these your father's people?" Alex asked; he was starting to get the nagging feeling that trouble was brewing.

"No, we are still well north of our lands," she replied, the light dawning in her eyes as well.

"Let's take a look in the hold after they are finished here," Alex suggested.

While they watched the activity on the docks, Alex noted that there was a lot of unloading with very little being sent the other way. It had the distinct look of a provisioning mission. The other thing that caught Alex's eye was the men with the wagons waiting to be loaded. They were all in civilian dress, but had the same look as all the Windfall soldiers he had seen.

Once the offloading was complete, Captain Hagen had her ship back in the river and on to her next port of call. Alex and the two women waited until everyone had settled into their routine before they headed below. Making excuses about checking on the horses, and with Kinsey at hand, the crew gave them a wide berth and allowed them to pass unrestricted.

As they wandered around the hold, each investigated different parts of the cargo area. With crates stacked all over, they had to take their time as they made their way from one end of the hold to the other. Collecting at the stalls where the three horses were stabled, they compared notes.

"The hold is filled with crates from Two Thorns," Abrianna said.

"There are only two more stops between here and Rivers Edge," Cassie added.

"I am getting the impression that someone is supplying an army on the border with Great Vale," Alex commented.

"We need to get to my father as soon as possible."

----*----

For the rest of the day, Alex, Cassie, and Abrianna kept watch as the riverboat made two more stops along the river. With each port of call, they watched as the crew offloaded more of the crates from Two Thorns. There were always wagons waiting, and the men receiving them doing a poor job of hiding their true nature. Even Alex could tell the difference between the dockworkers and the soldiers in disguise.

As evening approached, several hours after their last stop, the three were seated in the galley eating dinner. Cassie had been the last to arrive; she had just finished another pass through the cargo hold.

"Well, what did you find?" Abrianna asked, as Cassie seated herself next to Alex.

"There are still eight crates below deck," she replied.

"There are no more stops before Rivers Edge," Abrianna remarked while shaking her head.

"Would your father have ordered these?" Alex asked.

"We don't typically use Two Thorns weapons," Abrianna replied. "Father has....other sources. We have Elven blades for the palace guard and special units."

"And Rivers Edge is the last stop for the good captain?" Alex asked.

"Yes, I'm positive. The river continues bearing southwest for quite a ways before finally opening into the deltas near the sea. It gets so shallow there ships like this will go aground. That's why we were looking to align with Windfall and their deep water ports," Abrianna answered.

Although Alex wasn't a soldier, he had minored in history in college. He had a particular liking for military history and had a sizable collection of books at home on the subject. This had all the makings of a trap in his mind.

"I suggest we make a habit of keeping our weapons close," was all he would say on the subject without further information.

----*----

The four had retired early that night although Alex did not get much sleep. With every bump that vibrated through the ship's hull, he would sit awake listening for other telltale sounds indicating trouble. Kinsey shared no such concerns and slept soundly, curled upon the floor next to his bunk.

The following morning Alex was up with the morning sun, having had a less than restful night. As he left his cabin, he met both women in the passageway, armed as heavily as Alex himself. Since they intended to disembark later that morning, he hoped it wouldn't attract undue attention from the crew.

With Kinsey following along, they headed down to the galley, although none appeared to be all that hungry.

"We should be well inside our borders by now," Abrianna commented.

"Even so, we won't make landfall until later this morning," added Cassie; Abrianna nodded in agreement.

Breakfast was identical to the day before though Alex suspected the bread was a day older than yesterdays. No one but Kinsey finished it, and she got the leftovers from the others. After eating, they assembled on the main deck, in the bow behind the cargo access doors.

Alex wandered over to the railing, noting some activity behind the trees on the bank off the starboard bow. Suddenly the ship decelerated dramatically, sending everyone to the deck. Scrambling to his feet and assisting Cassie, who had been right behind him, Alex could see where a heavy braided rope had been strung across a narrow point in the river.

Weighted to rest just under the surface, it had been invisible to the ship's crew on approach. Now it was stretched tight and straining, anchored to the trees on both banks. As the crew started to take action to free themselves, both banks erupted in activity. Several small boats filled with men started rowing to intercept the riverboat.

"Alex!" Abrianna screamed, as she pointed to the far bank with more boats and men headed their way. He could see that all the boats held men with weapons.

Just then, several arrows appeared in the surrounding decking, fired from the nearest boats coming from the west bank. Having brought his own bow along, Alex began pulling the arrows up from the decking and returning them to their owners. He let fly with several in a row causing the archers to fall on the rowers and disrupting the control of the boats.

The river current carried the out-of-control boats into the rope holding the riverboat in place and created total bedlam on the water. Unfortunately, the boats on the other side had been able to cover the greater distance unimpeded and were close to boarding them.

Alex watched as Cassie dropped her sword and belt and then pulled her boots off. Confused at her actions, he started to move to her side of the boat when she suddenly jumped overboard. By now, the boats on his side had started to reorganize, so Alex let fly another volley of shafts to keep them from uniting.

Turning back to fend off the boarders from the east bank, Alex was at first confused, then thrilled to see a small water spout had formed right in the center of the oncoming armada. He could just make out Cassie's head and hands as she manipulated the whirlwind of water. She bounced it from one boat to another, spilling their passengers into the river.

With confidence that she had things well in hand, Alex turned back to his own troubles. The boats on his side were still clustered against the ropes, with about half of the various occupants sporting arrows or in the water clinging to the sides.

Alex concentrated on the visible section of rope between him and the boats. He visualized streams of sunlight energy fusing with the rope. He was relieved as a section of the rope exploded in flames and separated.

Satisfied with his handiwork, he sprinted to the far railing, and without waiting to see what happened to the little boats, Alex grabbed some line and flung the coil out into the water. "Cassie, grab the line!"

In short order, Alex had her up and back on deck. As he pulled her over the railing, he was rewarded with a kiss that neither was in a rush to complete.

"Ahem," Abrianna sounded, as she stepped up, "we are free of the snare and moving again."

Both Cassie and Alex turned their heads to her, but he continued to hold her tight.

"Well, I guess we know where the last delivery was intended," Alex commented before Cassie turned his head back for a second kiss.

Chapter 10

As the boat continued on its way, the crew was busy cleaning up after the attack. Several had been wounded, and the captain was beside herself with rage over the attempted pirating of her ship and cargo. Alex and Cassie had cleaned out their cabins of their meager possessions and had everything ready, though they still had a few short hours until Rivers Edge. Abrianna was busy with the wounded, healing those she could and assisting with the only crew fatality of the raid.

With Kinsey laying nearby, Alex and Cassie stood talking by the railing. Their possessions were piled to one side, out of the way of any traffic. As they talked, the captain approached them.

"Here, this is yours," she stated while handing Alex the sack of coins he had turned over to Abrianna to secure passage.

"I don't understand," Alex replied while accepting the bag, but holding it out questioningly.

"You saved my ship. I normally pay for that service, but didn't expect the need this trip."

"So you came to the same conclusion we did, that someone set you up?" Alex asked, including her in the conversation he and Cassie were just having.

"Yes, I was paid too well for this delivery. I see now they expected to recover the payment with the cargo."

With that, she turned and left, passing Abrianna as she was approaching the group.

"How are the wounded?" Cassie asked.

"All but one survived," she replied, "that one was dead before I even saw him."

"They were lucky," Alex offered.

"Yes, the crew all understand they would have been butchered had we not intervened," Abrianna replied.

"And I'm thinking having a Water Nymph around is pretty handy!" Alex said, pulling Cassie to him for a quick kiss.

"I bet you do!" Cassie replied smacking him in the chest with her open palm.

"In all seriousness," Abrianna added, "you have saved us twice now, Cassie. I know you have suppressed this part of you in the past, but you might reconsider."

Looking at Alex, Cassie said, "I'm seeing some advantages to it."

The three continued to lounge on the foredeck, talking while the riverboat approached its final destination. The closer they got to Rivers Edge, the more animated Abrianna became. It was clear she was anxious to get home to her father.

By midmorning, they could see the docks and structures that Abrianna identified as Rivers Edge. As this was an entry point into the lands of the Great Vale, she indicated a detachment of her father's soldiers would be at hand to process entry into the area.

Sure enough, as the riverboat nosed into the wharf, a handful of soldiers dressed in blue trim greeted the ship. They wore the same uniform as the men Alex had seen the first day he rescued the two women. He and Cassie stood back and watched as Abrianna crossed the loading ramp and presented herself to the men.

Alex actually laughed as the men scrambled to attention, having previously appeared far more relaxed and informal. He watched as she directed the detachment to assist with the wounded and take the report from the captain regarding the attack on the river.

Alex tapped Cassie who had been watching Abrianna and pointed to the ship's crew unloading the crates of weapons. The two of them followed soon after as the horses were brought up from below. Once they had disembarked, they collected their horses and crossed over to join Abrianna on the wharf.

"What's with the crates?" Alex asked Abrianna, who was standing next to the ship's captain.

"My shipper says to deliver these crates to Rivers Edge, and that's what I'm doin'," Captain Hagen said before Abrianna had a chance.

"I'm having the detachment gather some wagons and we are taking them with us," Abrianna added. "I've already had them dispatch a messenger. My father will know we are coming long before we arrive."

Alex and Cassie led the horses to one side to allow the soldiers to perform their duties. As they watched, several wagons appeared, and each wagon took several crates. However, it still required three wagons to handle the entire load.

The head of the guard detachment approached, and eyeing Alex and Kinsey with disdain, addressed Cassie, "Lady Cassandra, it would be a great honor for my men and I to escort you and Princess Abrianna to Great Vale."

Cassie smiled and replied in a loud voice so all could hear, "Captain, this Ranger has saved the lives of her royal highness and myself several times in the last few days. You are to treat his orders as my own."

The look on the man's face was one of serious doubt, one shared by Alex.

Suddenly, from one side of the assembled mass came a shout, "Or as mine!"

All turned to see Abrianna removing any doubts regarding Cassie's declaration.

"Yes my lady."

Looking at Alex, he tipped his head in a sign of respect, "Sire." He then turned and started barking orders to spur his men into action.

Alex, Cassie, and Abrianna all thanked the ship's captain before mounting their horses. Following behind a pair of mounted soldiers, the detachment's captain started onto the road to Great Vale. Behind them were the wagons full of weapons, bringing up the rear of the procession.

----*----

They had been on the road for several hours before the sun started to get low in the afternoon sky. As they rode, Cassie informed Alex about the route they would be taking. While it was almost a straight line west, it would still take part of the next day to reach Great Vale.

The surrounding country was low, flat, rolling hills with the occasional tree or stream. Cassie explained that most of what they could see was farmland. The king was very adamant that farmers rotate their fields to ensure they gave the land a chance to recover between usages. This meant that all the land they currently saw was recovering between seasons of usage.

She explained that, as he had encountered on their trip east to the river, there would be a small community ahead. Like the others he had seen elsewhere, it was located almost a day's ride from the river to cater to travelers. This time however, they were arriving as traveling royalty and there would be much pomp and ceremony. On the plus side, the food and accommodations would be the best available.

Another interesting development along the ride was in the change in attitude of the soldiers regarding Alex and Kinsey. Apparently in her many trips to the front to the column, Abrianna had informed the captain of Alex's exploits.

Of greatest interest to him, was Alex avenging the deaths of her guard, as well as sinking a shaft in the shoulder of the cowardly Crown Prince of Windfall. With each rest stop, Alex noted increased deference to himself and Kinsey. At one point, he and Cassie watched as several of the soldiers shared dried meat strips, similar to jerky, with Kinsey.

Tentative at first, she soon warmed up to the men and happily munched away on the gifts. By the time they reached the final stop for the night, she was happily trotting along between the wagons looking for handouts.

Well before dusk, they approached their stop for the night. The town consisted of several buildings on both sides of the road. Alex could see the store and the inn right away. Another building he mentally tagged had to be the military post, as it also included a sizable stable and barracks building. Almost all the one-story structures were of stone, with the two-story inn containing a wooden second floor, as he had seen before.

One of the lead guards had been dispatched ahead, so as they drew close, there were plenty of soldiers in attendance upon their arrival. Alex found himself catered to in a fashion that made him decidedly uncomfortable. Cassie couldn't contain her laughter as she watched him spin about in confusion with all the activity around him.

First one soldier took the reins of his horse from him as he dismounted. Before he could react, another had removed the saddlebags, while a third removed the saddle.

"Please come this way, Sire," the captain offered, leading Alex to Abrianna and Cassie. Several of the soldiers from the road had already coaxed Kinsey to the group. Those in residence here kept their distance from the wolf.

With Abrianna in the lead, the entire entourage was directed inside the inn. The room was fairly well lit, by both candlelight and the circular fireplace in the center of the room. Alex had to admit that the lodging house here looked far nicer than the one they stopped in outside the dark woods.

The room was rather large with several windows on three sides, front, back and left. The fourth side on the right had a long bar with stools along the entire length. Alex assumed it served the soldiers on a regular basis.

In the center was a large round stone fire pit with a flue that ran straight up. He assumed it passed through the second floor and straight to the roof. The exposed woodwork and the fireplace reminded Alex of a ski lodge. All the tables in the room were placed to permit easy access around the room. People could pass easily to, and from the central fire pit. To their right near the bar, was the assembled staff.

"Your highness, please allow me to welcome you!" A woman announced as they entered.

For the next several minutes, Alex watched Abrianna and Cassie do the royalty dance with everyone presented in turn. He admired the way they interacted with the staff without projecting arrogance or superiority. To Alex's surprise, as they were all being led to the table prepared especially for them, the woman approached him.

"Ranger, we would be especially honored if you would take the seat at the head of the table."

Both Cassie and Abrianna were smiling as he was led to the end of the table, with Cassie on his left and Abrianna on his right. Even Kinsey had a specially prepared spot next to the wall. A blanket had been provided, as well as a very large bone, meat still clinging to it.

Abrianna leaned in and whispered, "You are quite the honored guest!"

"What lies have you been telling them?" he whispered back as they started bringing out the platters of food.

At that, Cassie said, "They take the defense of the royal family very seriously here."

"But not half as serious as they regard avenging the cowardly butchering of their comrades," Abrianna added.

It was then that Alex noted the entire room was lined with the soldiers.

"You are receiving the gratitude of the garrison," Cassie explained.

Alex swore she appeared as proud of him as anyone in attendance.

"What do I do?" He asked them.

Abrianna answered, "Stand, then bow to your left, then turn and bow to your right. Once they return the bow, you can sit."

Alex performed the task as described. After all the bows were returned, the soldiers filed out, leaving a few honor guards to act as protection. Alex didn't actually take his seat until they'd left, thinking it rude.

"That was perfect," Abrianna said, while Cassie got up and kissed his cheek before reseating herself.

"That was improper behavior," Abrianna chastised Cassie.

"We aren't at court yet," she replied lightly.

"By the gods, father is not going to recognize you," Abrianna replied, rolling her eyes.

The three ate a grand meal, thanking everyone in sight. For Alex, the constant attention was all a bit much. If he could have chased everyone out of the room, he would have. Remembering it wasn't his place to do so, he simply went along for the ride.

It was quite late by the time they finished the meal. So, with guards as escorts and guards at either ends of the hall upstairs, each was shown to his or her own room. Cassie blew him a kiss as he wished her a good night. Alex and Kinsey's room was quite spacious. He was also surprised to discover a large metal bathtub filled and waiting for him. As he was preparing to get undressed, there was a quiet knock at his door. Half expecting to find Cassie on the other side, he was surprised to find a young woman there.

"Sire, if you please. I am here to collect your clothes for laundering," She said without actually looking at Alex.

"One moment," Alex replied, closing the door.

Looking around the room for his saddlebags, Alex noticed a rather gaudy looking robe had been laid out on the bed for him. Quickly undressing, he put the robe on and went back to the door.

"Here you go," Alex said, handing the bundle to her.

"Um, your boots, too, if you please, sire."

Not bothering to close the door this time, he grabbed his boots and handed them over to the young woman.

"Thank you, sire. Have a good night." She backed away and closed the door behind her.

"Wow, now that's service," Alex said to Kinsey as he went back over to the tub.

Alex wasn't sure if he was to use the robe to dry, but on a stool at the far side of the tub was a folded thick towel ready for his use. Testing the water, he found it lukewarm at best. He liked his bath hot, so he decided to try a little magic.

Placing his hands in the water, he closed his eyes and visualized small rays of energy flowing into the water. He quickly dropped the vision when his hands got decidedly hot rather quickly.

"Gotta work on my control," he said to himself, as he dropped his robe and gently slipped into the tub of rather hot bath water. Not wanting to risk any more manipulations while he was in the bath, he simply soaked in the hot water, feeling it ease the tension out of his aching muscles.

Kinsey, never enjoying the concept of baths, had chosen a spot as far from the tub as possible and lay curled up on one of the many floor rugs. After a good long soak, Alex climbed from the tub and, using the towel on the stool, dried himself. Grabbing the robe, he threw it on and started looking for something to sleep in.

Discovering what looked like a nightshirt folded and placed at the head of the bed, he decided that it reminded him too much of a Dickens story. All he needed was a sleeping cap to play Scrooge. Removing the robe and laying it at the foot of the bed, he slipped under the blanket and slept au natural.

----*----

The following morning, Alex woke well rested, and more comfortable than he had been in quite a while. He wasn't sure exactly what time it was, but he thought it was still early, as things were still very quiet. He sat up to find his clean clothes folded and resting on a table near the door. His boots were on the floor next to the table.

After dressing, he had an urgent need to address. Surprisingly, he discovered one of the doors he assumed held a closet was in fact a toilet. Rather than a pedestal toilet, it was a bench along the back wall with the traditional seat, however there was a porcelain tank with a pull chain for flushing on the wall above the seat.

Curiosity overcoming caution, Alex looked in the hole to see a deep recess. What confused him was there was no means of draining the recess. Pulling the chain, Alex watched water from the tank above flow into the recess, as a flapper valve at the bottom opened to allow the contents to drain away. Once empty, the flap closed to block any noxious fumes from returning up the drainpipe.

Impressed and happy to have working plumbing again, he quickly completed his business. Suspecting that Kinsey had the same needs, he hurriedly finished up and headed to the doorway. As they stepped into the hallway, he found two new guards in place exactly where the previous night's attendants had stood.

Both snapped to attention at his appearance and Alex acknowledged them as he headed out. Once downstairs, he found more soldiers in the dining room, eating. The entire room stood at his entrance and he had to wave them back into their seats as he passed.

"Just taking Kinsey out," he explained as he passed. He was rewarded with a few chuckles as he left the room. Outside he found even more soldiers in various modes of preparation for the day's travel. He suspected that either the entire garrison had turned out, neglecting all their usual duties, or more troops had been sent in the night from Great Vale to escort their wayward princess home.

As he passed, he noted several soldiers whispering back and forth with nods of agreement. All the attention was getting a bit tiresome and he wondered how Cassie and Abrianna had handled a lifetime of living under everyone's watchful eye.

He watched Kinsey run out into the open countryside behind the inn and, after sniffing out several scents, do her own business. He laughed to see a two hundred pound wolf behave like a fifty-pound house dog, chasing around the open field.

By the time they returned to the dining room, he found the women had emerged from their rooms and were seated for breakfast.

"The guards said you had just taken Kinsey out, so we decided to wait for you," Cassie announced at his return. She pulled out the chair next to her so he could sit.

Slipping in next to her and receiving a quick kiss, he surveyed the table's contents. There were several meats of differing cuts and freshly baked bread and sweet pastries. He could see why the women had considered the ship's fare spartan.

"I hope you are planning on sharing with someone because the three of us can't eat all of this."

"It is custom that after we finish, the staff and troops are permitted to eat. My father says that always guarantees he will never go hungry," Abrianna said with a laugh.

While they ate, Abrianna described their destination. Alex listened intently, eating sparingly as they still had half of a day's ride. Alex noted Kinsey had her own little banquet in the corner. Soon enough, everyone had eaten their fill. As if on cue, the captain approached the table. "Your Highness, my Lady, Sire, we are ready to depart at your convenience," he stated, paying deference to all three.

Stepping outside, their three horses were saddled and ready. Alex noted his black mare had been groomed and his gear was neatly arranged. Slipping in between Cassie and the soldier attempting to assist her, he helped her mount before mounting himself.

He caught a wink and nod of approval from Abrianna before the entire column started moving west. Looking fore and aft, Alex counted twice the number of riders now than from Rivers Edge. He was sure daddy was taking no chances.

Chapter 11

Alex sensed that the last leg of the trip to Great Vale seemed to take forever for Abrianna and Cassie. Both appeared antsy and restless with each stop along the way. Considering their trip had started as a diplomatic mission and became a run for their lives, he understood why. The only one who seemed to be enjoying the trip was Kinsey as she wandered between the troops and the countryside.

By late in the morning, just before noon, they could see their destination as they crested a rise in the road. Alex had to admit the name fit the destination. The valley below was expansive; it seemed that the city lay in the center of a huge bowl in the earth. There was an outer wall circling the city although there were buildings outside its boundaries. The civil engineer in him suspected that the location allowed for the collection of rainwater, providing there was a sizable reservoir somewhere under the city. Off to one side of the city, a small river ran the length of the valley from north to south.

In the center of the city was a rise, likely man made, containing a large stone castle. It was all very medieval. Alex could see the road they occupied was only one of several entering the valley, all terminating into the city at different points. Considering all the traffic he could see on the roads, Great Vale appeared quite prosperous.

With the entry into the valley, the mood of both women improved immensely. Cassie pointed out several large structures in the city to Alex. The main square, the market district, warehouse district, and the Ranger's Guild were all ticked off as she chatted excitedly.

Alex had no idea what he was going to do about the Ranger's Guild. The phrase, "I'm not a doctor, but I play one on TV" came to mind. He also doubted that the Guild was going to be all that thrilled at his impersonation, not that he had ever been consulted on the choice to begin with.

As the column entered the city through one of its gates, he watched as several of the escort riders peeled off in other directions. That left a core guard, and the wagons loaded with crates, headed to the castle. The streets had been cleared of traffic and there were lots of locals watching as they passed by. He noted Abrianna and Cassie waving frequently to people along the way.

It impressed him that the two seemed to be very well thought of. Maybe he had read too many stories of evil monarchs, but the people of

Great Vale appeared to love their royal family. It was also quite obvious that Alex and Kinsey were known to the people as well.

With all the new people and enclosed spaces, Kinsey had taken to sticking with Alex. As they passed by, people were exchanging comments and pointing at them excitedly.

"Cassie, why are they pointing at me?" he asked.

"There was a troop exchange last night, I suspect the soldiers reported in once they returned here," she replied after a moment's thought.

"Reported what?" Alex asked, afraid of what embellishments were being created at his expense.

"Relax," replied Cassie, waving to some girls on a street corner, "you are a hero. You saved the Crown Princess and a member of the royal family from assassination."

Alex didn't exactly remember it that way, but he could see her point. Either way, the deed was done and his reputation was fixed. He was more concerned about what the king had heard. As the thought entered his head, they turned the corner and there were the main gates to the castle itself.

Passing through the gates, they entered a courtyard lined with troops. This was about as much pomp as Alex could take. Kinsey was not thrilled with all the activity and clung near his right foot. Alex looked around, taking the castle in.

They were inside a walled courtyard, where the area over the main gate held a parapet for the defending troops. On his right, as they entered, were areas for stalls and he could see where a passage led back to more enclosed stables. Directly in front were the stone steps and wooden double doors leading into the main keep. On his left were several smaller structures that had the look of workshops and other military offices.

At the steps of the keep, several soldiers came forward and took their horses as they dismounted. Alex waited until Cassie and Abrianna took the lead, and then he and Kinsey fell in behind them. The captain who had escorted them followed Alex and several soldiers followed him, carrying one of the crates.

After entering through the double doors, the entire party turned left and entered a long room lined with people. At its end on a raised dais was a man seated in a simple large wooden chair. Alex assumed it was Abrianna's father, the king.

Alex noticed several men standing to the king's left. All wore the tan and green of the Rangers Guild and were scrutinizing Alex as he entered.

Those men to the king's right bore the blue tunics of soldiers, and spread throughout the room. The sight of the Rangers made Alex very uncomfortable; he was sure he wasn't going to fool anyone.

"Father," Abrianna said, while she and Cassie curtsied, "I bring bad news from the north."

Alex followed the lead of the men around him by bowing.

"My mission to Windfall was ambushed," she continued. "The assassins were led by Crown Prince Renfeld himself. Only by the grace of the gods, and the intervention of this Ranger, were we able to escape death and return unharmed."

There was a murmuring throughout the room. One of the soldiers next to the king whispered something to him followed by one of the Rangers on his left. Alex had the distinct impression the man had denied any knowledge of his identity and wasn't at all happy to see him. Finally, the king held up one hand, indicating a need for silence.

"Ranger, present yourself," the Ranger next to the king announced.

Alex saw Abrianna waving him forward, so he stepped up to the right of the two women.

"Your name?" the Ranger asked.

"Ah, yeah. My name is Alex Rogers..." he started, but the king held up a hand, halting him.

"Please clear the room," the king asked in a quiet voice. Those around him looked confused.

"Sire...." The soldier next to him started.

"Go," he said in a gentle tone, "I'll be quite alright. Just these three will remain... well four," he finished while pointing at Kinsey, who indicated she did not intend to leave Alex's side.

As the room cleared, Cassie slid sideways, next to Alex, and took his hand. If the king noticed, he said nothing as he watched the room clear. Once they were alone, he looked down at them.

"Ok, so you are no Ranger, are you?"

"No sir," Alex replied.

"Father..." Abrianna started, but the king put up his hand to silence her.

"Cassie?" he asked, indicating her attachment.

"Uncle, I like him."

Apparently, the meaning was all too clear. "You two may leave. I will meet with you privately later."

As if to reinforce her statement, Cassie kissed Alex on the cheek before another curtsey and the two women departed, leaving Alex and Kinsey alone with the king.

The two men appraised each other for a long while. Alex saw a man in his 50s, graying but fit. He was around six feet tall and had a stocky build. Suddenly the king stood and stepped down from the dais.

"Follow me," he said leading Alex and Kinsey to a door on the right of the room.

They entered what looked to be a study. Three of the walls held floor to ceiling wooden bookcases, and all were filled with books and other artifacts. There was a desk on the right of the door, while on the left were two overstuffed leather chairs with a small table in between. Straight ahead, the bookcases framed a fireplace.

To Alex, it had the look of a Victorian study.

"Sit," the man said pointing to one of the overstuffed chairs.

As Alex watched, the man pulled out a cigar, and offered one to Alex, which he politely declined. He then grabbed a bottle off one of the shelves, and filled two glasses, handing one to Alex before seating himself in the other chair. Kinsey had found a spot to lay next to Alex's chair.

"Here's mud in your eye," the man said toasting Alex.

Taking a sip, Alex coughed at the strength. Before he could say anything, the man asked him a question.

"Have you slept with her yet?"

"Pardon me?"

"Sex, man. Have you had sex with Cassie?"

"Ah, no sir."

"Thank God for that. You have no idea what you are playing with there," he replied in a casual tone.

Unable to restrain himself, Alex asked, "Who are you?"

"Name's Ben Griffin," the man replied extending a hand to shake with Alex.

"Where you from?" Ben asked while Alex recovered from the shock.

"Seattle," Alex answered. "I was hiking in the Cascades when I fell in a sinkhole and woke up here."

"Yup," replied Ben, "I was prospecting in the Superstition Mountains of the Arizona Territory when the same thing happened to me."

Something about the statement rang strange to Alex, "Prospecting?"

"Yup, after the war, I worked for a while as a Geologist, but decided to try my luck on my own."

"War?" Alex asked, trying to tie the man to a generation. He looked too old for the Gulf War and too young for the Vietnam War.

"The War for Southern Independence."

"The Civil War?" Alex asked, astonished.

"Oh yeah, I heard they called it that later," he replied after taking another sip.

"What year did you come here?" Alex asked.

"1870. What about you?" the man replied, while watching Alex closely.

"2015." Alex shook his head in disbelief.

"Funny, huh?" Ben said. "Time doesn't seem to track here like back home."

Alex nodded as Ben continued, "Like I said. I was prospecting in Arizona when I fell down a mineshaft. Woke up in time to save this family from an Orc raid. I had been a cavalry officer in the war and was pretty handy with a saber."

With that, the man stood up and pulled a blade in its scabbard from the wall. Handing it to Alex, he drew the blade out far enough to see the metal was identical to the sword in his possession. This had more of a gentle curve favored by cavalry.

Alex returned the sword, and while Ben replaced it, Alex extended the one in his possession, having removed it earlier to sit. Ben inspected the blade before returning it.

"They sure make fine weapons, don't they?" he commented absently.

"They?" Alex asked.

"Elves man, I am sure you know by now we are far from home. I am told you have saved my kin from Windfall troops, Orcs, Gorm Orcs, and bandits. Truth be told, my men consider you a war god," he said with a laugh.

"As you might expect there is more to those stories," Alex replied.

"I would expect so, but we are running short of time and my daughter and your girlfriend are probably fretting about now. For the time being, understand two things. My daughter and Cassie do not know I am not from here. Cassie's mom was part of the family I saved. She is sworn to secrecy on this, as are you now. Number two; do not have sex with Cassie. She is more nymph than she knows and we don't know how it will affect her. Either she will bond to you for life, something you need to think hard on, boy, or she will go native on us and disappear into the wild."

As they were preparing to leave, Alex asked, "What do I call you?"

Ben stopped for a minute considering the question, then replied, "If you're not careful, uncle."

"How about sire?" Alex replied as they walked out of the room.

----*----

Alex and Kinsey were shown to a room in the castle provided specifically for them. He suspected the king had chosen the location, as it was right down the hall from his personal chambers. That meant there were more guards per square foot watching his every move than anywhere else in the castle.

The orderly who had been assigned to service his needs laid out a clean set of Ranger attire.

Apparently, the charade was to continue, and he was to present himself as a member of the guild.

"Dinner will be in an hour, sire," the boy pronounced before backing out of the room and closing the door behind him.

Alex looked around the room, scratching Kinsey between the ears as he did so. It was larger than any bedroom he had ever slept in. He laughed as he considered it was bigger than his first apartment.

To his left, a large four-poster bed extended from the wall. There were oil lamps on stands on either side, not currently in use. Directly across from the door was a huge glass window framed in heavy fabric drapes. To his right was a fireplace with overstuffed chairs creating a sitting area. The walls were all finely crafted wood panels, stained a dark brown.

As it was at the inn, there was a metal tub in the far right corner for bathing. The door beyond held a toilet, tank and chain assembly, identical to the one he used earlier that day. Using the washbasin near the tub, he washed up rather than a full bath and then changed into the fresh clothes provided.

If what Cassie had told him days earlier was true, the change of clothes was an extravagance. While changing, he inspected each piece they had provided him. It was of identical manufacture to what he wore coming here. The one difference was the boots. Rather than the soft-soled rough leather boot he woke up with so many days ago, these were polished black leather, with a firm, stiff sole. He supposed these were better suited for the stone streets of the city.

In due time, he was summoned to dinner, with Kinsey's meal delivered to the room. Alex didn't blame anyone for not wanting her in the dining hall. Besides, she preferred to avoid crowds of people anyway.

Following the orderly, he was led back downstairs to the ground floor and to the side of the castle opposite the hall, where he had been received earlier that day. Entering the dining hall, he saw rows of tables in front of him, while a long table on his left was raised above and running perpendicular to the rest. The room was filling with guests, some in uniform while the majority was in fanciful dress.

Already seated at the long table on his left, and watching the procession entering, he could see Ben front stage center. As various groups entered, they would go forward to pay their respects before finding a place among the rows of tables. Alex could see Abrianna on her father's left, with Cassie to Abrianna's left, both in amazing dresses. Rather than seating Alex next to Cassie, farther left from center, the orderly led him to the empty chair on the king's right. Alex was sure there was more than one significance to this, but he was never good at politics. He was sure the seat to the left of the king was for the queen or hostess and at the right of the king was a place of honor. As Ben was more of a father than uncle to Cassie, he completely understood the separation from her.

Acknowledged with a nod from Ben, Alex sat quietly, waiting for the events of the evening to unfold. Both Cassie and Abrianna caught his eye, each gracing him with a smile, though Cassie's was much warmer.

Scanning the room, Alex again identified several members of the Ranger's Guild mixed in with the guests. He had no idea regarding Ben's intent on continuing the impersonation, but he had to trust the man knew what he was doing.

In due course, everyone found a seat and the room quieted to allow for introductions. As Alex sat, he was introduced to the local businessmen and women, military leaders, and Masters of the Guilds. Of particular note was the Ranger's Guild Master, as he had been on the dais next to the king in the earlier reception. The man radiated his animosity toward Alex.

Ben had chosen to introduce Alex as just that, Alex, with no surname included. After all the official ceremonies were completed, food was brought forth and the mood lightened considerably. Ben ran a very informal royal court, and everyone, regardless of class, was encouraged to participate. There were several questions from the gallery regarding the events around the Princess's mission and the resulting flight from Windfall. Alex did his best to look invisible during the entire exchange.

Suddenly, a young officer who had been sitting next to the Master of the Ranger's Guild came forward and announced to the gathering, "I have heard many unbelievable stories about this supposed Ranger. Perhaps he might choose to clarify them."

Alex had never seen the man before, so he suspected he was part of the castle guard. He judged the man to be about 5' 8" or so with short dark hair. He had a stocky build, but moved with a smooth grace that reminded Alex of a cat.

"You would question my recount or his identity?" Abrianna said before Alex could respond, indignation evident in her tone.

"No your Highness, no one doubts you believe what you saw. I only question because a warrior's eye is more keen in such observations," he replied with a smile and a flourishing bow.

"You doubt my warrior's eye, Captain Leander," Cassie countered, sounding even angrier,

"Especially as I have bested you with a blade?"

The man blushed before replying, "I only suggest that a demonstration might be in order."

Ben leaned into Alex and whispered, "You're being called out, my boy."

Alex could see every eye in the room trained on him, as well as the red flush of anger in Cassie's face at the perceived insult to her love interest.

Standing up slowly, Alex walked to the open area between king's table and the rest of the seating. The young soldier made his way to the front and drew his blade in preparation.

As Alex passed Cassie, she whispered, "Be cautious, he is an excellent swordsman."

Standing weaponless and facing the soldier, Alex debated his course of action, then turned to the wall where an assortment of weapons were available. Grabbing a battle-axe from its hangars, he continued on to a row of poles containing various banners that surrounded the room.

Pulling up one of the banner poles, he walked over to the Ranger Guild Master's table, and marking off a measured distance on the pole, he cleanly cut the pole in two, leaving the axe squarely embedded in the table in front of the man. As he turned, everyone could see he had provided himself a staff about seven feet long.

He walked to one side of the open space in front of the king's table, twirling the staff, first in one direction and then another, until he had a feel for its weight and length. Turning to face Leander, he continued to spin the staff in a continuous motion.

Watching the man's face and not his blade, Alex let the man come to him. With his first lunge, Alex parried the thrust with his staff and slapped the man's wrist with the opposite end of the staff as it twirled. The man's sword went skidding across the floor, as he grabbed the wrist Alex had just slapped.

Stepping back, but saying nothing while watching as Leander rubbed his wrist, Alex motioned for the man to retrieve the blade while continuing to twirl the staff. Moving quickly, the soldier retrieved the blade, looking for a trick as he did and then retreated. Alex waited patiently until the man appeared ready.

Again, he waited for the man's lunge before sidestepping, then parrying in the opposite direction, while again freeing sword from swordsman. Quickly spinning the staff a second time, he connected with the falling blade in midair. The swat sent the sword flying across the room, narrowly missing the Guild Master. Alex gave a sheepish grin, a mock apology to the man for the narrow escape from the flying blade.

Alex again stepped back and indicated that Leander should retrieve his blade. The soldier retrieved his sword, as one of the spectators handed the blade to him. This time he charged quickly, trying to catch Alex by surprise. Instead, he was treated to repeated blows from the staff, the first disarming him and the next to the side of the head. Stunned, a third blow swept his feet out from under him, landing him flat on his back and out cold as his head hit the stone.

Alex stepped back, retrieving the dropped sword, and then sheathed it in the unconscious man's scabbard. As several others came forward to help the fallen captain, Alex moved back around the table. Before he could pass, Cassie stood and planted a kiss on his lips, in front of the assembled mass. The action removing any doubts about her feelings.

Chapter 12

The rest of the evening meal was anticlimactic after Alex's demonstration. The captain was able to return later that evening, but selected a seat far from the Ranger Guild Master who had set him up. At one point Ben did ask Alex where he had learned to fight with a staff like that.

"Elves," was all he had to say in reply.

At several points during the evening, Cassie came to sit by Alex, chasing away whoever happened to be sitting by him. Her uncle interceded repeatedly and had to remind her they had guests to entertain, and the event wasn't for her personal enjoyment.

By the time they were all ready to call it a night, Ben grabbed Alex and led him back into his study. Indicating Alex should take a seat; Ben took the other, and let out a heavy sigh.

"First, I want to apologize about the little challenge tonight," Ben started a bit sheepishly.

"Needed to separate fact from fiction?" Alex asked, a bit indignant.

"That wasn't my idea, boy," Ben replied to the insinuation, "but yes, I allowed it to see if you have what it takes to survive here."

As Alex considered the statement, Ben continued. "I got word tonight that the pirates you thrashed on the river were indeed Windfall troops."

Alex nodded in understanding, and then asked, "Are you equipped for war?"

"They outnumber us three to one, but that's always been the case. What the damn fool's father knew that he doesn't, is it's magic that's kept us free all this time."

"Abrianna mentioned that you are an accomplished wizard," Alex said in reply.

"And she tells me you have more power than the two of us combined," he said flatly.

"Did she also tell you I almost boiled myself trying to heat my bath water?"

That brought a laugh from Ben, "A little control problem, huh?"

"No, a big control problem," Alex replied. "Abrianna has helped me some, but she seems to think I'm some great white wizard."

"Yeah, she told me about the Orcs and the fire lance. You think you can start that fire?" He asked pointing to the stack of wood in the fireplace.

Alex started to get up when Ben said, "From here."

Alex sat back in his chair and then concentrated on the wood in the fireplace. He envisioned energy streaming into the wood until it burst into flame.

Turning back to Ben, he heard, "White as snow. You hide it well though. Any idea how?"

"At this point I can boil water and start a fire. Beyond that I have no idea what I am doing," Alex replied in frustration.

Ben gave it a moment's thought, and then said, "Could be your natural personality; were you a quiet boy?"

Now it was Alex's turn to think. After a bit, he replied, "I was an only child, so I spent a lot of time on my own. I was never a ladies man either. Those guys that chased women were way too flakey for my tastes."

"Well that's good news for Cassie," he said with a laugh.

"I suspect you have a natural talent for hiding your abilities. The things you did back home translate to talents here. I grew up on a farm outside of Charleston, where I learned how to live off the land. After that, I graduated from The Citadel, in Charleston, before the war. Worked as a geological engineer, building forts. Learned to fight in the war, was at Fort Moultrie when we fired on Sumter. Went to the cavalry after that. From others I've met since, it seems those with science and engineering skills transfer to magicians here. Fighting is fighting, here or there."

"Others?" Alex asked.

"Oh yeah, none as powerful as you, and most never survived past the first few weeks," he replied in a matter of fact tone.

"That's great to hear," Alex said sarcastically, better understanding Ben's desire to test his survivability.

Ben waved it off. "You've already passed the test they all failed," he replied while tapping his head.

"It's smarts that keeps you alive here, not talent, or power."

Alex gave him a confused look, so he continued.

"Take that little show you provided tonight. Someone less intelligent might have gone up against that soldier, blade for blade, and gotten skewered. Accidents happen, and they all train with a sword from childhood here. You created a non-lethal weapon and took him apart. Granted, there was Elf magic involved to boost your natural abilities, but the soldier underestimated you and that gave you the advantage."

Alex listened, thinking Ben was giving him way too much credit, but he did admit he chose the staff because it was familiar. Like the foil in fencing, he had sparred with a staff before and knew its flexibility as a weapon. As a boy, it had been one of his favorite activities.

"Abrianna also told me you were the one who linked the Two Thorns deliveries to the Windfall plot. All but predicted the attack on the river, she said."

"So where does all this get me?" Alex asked.

"Depends on you," Ben replied.

"You wanna go home or stay here?"

Alex had to think hard on that question. Until the day he saw Cassie in the stream, he would have opted out in a heartbeat, asking to return home. Now, he asked himself, to what end? A three bedroom, two bath, house in the Renton Highlands? Six day work weeks and the occasional date on Saturday night?

Here he might die tomorrow, but there was excitement and he had the potential to influence things. Then, there was Cassie. A cross between the redheaded girl next door and Xena, the warrior princess, she was nuts about him and he her. On the other hand, maybe she was just nuts. That much was yet to be determined; Ben had indicated she was part nymph and could go native on them all.

"What do you have in mind?" Alex finally asked, with a smile on his face.

"Good man," Ben replied. "So, here is what I was thinking..."

The two stayed up late into the night as King Ben and Ranger Alex plotted their future together.

----*----

Cassie woke the next morning, anxious to see Alex. After his little demonstration last night, she was sure no one would question his abilities and her uncle would be thrilled for her. Deep down inside though, she was still at war with herself.

Since that day at the spring, where the nymph had explained everything she was going through, she had been struggling with the two very different parts of herself. The warrior in her was disgusted at the way she gushed over Alex. Constantly concerned about her appearance, she had worn a dress last night for the first time since she was thirteen.

The nymph in her struggled to be set free, to embrace her femininity and sexuality to it's fullest. She had discovered her power to control water and men. The excitement it generated within her was intoxicating. It was also unsettling. She felt she could lose herself completely if she wasn't careful.

Putting all that aside, she was up and dressed in no time. Checking her appearance before leaving her room, she again cringed. Before this man, she hardly ever gave her looks a consideration, now it was her first thought.

Almost skipping as she headed down the hall and then the stairs, she headed to the rear of the first floor. Near the kitchens was a smaller private dining room maintained for the Royal Family and guests. Entering the room, she was delighted to see her uncle and Abrianna already seated and in conversation.

Cassie noted the conversation between the two ceased as soon as she entered. Hurrying over, she kissed her uncle on the cheek and then took the seat next to him and across from Abrianna.

"Where is Alex? Not up yet?" she asked.

Abrianna looked at her father, who replied, "Oh no, he is up and gone."

Cassie's face dropped.

"Gone where? What have you done, Uncle?" she asked in a serious tone.

Before her father could reply, Abrianna jumped in, "Cassie, do you remember the crates from Two Thorns?"

"Yes," Cassie replied cautiously.

"Father has asked Alex to lead a small group to find out exactly what the Windfall troops are up to."

"That's dangerous, how many men did he take with him?" Cassie asked after thinking on it.

"Captain Leander," her uncle replied.

"The ass from last night? Are you crazy?" Cassie blurted, ignoring the fact that her uncle was the king.

"Captain Leander was a Ranger before joining my guard, and is a very good swordsman," Ben answered, ignoring the outburst.

"One I have bested," Cassie replied. "You should have sent me in his place."

"Only sparring," Ben replied, "and you are royal."

Cassie bristled at the implication that the captain might not have done his best in their contest, but held her tongue.

"Besides, you are going to be very busy right here."

"How so?" Cassie snapped, irritated at the turn of events.

"Do you really love that boy?" Ben asked curtly.

"Yes," Cassie replied in a small voice, almost surprised to hear the words escape her own lips.

"Then you have a lot of work to do," Ben replied, pointing to a handful of people entering the room.

"I won't have my niece living in a spring."

----*----

Alex was tired and grumpy. He had actually been looking forward to spending a few days in the castle. Soft beds with warm baths, and regular hot meals were very appealing right now. However, after he and Ben had stayed up late reviewing the situation, it became clear they needed more information.

While Alex was not the military man Ben was, he was an outdoorsman. He was also observant and resourceful, things Ben highly valued. There was also the fact that it looked very much as if someone inside the castle had been feeding the Crown Prince information.

Abrianna's mission to Windfall had not been publicized outside of a very tight circle of people. There had been very few who knew she was going, and even fewer that knew the exact route. They hadn't even notified Windfall of the exact date she would arrive. With these limitations, someone had still been able to plan and execute an ambush. Were it not for Alex's appearance, Ben would have been without heirs.

Captain Leander had been selected as Alex's companion for several reasons. He was a former Ranger, a relationship that had caused him some grief by Alex's hand the previous evening. As a former Ranger, he knew the areas they were to travel very well.

He was also an orphan, his family massacred in a border skirmish with Windfall in the early days of

Ben's reign. His distaste for anything Windfallian was well known. It placed him very low on the suspicion list for informants, paid or otherwise.

Once the plan was set, Alex expressed concern over Cassie's opinion of their strategy. Ben assured Alex that he understood his decision to remain indicated more than a passing interest in the girl. He would ensure that their time apart would be spent constructively.

So that very night the Captain had been summoned and informed of their mission. He had been both surprised and appreciative. He had presumed a demotion might lay in his future after his display, egged on by the Ranger Guild Master.

"What's with that guy?" Alex had asked when the subject came up.

"He prides himself on his total control of the Rangers in his region," Leander replied.

"That was a big reason why I left the Guild."

"You appear here as a complete unknown to him, and with a reputation that overshadows his entire jurisdiction. He fears you," Ben said.

"I am the finest swordsman in the region, so when I left to join his majesty's service, it was unpopular with him. The only reason I was allowed to leave in good standing was my assignment in the King's Guard," Leander said with less humility than was probably proper.

Then after a second he added with more humility, "Rather, I was the finest until last night."

"Oh, yeah, sorry about that," Alex replied sheepishly. "I really didn't want to fight at all."

"No, you were a generous opponent. I was a fool to listen to the whispers in my ear," Leander said, referring to the Guild Master's manipulations.

With their past behind them and a mission ahead, the two men pulled what little supplies they needed together. Gathering early before breakfast, they ate and headed north. Kinsey had taken to the Captain well enough, but the captain's horse did not care for her at all. Alex tried to keep his mare, the same one he'd awoken to in this world, between the two.

As they rode, Alex thought about Cassie and everything that had happened to him since his arrival. It was hard to believe he had been here for almost a week. He had nearly died on several occasions, found love and was now on a mission for a king who was really a vintage 1800's prospector.

Although, Alex did have to admit, Ben had done quite well for himself. King of an apparently prosperous kingdom and admired by friend and foe alike, the man was a success.

Changing his focus to the now, he considered his current situation. Both he and the captain had selected the tan and green of the Ranger's Guild. As Rangers, they would be less conspicuous than civilian travelers, who were typically viewed with distrust. In addition, Rangers found people far more accepting wherever they went. For Alex, it was a continuation of his existing garb, while Captain Leander found it a return to his past.

The two had hardly spoken more than a few words since leaving Great Vale. Accepting Leander as the local expert, Alex had no issues with him taking the lead in their route selection. Honestly, as a man with absolutely no military experience, Alex questioned why he was even on this adventure.

Ben had told him not to worry about his lack of experience; just go out and investigate, he said. He assured Alex that the good captain would supply all the military experience he needed.

Alex took him at his word. Ben was a former Confederate Cavalry officer after all. Leander and Alex had decided to travel as directly North as possible, looking for any indications of troops massing on or near the border with Windfall.

They had chosen to enter the great forest just south of the dark woods that Alex had traveled through days earlier. Leander thought that this would be a choke point for east-west travel because of the superstition of the soldiers. If they were receiving weapons deliveries from Two Thorns via the river, they would stay south of the dark woods and north of the border with Great Vale.

This area was no more than a few miles wide and easy to monitor, as there were a limited number of routes capable of wagon traffic. The two men rode in silence, both scanning the countryside, and Alex wondered again how Cassie was taking the news.

----*----

Cassie was fit to be tied, more than frustrated at her situation. During breakfast, her uncle had introduced her to a small group of people that would be her tutors for the foreseeable future. There were two women, both part Wood Nymph, and a minor green wizard in the king's employ.

There were also Abrianna's former tutors, all from her younger years and whose specialty was taking young women of royal birth and preparing them for life at court. Cassie recalled Abrianna called them the dungeon masters.

While the nymphs held a particular interest to Cassie, the rest could go jump in the river, as far as she was concerned. She had skipped out on all that as a young girl, and she now had no desire to play catch up. However, her uncle explained, and Abrianna confirmed, that the ladies of the court had to exert far more self-control than any man. The skills she acquired from these people would serve her well in managing the internal battles she would face.

Thinking of Alex and all she had already struggled to control, she begrudgingly accepted. Abrianna had smiled and gushed, excited to help her cousin. Her uncle simply nodded, as if the whole thing was never up for debate to begin with.

----*----

Alex and Captain Leander had traveled the entire day without seeing more than the occasional farmer working in their fields. Earlier, both men had agreed to stop just before dark. They were still more than two day's ride from the border, with the Great Forest starting just before the boundary. As evening approached, they selected a stand of trees to spend the night.

With the horses cared for and Kinsey settled in with her own food, the two gathered wood and set up a small camp just inside the tree line. From their location, they had an expansive view of the surrounding countryside.

For that same reason, they set the fire pit back from the tree line and made it smaller than usual, digging it into the ground. Otherwise, it would be visible from afar and that was unacceptable. After collecting a fair amount of wood, the two set to spreading their bedrolls.

"If you please," Leander said while pointing to the wood in the fire pit, "I have no talent for such things."

"I thought all Rangers had some magical abilities," Alex said igniting the fire. It took him a second to realize he had performed the task with little effort.

"Most Rangers have a very limited ability," the captain replied. "They promote the perception they have far more, as it has its advantages. Those with more talent usually end up a mage."

Alex could see where the implications of a magical opponent might deter unwanted confrontations. It also gave Alex a huge respect for those Rangers that slayed foul creatures, as Cassie had described. So far, he was running odds-on for needing magic in such encounters. He was also starting to get a better understanding of the Guild Master's concerns. The man likely feared for his job as a magical Ranger Guild Master could be quite popular.

Both men settled down by the fire, as Captain Leander unwrapped some meat strips similar to the ones Cassie had purchased outside of the dark woods. Skewering one, he handed it to Alex and then repeated the task for himself. The meat was followed by bread and soon both had dinner roasting over the fire pit.

"Go ahead and ask your questions," Alex said watching his dinner cook. While not the most observant person when it came to seeing people's discomfort, Alex had noticed the man's awkwardness all day long. It was obvious Leander had many questions, but was afraid to ask them.

"Castles have many rumors flying about at all times. While most are of no interest to someone like me, since your arrival there have been stories," he stopped without completing the thought.

"Stories?" Alex asked.

Clearly uncomfortable with the question, Leander finally just asked, "Is Lady Cassandra really part Water Nymph?"

Alex laughed, wondering what stigma that association held. While only knowing the captain a very short time, he didn't appear to hold any prejudices so he came clean, "Yes, and that saved our lives several times."

Leander shook his head before replying, "She is quite proficient with a blade and, honestly, not very demur or ladylike. Nymphs are not known to be either."

"I suspect she does that on purpose," Alex stated, getting a nod of agreement from Leander.

"I understand she has taken a liking to you as well?" he asked.

"The feeling is mutual," Alex replied with a smile.

"I certainly meant no offense..."

Alex held up a hand, stopping him.

"None taken. I guess she spent her life hiding that fact from everyone. Now that it's out in the open, there are likely more than a few who are surprised."

The two men talked while they ate, and Alex found his companion quite pleasant. Slowly, Alex drew out the man's life story, apparently gaining his trust as they talked. Leander had grown up in less than positive circumstances and done extremely well in spite of it. Before calling it a night, Alex decided Ben did know what he was doing, after all, in pairing the two men up for this mission.

The following day was much like the last, with both men riding the entire day without incident. They did see the occasional farmer, but as they were well off the roadway, there were no travelers in sight. Kinsey was enjoying the outing, darting about, chasing things and catching something that looked like a fox just before dark.

Again the men chose to camp in a sheltered area, minimizing their exposure to the evening breeze and limiting the visibility their fire created in the darkness. As he fell asleep, Alex lay watching the star filled night sky and stroking Kinsey next to him.

Chapter 13

The following morning, both men rose with the sun and after a light meal, headed north. As they rode, they again scanned the countryside looking for anything amiss. Alex wasn't exactly sure what that might look like, but he put his best effort into it nonetheless. By mid-day, they could see the Great Forest in the distance.

Alex was amazed at how large Ben's kingdom really was. He could see now why Abrianna had suggested the river route instead of the more direct southern path. While the distance had been greater, the ship traveled for 24 hours, thus reducing the overall journey time.

The men talked as they rode, developing a comfortable relationship with one another. By that afternoon, they reached the edge of the Great Forest.

Entering the woods, they were eventually forced to ride single file, picking their way between the trees. With Captain Leander in the lead, they rode quietly north. Kinsey continued to wander in and out of sight as she shadowed the two riders.

Twice, they crossed trails that showed little indication of usage.

"We are well out of Great Vale by now," Leander said during a rest stop. Suddenly there was a commotion just ahead. Leaving the horses, the two slipped through the undergrowth while attempting to remain unseen.

Crouching to hide amongst the heavy undergrowth, they discovered a path wide enough for wagons to pass. As they watched, there were men loaded into two wagons with riders in the lead and trailing behind the wagons. Alex had to quiet Kinsey as she started a low growl when they passed.

Alex counted twenty men in all, heading from east to west. After they had passed, Leander indicated they should move back. "Let's go west paralleling the trail and see where they are headed," he said, mounting his horse.

Alex nodded and followed suit. The two riders stayed in the trees and started west, moving slower than the wagons but still making good progress. It turned out they didn't have far to travel as Leander reined up and waved Alex back.

Dismounting and leading his horse, he led Alex back and retraced their path a good fifty feet before stopping.

"They are camped in a clearing back there, I didn't get a good look, but there were a lot of them," he explained.

Securing the horses, the two moved forward cautiously, Kinsey insisting in coming along. Again, staying close to the ground and hidden in the undergrowth, they were able to get within sight of the camp. They could see sentries posted on the trail at either end of the camp and around the perimeter near the wood line.

They could see a small meadow crowded with tents and men, all dressed in civilian garb. Even to the untrained eye, the precision in the alignment and spacing of the tents alone was a dead giveaway. Alex noted that more than one of the men also sported chainmail under his shirt, poorly concealed.

They could see the wagons they had spotted earlier as crates of food and casks were unloaded from them. Alex assumed they held something to drink, as there was no stream nearby for a water source, and made mental notes on what he saw as they watched. Finally, they retreated and returned to their horses. Mounting, they turned east and started back on their original route.

Once he was positive they were far enough away, Alex spoke.

"Shouldn't we do something about them?"

Leander thought for a moment.

"We can wait until tonight and slip into that camp. Maybe set some fires or poison their water. Then what?"

"There would be 300 less men to fight?"

"And then the eight or ten thousand men spread all around these woods would know something was amiss. The toughest part of military reconnaissance is not taking action. We are here to gather information that gives us the advantage over the enemy. If we act, we lose that," Leander replied.

Alex could see the logic of the explanation, but still hated the inaction. The two continued for the rest of the afternoon, staying in the woods rather than using the trail the soldiers traveled. It was almost dark when they found the second camp. This one was slightly larger, containing as many as 400 men, again all in civilian garb.

Rather than risk detection by stopping too close to the camp, the two men dismounted and continued on foot in the darkness of the woods. It was late when they finally stopped, agreeing on a cold camp for the night. The risk of detection was too great to permit a fire.

Dinner was dried meat and bread, Kinsey being the only one ambivalent to the choice. Speaking in hushed tones, they compared notes and affirmed each other's observations. Before they left Great Vale, all had decided that they would not record their findings on anything that might incriminate them should they be stopped and searched.

As it wasn't typical for Rangers to need maps to navigate, possessing one would raise questions. The Ranger apprenticeship revolved around learning and memorizing their surroundings. For Alex, that meant nothing, but Leander was very knowledgeable about the area. That should allow them to report back accurately by memory.

The following morning they moved out early, only to discover a third camp just inside the forest's eastern edge. This one was substantially larger than the other two; all combined they counted over two thousand men between the three locations.

This created a big problem for the two men, as there was no way for them to emerge from the forest without being seen. In the end, they decided to backtrack yet again, first heading west and then north. This would allow them to move around behind the big camp and exit the woods far north of the group.

They had to wait for quite a while to confirm the trail was vacant, and then Leander returned to cover their tracks after crossing the trail. Positive these camps continued to spread along the border throughout the forest, from east to west, they agreed to head to the river to investigate the supply lines. Alex was confident some of the crates they had seen in the camps were identical to ones he saw offloaded from Captain Hagen's river barge.

Both agreed that river barges made more sense than wagons in supplying large troop deployments. As such, they continued north until they felt safe enough to turn east to the river. Before they left Great Vale, Ben had suggested that, should they be stopped by anyone, they present themselves as Rangers of Westland, rather than Great Vale.

Leander had been there many times, so he knew enough of the area to fool anyone not from the region. West of Great Vale and South of Windfall, Ben had described Westland to Alex as very similar to the Scottish Highlands, with very rough and rocky terrain. There was little land to farm there, so they were mostly herders who traded extensively with Great Vale.

There really wasn't a major city there, it was more of a confederation of small villages. Alex laughed at Ben's use of the word confederation, given his association with the south in the Civil War. Their cover story was they were on a trip to Two Thorns to place a weapons order for the Westland Ranger's Guild.

Both Ben and Leander agreed the story should hold up under questioning. It also gave them cause to go as close to Two Thorns as needed. With Windfall taking such large deliveries from the mountain city, it was considered a location of interest.

After finally turning east, they emerged from the woods to find a large amount of activity along the riverbank in the distance. Both men could make out what appeared to be forty to sixty men spread along the riverbank, tents pitched, and horses nearby.

Alex looked at Leander and the captain tipped his head indicating a change in direction. Rather than continuing east, the two, with Kinsey trotting alongside, turned north again. This allowed them to hug the tree line and avoid close contact with the men on the riverbanks.

"Do they really think they are fooling anyone?" Alex asked after passing the third such grouping of men.

"People will always ignore the obvious if they wish to avoid the truth," Leander replied. "If we were to go down and question the activity, I am sure they would have some story concocted just as we have," he said with a laugh, "like it's a soldier's reunion."

Alex laughed as well, and the two continued their trek north. At one point, Leander had them retreat into the trees, so they could watch a riverboat being pulled to the bank and several crates and barrels offloaded.

"That's a supply drop," Leander commented, "enough for a few days, but not more."

They waited until the boat had gone before emerging from the woods again and resuming their trek. After a bit, Leander stopped his mount, turning to Alex.

"I'm thinking we need to send word to the king before we continue much farther north," Leander said thoughtfully.

"Great, but how?" Alex asked.

Reaching into one of his saddlebags, Leander pulled out a small leather pouch, similar to the one Alex had, full of coins. Leander's pouch contained a small parchment roll and a lead pencil. There was also an acorn. As Alex watched, Leander wrote a short message on the parchment, and then handed it to Alex for review.

It read: "2000+ men camped north in woods. Supplies coming down river. Going north to Two Thorns."

"Looks about right," Alex commented, handing it back to Leander. "Now how do we get it to the king?"

"With this," Leander replied, holding up the acorn, "The Ranger's Guild commissions these from various wizards; it takes a special kind of magic to make them. They are very rare, and the king had to pressure the Guild Master into providing me this one. After that argument, I think he intends to bypass the Guild and get his own. You think about who you want to receive the message," he said while placing the message and acorn in his palm and then covering both with his other hand.

Alex watched Leander stand there for a second or two with both hands clasped. He then removed the top hand and in his palm was a small bird, the message nowhere to be found. As both watched, the bird flew up and headed south, presumably headed to Great Vale and King Ben.

"We won't make Portsward until later tomorrow," commented Leander, "but a trip to Two Thorns might prove valuable."

"Talk to the weapons suppliers?" Alex asked.

"Yes, we might get an idea of how many were ordered and who else may be involved in the support of this effort. I'm surprised Windfall would even attempt this after the last war."

"Where your family was killed?" Alex asked cautiously.

"Yes," Leander replied, "we had a farm north of Great Vale. This was before King Ben. As a matter of fact, it was because of his efforts in that battle that he was permitted to marry the princess and became king."

Alex had wondered how Ben had ended up as king, now he knew. Abrianna's mother was apparently the prior King's daughter and royal heir.

"Anyway, the King of Windfall invaded the Vale, killing many along the way. When they finally reached the outskirts of the city, King Ben, in the service of the King at the time, mounted an attack on horseback. That tactic had not been seen before, and in combination with his magic, he defeated Windfall on the field of battle."

From what Alex knew of Ben, cavalry officer and all, it wasn't a surprise. The Civil War had been a brutal conflict. Cavalry used directly against ground forces though was not that unusual.

"Ben...sorry, King Ben...led direct cavalry assaults against the infantry front lines?" Alex asked, seeing Leander flinch at the familiar reference to his king.

Leander answered, "No, the Vale ground forces were greatly outnumbered. King Ben led the riders and flanked the Windfall lines from both sides, attacking the rear. This, in conjunction with the frontal attack of the Vale infantry and the magic of the mages, collapsed the attack."

"I thought you said it was King Ben's magic?" Alex asked.

"King Ben was the King's Wizard and head of the Mage's Guild. They all acted under his direction, and he was the most powerful on the field of battle," Leander replied.

Alex nodded at that, giving thought to his own circumstances. Ben had been brought here, as had he, in support of some grand Elf vision. It seemed obvious that Ben had been selected to turn back the Windfall invasion and thus maintain the status quo.

Was it coincidence that, at a time when the same scenario was beginning to play out once more, Alex was hijacked and brought here? Why would they need him, however, if they already had Ben? Alex wasn't a military man, and even though everyone said he held great potential as a wizard, he wasn't seeing it.

The two rode on for the rest of the afternoon, noting that the number of troop camps diminished substantially, indicating a massing along the border. Near dark, they retreated into the woods as usual for the night's camp. They ate mostly in quiet and soon went to sleep.

The following morning, as they were breaking camp, something occurred to Alex.

"We are heading into Portsward today aren't we?" he asked Leander.

The captain turned from tying his bedroll to the back of his saddle and replied, "Yes, we need to use the ferry in Portsward to cross the river."

"Likely quite a few Windfall troops there?"

"Yes, if they are using it as a staging area for supplying the troops down river, I would expect a rather large contingent there," Leander replied without turning this time.

Alex rummaged through one of his saddlebags until he found what he was looking for.

"Here," Alex said as he tossed something to Leander.

"Sire?" the captain replied, reverting to the title of respect, while he held the Elf made tan shirt before him.

"Alex," he replied, realizing neither man had addressed the other by first name until now.

"I cannot accept this," Leander said, handing the garment back to Alex.

Waving him off, Alex indicated the one he wore.

"I have two. Besides, I am told that shirt is as good as or better than chain mail, and we are headed deep behind enemy lines. It's in my personal best interest to ensure you should have the finest protection available," he said with a smile.

Alex watched the captain consider his words. Finally, he slipped off his shirt and the mail vest he had under it, and pulled the other on over his head.

"Thank you, sire," Leander replied.

"Please call me Alex, and, by the way, all I know you by is Leander," Alex answered.

"I was very young when my family was killed. I only know my first name, Leander," he stated.

With that, the two mounted up and headed off, with the ever present Kinsey trotting along.

----*----

They rode into Portsward after being stopped twice on the road by soldiers in Windfall colors. As expected, the soldiers relaxed and lost interest once they declared themselves from Westland, and sent them on their merry way.

As this was his only visit to a town of any size, other than his brief view of Great Vale, Alex was rubbernecking while they rode through the street.

"You do that well, Alex; to all you appear a country boy in his first real city," Leander commented.

Alex would have flipped the man off, but he doubted the gesture translated well here. Besides, the comment appeared genuine, so he just smiled and nodded.

There were quite a few Windfall soldiers everywhere they looked. Most seemed bored and disinterested in them. Kinsey however, drew her usual points and stares. In all, none impeded their progress, allowing for an uninterrupted trip to the ferry dock.

The three arrived in time to see the ferry in mid river, heading away from their side.

"Looks like we wait," Alex said.

"I suggest we find a place to eat. It will be several hours before they return and are again ready to cross in our favor," Leander replied, while pointing to several buildings along the waterfront. From the foot traffic in and out, Alex assumed they were restaurants or inns. Indicating that Leander lead, Alex fell in next to him.

Leander selected a place with a watering trough out front. To Alex, it looked like something right out of a western. The one difference was the hitching posts were vertical with iron rings to tie the reins off with. Leaving the horses, the two men entered, with Kinsey at Alex's heels. They selected a small table against the wall and away from the soldiers seated to their right.

Before the server arrived at their table, Alex had Kinsey find a place out of the way of any foot traffic. Soon enough, a man in an apron appeared, not looking overly thrilled.

"Rangers eat free," the man declared in a less than enthusiastic tone.

"We pay our own way," Alex said, setting a silver on the table, but away from the server's grasp. At the sign of the coin, the man's attitude improved greatly.

"We have red and white fish, fresh bread, and day old," he said brightly.

"Dark or light," Alex asked Leander.

"Fresh light bread and the red fish," Leander replied.

"Dark bread and strips for me," Alex added, not sure he wanted to try anything new on this trip.

"Ale, wine or water?" the man asked.

"Water," Leander replied, with a nod of agreement from Alex.

"Bone for Kinsey?" Alex asked while pointing to the wolf in the corner.

"I'll check," the man said a bit nervously, apparently not seeing her there before now.

"If not, a good hunk of meat will do, I'll pay the going rate," Alex replied. Both watched the man retreat before speaking.

"Thank you," Leander said, "while I understand why Rangers eat free, I am uncomfortable taking meals under false pretenses."

Alex smiled and nodded, agreeing with the man's sentiments.

"Anything our new friend might know, that a few coppers could secure?" Alex said while spinning the silver like a top on the table.

That brought a smile to Leander's face. In due course the man returned, carrying bread, a water pitcher, cups, and Kinsey's bone.

"A water bowl also, if you please," Alex said while pointing to the wolf. He kicked himself for forgetting earlier, but Kinsey was delighted with the bone.

"Sir," Leander said as the man prepared to turn, "I haven't been through Portsward in quite a while. Why are there so many soldiers around?"

As the man looked at Leander, Alex slid the silver in the server's direction without releasing control of the coin.

"Don't know exactly," the man replied quietly, while leaning into the table, "been building up over several fortnights. Then about a month ago, them shipments started coming down from the mountains. Someone said it was arms from Two Thorns. Dwarf forged blades."

"Going to whom?" Leander pressed.

"Only see Windfall soldiers these days," the man replied with a knowing wink.

Alex released the coin and said, "Keep the change."

Snatching up the silver, the man hurried off before Alex could change his mind.

"Why would the Dwarves be making weapons for Windfall?" Alex asked.

"The city of Two Thorns resides in the middle of the Dwarf kingdom. Like the Elves, the Dwarves don't usually interact with others unless they must. In this case, they use Two Thorns as their intermediary, have for ages. Unlike the Elves, Dwarves can be convinced to sell weapons for the right amount of gold or gems."

Leander continued, "Besides, it may not be the dwarves, themselves. The smiths of Two Thorns do much of the work that is attributed to the Dwarves."

Satisfied with that answer, Alex took the water pitcher in his hands, as he had seen Abrianna do. Closing his eyes, he tried to let his senses reach out into the water. Sure enough, in his mind's eye, he could see the impurities in the water. Concentrating energy at them, he watched as each was consumed. Unfortunately, he could also feel the pitcher warming in his hands. He removed everything he could, then worked on removing energy from the water. Suddenly he felt Leander's hand on his arm, breaking his concentration.

"It's starting to freeze," he whispered as Alex opened his eyes.

Sure enough, there was a small amount of ice forming across the top of the pitcher.

"Sorry," Alex replied while pouring Leander a cup full and then one for himself.

"Fresh ice water is a treat," Leander replied with a smile.

"Just don't ask me to heat your bath."

Chapter 14

The two men finished their meal and were at the docks in plenty of time to make the next crossing. The ferry had returned while they were eating, and the waiting passengers were preparing to get on board after the occupants from the opposite side finished unloading.

As they watched, Windfall soldiers escorted wagons filled with crates from the ferry and over to the docks for loading onto river barges. They counted another 12 crates bearing Two Thorns markings mixed in with other items.

Once the ferry had emptied, the two men led their mounts on foot, boarding the ferry when summoned. Following the loadmaster's directions, they tied the horses up on one side of the deck. Alex noted there seemed far less traffic headed east at this point, versus what they had seen on the westbound run.

For the first time, Alex got a good look at the ferry operation. A large flat deck allowed for a substantial amount of passengers and cargo. Each side of the river contained two large rope reels and turnstiles. Heavy ropes were attached to each end of the ferry, drawing it to one bank or the other.

Horses on the turnstile turned the reels, which pulled the ropes as they spooled up the loose line. Horses on the slack side were removed, allowing free movement for the lines to play out as the ferry departed. Because the heavy rope sank, any river traffic was free to pass behind the crossing ferry.

"What is directly east of here?" Alex asked, as the ferry let loose from Portsward and started across the river.

From his vantage point, Alex saw only a small number of buildings supporting the ferry on the far side.

"Over there is the ferry dock and a few support structures," Leander replied.

"There is an inn, a stable, and a dry goods store for supplies."

Pointing to the mountains in the northeast, he said, "Two Thorns is that way. The mountains and the city share the same name."

Alex could just make out the two ragged spires contained within the rugged looking range.

"Straight east, and to the south, the land is far more arid. Those people are more nomadic, roaming their herds from place to place, as the seasons dictates. That is what makes Great Vale so important. For hundreds of leagues in all directions, it is the largest single consistent source of farmed goods."

Alex had wondered about the Windfall fascination with Great Vale. He assumed it was a medieval power grab, but with that explanation, he could see it was a lot more than that. Controlling Great Vale meant you controlled most of A'nland.

"So Windfall is the shipping power, but ship to where?" Alex asked, trying to get a better grasp of the power dynamics and world geography.

"Across the western sea are several ports of call," Leander replied, "goods from all over A'nland are shipped through Windfall, both in and out, as it has the only serviceable ports on that coast."

"Westland is on the coast, isn't it?"

"Yes, but the coastline is rocky and rough, mostly high cliffs. There are a few places where you can land a boat on the beach, but no heavy shipping is possible. It is quite popular with smugglers bypassing the Windfall tariffs."

Alex felt a bump as the ferry reached the east bank of the river. Looking down, he watched Kinsey rise to her feet, having sat quietly during the entire crossing. It still amazed Alex at how well she had adapted to her new form. He was just happy she remained as obedient and loyal as ever.

When their turn arrived, the two men led their horses off the ferry and onto the docks before finally reaching the roadway on the other side. The two had agreed over lunch that they would press on to Two Thorns even though it was late in the day and the city was a day's ride from the ferry docks.

Traffic on this side of the river was sparse at best. The men mounted and headed out of town, alone on the road. The other ferry passengers were heading directly east or chose to spend the night and leave in the morning.

As they rode along, Alex studied the mountains ahead. The two craggy spires that inspired the name were prominent against the skyline. The rest of the mountain range reminded him of some of the areas he had frequented in the Cleveland National Forest of Southern California. That area contained extremely rocky scrubland; he often joked that it looked more like a rock garden than a forest.

Alex also noted that there would be no retreating into the trees for tonight's camp. The area around the roadway held local plant life of no more than two or three feet high in all directions.

----*----

Cassie knew her cousin meant well, she didn't have a mean bone in her body. However, she was starting to feel like Abrianna's personal dress up doll. As part of her education, Cassie had received an entirely new wardrobe. Abrianna had taken it on as her own private task to certify Cassie had feminine attire to fit every occasion.

Cassie had never seen so many pastel colors on clothing in her life. Well, that wasn't entirely true, Abrianna had a closet full. Between the pastels and the lace, she was overwhelmed.

Then there were the fabrics. She was being draped in weaves so exotic that she even dreaded to ask the cost. What all this had to do with controlling her inner nymph, she had no idea. Besides, what was taffeta anyway?

----*----

Following a rather rough night, Alex and Leander woke feeling less than rested. Alex discovered that the eastern side of the river, so close to the mountains, was windier than the west. With no trees to shelter them, the brisk wind buffeted both men all night long. Even the horses had dropped down to try to use the brush as a wind block.

With a quick meal behind them, the men set out to reach the gate at Two Thorns by mid-afternoon.

Alex opened the conversation about an hour into their ride, "We seem to be the only traffic in sight. On our return to Great Vale, I could see travelers on roads all over the valley."

"Great Vale has a very diverse economy with a tradition of neutrality. Centrally located, people come from all over the realm to trade. Two Thorns, on the other hand, is a remote location in inhospitable mountains. They specialize in metalworking and weapons manufacture, which they export all over the realm. This is not exactly the place one comes to visit on a whim."

Alex laughed and asked, "Did you swallow a tour guide?"

"I'm sorry, I don't know what that is?" Leander replied, confused at the question.

"Just a joke," Alex replied, waving it off.

"It sounded like you read something out of a book."

"Ah," Leander said, as if he understood, "after my parents were killed, I was taken in by the Ranger's Guild. They have strong traditions around learning. Not all who are taken in become Rangers, but all are well educated. Those not selected for Ranger service are highly sought after by the other guilds."

"Why did you leave?" Alex asked after a bit.

Leander appeared to consider the question before answering, "As you know, the Guild Master in Great Vale was quite controlling. However, that was not the only reason I left the Rangers, though it was a big one. The Guild is supposed to be politically neutral. Since it resides in all cities in one fashion or another, it is based on the principle of protection for all."

"Yes, protect nature and slay foul creatures," Alex replied, repeating Cassie's description.

"Exactly, legend states that the Rangers were founded by the Wood Elves to instill in man a sense of ownership for all nature. There are rumors that the real reason was to counter the foul creatures spawned from Dark Elf magic."

"So the two don't get along too well?" Alex asked.

"There are actually many Elf clans. Dark, Wood, Sea, Mountain, and even Winged, but the predominant sects are the Wood and Dark. And yes, I am told they disagree on many things," Leander replied.

"Anyway, I was seeing more and more bias in the daily business of the Ranger's leadership. They were inserting themselves into local politics at alarming levels. There were rumors that it was happening elsewhere, in other cities. When the Great Vale Guild Master insisted on a seat at the table of the king's council, I knew it was time to leave."

"Would the Guild Master have been involved in the planning of the princess's trip?" Alex asked, suddenly sensing a connection.

"Most certainly, his seat on the council is specifically involved in such things," Leander answered, catching the implications and shaking his head sadly.

Alex considered this new development as the two men rode along quietly. From all the information he had gathered to date, he had been transported here by one of the many Elven sects for a reason. The popular guess was to help restore the balance, and with war looming, it seemed logical something was definitely out of sorts. As he was dropped here in Ranger's clothes, it could be argued the Wood Elves were at work. It was also troubling to hear that the same Ranger group was potentially corrupt.

But why him? That had Alex confused. While everyone talked about his great power, only he knew the truth. So far, he had stumbled his way through several small conflicts, surviving by the smallest of margins. The saying, "I'd rather be lucky than good" seemed to be at play here.

Turning his attention back to the roadway, he noticed that they had moved off the dirt road of the low lands near the river and onto a stone causeway. By now, they were into the foothills of the Two Thorn Mountains and the grade was increasing in steepness with every step. Since it needed to accommodate heavily laden wagons traveling to and from the city, he had little fear of it becoming too challenging for their horses.

One of the interesting aspects of the road's construction was the fact that the roadway had drainage ditches cut into the stone on either side of the main causeway. The more surprising characteristic was everything was cut out of solid stone. Alex suspected it would take modern machinery years to cut this road all the way up into the mountains.

"Do you know how they made this road?" Alex asked.

"It was done long ago. Legends say the Dwarves of the Mountains formed the original roadway by hand. Once men came and created the city, the mages finished what we see here today. It is said it took them over one hundred years to complete. This is the only road in or out of the city, and it has never fallen to an enemy."

"Mages, not stone masons?" Alex asked, confused at the reference.

"No, it would have taken stone masons far longer to complete. The mages worked together to burn through the stone, creating the shapes as they went," Leander replied.

"I am told you have the power to burn down a dozen orcs with a wave of your hand."

Alex laughed at the comment, "So that's the story, is it?"

"You did no such thing?" he asked Alex curiously.

"Did they mention I passed out afterward?" Alex asked in return.

That brought a laugh from Leander.

"Great magic pulls hard from within. Yes, Lady Cassandra said you cut down several more with your blade before collapsing from exhaustion."

"I'll take her word on that," Alex replied, not wanting to belabor the point.

"After the blast I don't remember a whole lot."

By now, they had ridden well up into the mountains, with canyon walls raising high above them on either side. While not a military man, Alex noted this would be a great place to rain death from above. He suspected there had never been a successful assault on Two Thorns for that very reason.

By mid-afternoon, they finally reached the main gates of Two Thorns, right on schedule. The stone causeway they had been following led up a steep, straight canyon. It ran for several hundred feet with a massive stone wall at its end. Two huge gates opened outward at its center. Looking up as they approached, Alex could make out figures high above, likely guards watching the riders as they neared.

Passing through the gates unchallenged, Alex noted the walls were ten feet thick. The stones were finely shaped, with nothing more than a thin seam identifying where one stopped and the next started.

There was a second set of gates on the inside of the wall. These opened inward, providing additional protection from a gate breach. Once inside the wall, Alex could see the street widened out in front of them. Lining each side of the street were more stone structures that tiered up and away from them. He could see where the first level, closest to them, had flat roofs that supported a more narrow parallel roadway on top for foot traffic on either side. A second set of buildings were pushed up and back behind that.

Above that, a third tier mimicked the second and so on. It was level after level of buildings and roadways sloping up both sides of the broad canyon. Reaching the first intersection, he was surprised to see it only contained switchbacks allowing movement up or down from one level to another.

Noting Leander watching him, he heard the man say, "Two Thorns is like no other city in all the realms. It continues straight back, down this canyon, with buildings going up both canyon walls. There is no space for it to spread out as in Great Vale. There is far more you don't see carved back into the mountain itself."

They continued to ride up into the city, with Leander pointing out various structures on the different levels. Most of the travelers inns and merchants were on the first two tiers near the gates, while the Guild houses and other more personal residences where higher up on either side and more to the rear of the canyon.

Leander explained the armorers they were seeking existed far up the canyon, closer to their sources of materials. That meant nearer the Dwarf's caves and tunnels. As the Dwarves tunneled throughout the mountains, they mined the metals they unearthed. Precious metals like gold and silver they kept for themselves, but ore like iron and copper they sold to the metalworkers of Two Thorns.

Those profits, in turn, were used to purchase food and other supplies the Dwarves needed. The arrangement had existed for hundreds of years and had served both humans and Dwarves well.

"Let's try here," Leander said as they pulled up in front of one of the many stone structures. Alex could see nothing that indicated it was a smith's shop, or that it was any different from the rest. It was all stone with windows of glass and wood. The large wooden door, bound with iron bands, stood open.

Entering the first room, Alex could see the structure went far deeper into the side of the mountain than he had expected. The front room consisted of several long tables, with benches for seating. There were several men moving between the tables, going through loose parchments stacked in small piles.

Behind the tables were stacks and stacks of crates, with some of the stacks piled above head height. Beyond the crates, he could see another wall of stone, with a large opening in its center. Between the stacks, Alex could make out men working in the back, and the hammering of metal on metal.

As Leander and Alex entered, with Kinsey on their heels, one of the men stopped what he was doing and approached.

"Rangers," the man said, somewhat in surprise, "what can I do for you?"

Deferring to Leander, Alex stepped to one side.

"We are from Westland," Leander began, "and we find ourselves in somewhat of an embarrassing position. We have a class graduating and find the Guild armory short a few blades."

"Well you would be," laughed the man in a knowing fashion, "but why the trip? Surely you know our entire production is already committed. In addition, we are shorthanded due to the loss of our journeyman mages."

As if to commiserate with the Ranger's shortfall, the man continued, "As it is, our production commitments to the effort are falling behind. The junior mages left behind do not have the control we need for tempering and strengthening the metal in a reasonable time."

Leander and Alex exchanged glances before the captain cautiously said, "We had hoped a few coins might secure some older inventory."

"Why not wait for a few weeks?" the man replied with a confused look, "by then you all will be sporting new weapons to go with the new uniforms!"

As the man was speaking, Alex noted one of the men at the tables beyond had slipped out the front door while the third was listening intently to the discussion.

"Have you boys checked in with the Guild yet?" The man at the table asked, cutting off the other before he could continue.

On the way to Two Thorns, Leander had explained to Alex the normal protocol for any Ranger visiting a major city. They were to check in with the local Guild house upon arrival, receiving an orientation to local customs, provided updated orders, and informed of the latest relevant news.

Catching a whiff that something was amiss, Alex replied, "No sir, we had hoped to complete our business, get a hot meal and soft bed, and then head home tomorrow morning."

"You make a good point," Leander said to the first man, "Let's go check in then."

With that Leander spun in place and started heading out, picking up on Alex's concerns. As both emerged from the building, they went directly to their horses. However, before either could mount, Alex exclaimed, "Oh shit!"

Coming up the street, and blocking their exit from Two Thorns, were at least twenty armed men, some in Ranger colors.

"Those two!" the man who had slipped out earlier cried, while pointing at Leander and Alex.

"Follow me!" Leander said pointing his horse at the oncoming group and slapping its rump, sending it running into the mass of men.

Grabbing his bow and quiver, water skin attached to both, Alex followed suit while yelling, "Go Home!" to his mount.

He then spun and followed Leander back into the building, with Kinsey in the lead.

Back inside, he found one man on the floor, out cold, and Leander engaged with the second. Shutting and barring the door, he then shuttered the windows. Once finished, he found Leander standing over the second man. The form on the ground was motionless, and Alex didn't care to spend the time to see why.

"What now?" he asked Leander, as the shouting outside grew louder.

"We head out the back way," he replied leading Alex into the area with all the crates. He could hear pounding on the door behind them now as he left. Following the captain, Alex and Kinsey weaved through the stacked crates and into the work area behind them. As they reached the opening, Alex could better understand why nobody had come forward to investigate the disturbance up front.

The crates masked a good part of the commotion behind them and the noise inside this room was overpowering. Slowing to a walk, the three entered the room and continued to the rear of the work area. Several of the smiths glanced up from their work, but only nodded at the Rangers and then continued their work.

The work area itself was as large as the previous two spaces combined and had torches and oil lamps on the walls and in stands throughout providing additional light. The space contained five teams working at tables and flat metal blocks that Alex took to be anvils. Each team of two or three had one smith working a metal blade with one or two mages heating between hammerings. Alex was surprised to see a couple of women in the mix as mages.

At the rear of the room was another large opening, allowing entry into a passageway that ran both right and left. The passage was less well lit than the work area with only wall torches evenly spaced on the far wall.

"They use this as a service access and to permit ventilation. Its keeps traffic off the streets and goes directly to the Dwarf mines," Leander explained.

"They bring the materials in here from the mines, and finished weapons go out the front."

Turning right, he said, "We can head back toward the main gate this way and slip out after dark."

He suddenly pulled up short as a loud commotion ahead of them indicated pursuit had found an entrance into the same passage from the neighboring business.

"This way," Leander said while doing a 180 degree turn and breaking into a run. With bow and quiver in hand and Kinsey at his heels, he followed Leander at a dead run himself. They passed the occasional opening on their left with uninterrupted stone on their right.

Not knowing whether the two men had cut into one of the many openings, the pursuit had to slow to check each. Pausing to check the pursuit after a good distance, neither Alex nor Leander could hear the sound of men behind them. By this point, they had traveled quite a ways down the passage and back into the mountain tunnels.

Turning back to Leander, Alex pointed ahead at the passage walls, "That's not stonework."

"Dwarf tunnels," Leander replied, pulling a torch from the wall and heading off into the dark tunnel.

Chapter 15

Ben had received his feathered visitor from his personal Rangers two days ago, and had immediately called his private council together. Still unsure of who he could trust after the attempt on his daughter, Ben had reduced the number of attendees to his core advisors.

Once he shared the message, while not disclosing the source, his military commanders wanted to call up the troops in preparation for the impending attack. The Guild Master of the Rangers however, preached caution to the King. He speculated that this was nothing more than the posturing of the young prince, and sending troops into the field would only escalate matters. He assured Ben that his Rangers were reporting no visible troop buildups in Windfall.

Ben knew all too well that it took time to muster and deploy his army, both cavalry and infantry. Most would need to come in from the countryside for outfitting before they could be fielded in defense of the city. In the end, he agreed to a few more days delay while he waited for additional information. Only he knew about Captain Leander and Alex's mission, and he intended to keep it that way.

----*----

Alex, Leander, and Kinsey had moved deep into the tunnels before selecting a small side tunnel to rest and plan their next move. As Alex had accidently grabbed a water skin in his haste, they avoided a thirsty night. They sat quietly for the longest time, listening for any sound and insuring they hadn't been followed into the tunnels.

Leander had secured the torch he carried in a crack in the tunnel wall, blocking most of its light. This reduced the telltale glow of its flames down the tunnel to no more than a few feet in either direction. Sitting on the ground and making themselves as comfortable as possible, they rested in silence.

Finally, Alex whispered, "Is it ok to speak?"

Leander nodded, "Quietly. I believe they are gone, but now we have other concerns. Dwarves do not take kindly to those they find in their tunnels uninvited."

Alex returned a nod of understanding before changing the subject, "So did I misunderstand, or did we get confirmation that the Rangers are in on this too?"

"It appears the Guild is compromised. This is very disturbing," Leander replied solemnly.

"Why would all the Rangers turn on Great Vale?" Alex asked.

"They wouldn't," replied Leander.

"There has been an ongoing issue of Rangers disappearing while out in the wilderness. Now that I think about it in these terms, I suspect the regional Guild Masters sent those men to their deaths."

"Removing those they knew wouldn't go along?"

"Yes and then recruiting those more sympathetic to their goals. Apparently, I was fortunate enough to be allowed to transfer to the king's service instead. I would have never agreed to this," Leander said firmly.

"He also mentioned that the senior mages were all gone?"

"I suspect Windfall has recruited those of sufficient skill to act on the battlefield. Prince Renfeld will not repeat his father's mistake and take to the battlefield ill-equipped to deal with magic," Leander replied.

"Now, it is imperative that we need to get back as soon as possible and warn the king."

"We need to get out of here first," Alex observed.

Leander considered the statement before he replied, "I am told some mages can use their magical talents to divine doors or passages. Maybe if you can reach out with your senses, like you did with the water, you can find the way out?"

Alex wasn't exactly sure what he meant, but the visualization he got with the water was a start. Closing his eyes, he placed both hands on the wall opposite him and let his mind wander beyond the wall itself. Slowly he could visualize the stone and earth in the wall, small amounts of free energy trapped in spaces in between. As he began to travel through the wall, parallel to the passage, he expanded his senses to see if he could find voids, representing other tunnels.

He was suddenly stopped by a huge mass of solid metal. As his senses explored the object, he got a sense of purity. He could see the tendrils radiating from the gold nugget as they radiated out in several directions.

Moving on, he continued down the passage until he ended in a huge cavern. The chamber was several hundred feet from their current location.

"There is a huge cave a few hundred feet that way," Alex told Leander, while pointing off to his left. After a few more minutes, all three got to their feet and Leander retrieved the torch. Taking the lead, Leander headed off in the direction Alex had indicated. Stepping cautiously, the men moved down the tunnel, trying to make as little noise as possible and constantly listening for any indication of others.

Soon enough, they reached the place where the tunnel opened up into the cavern that Alex had sensed. As they stepped into the void, both scanned the darkness, but the torchlight wasn't powerful enough to illuminate the huge expanse.

As Kinsey let loose with a low growl, figures slowly emerged into the torchlight.

"You Rangers shouldn't have come!" one of the Dwarves barked.

Looking around, Alex discovered at least twenty men surrounded them, all no more than five foot tall but almost as wide. Each held some form of weapon, pick, or shovel. He suddenly suspected Mountain Dwarves could see in the dark.

"Couldn't sense the Dwarves?" Leander asked quietly.

"Nope," Alex replied.

"Need to work on that."

"Yeah," Alex replied sarcastically.

"We have told your master we want no part of your politics!" another Dwarf snapped.

"We aren't with those guys; these are disguises," Alex answered.

"Then why are you here?" asked a Dwarf moving to the front of the group. From the way the others parted to allow him passage, Alex assumed he was the leader.

"To avoid death," Alex replied.

That brought a laugh from the group.

"You chose to come here to avoid being killed," one commented, "that's poor decision making!"

"Who is trying to kill you?" asked the leader, mildly curious.

"We serve King Ben of Great Vale," Leander answered, "and we have unmasked a plot against him. They have corrupted the Ranger's Guild and seek to lay waste to our lands."

"More politics!" one of the Dwarves stated.

"What do we care about the tools of the Elves? You Rangers should have sought their help," the leader replied.

"You two need not worry anyway," replied another, swinging his axe back and forth.

"Kill them," the leader said calmly, turning away.

"Wait!" Alex bellowed, as Leander drew his sword and Kinsey prepared to leap on the nearest Dwarf.

"I am told you value gold," Alex yelled.

Everyone stopped. As he watched, the leader turned back and faced Alex.

"Yes," he replied simply.

"How much to buy our freedom?" Alex asked.

That brought another laugh from the group.

"Boy, we aren't interested in what you have in your coin purse," the leader replied, and began turning away again.

"What if I can lead you to a nugget as large as several men?" Alex asked lightly.

The Dwarf stopped in mid turn. Without turning back, he asked, "And where might that be?"

"In your own tunnels. I found it on the way in. You let us go and I will show you where it is."

"Liar. We have exhausted this side of the mountain," one of the others shouted. The leader turned back and stepped up to face Alex directly.

"Are you lying to me, boy? If you are, your death will be painful!" he said quietly.

"No lies," Alex said calmly, "you agree to let us go and I will take you right to it."

The Dwarf stared into Alex's eyes for a minute before saying, "Deal."

Leander gave Alex a confused look, but followed him back into the tunnels with the Dwarves close behind. Every so often Alex would stop and place both hands on the tunnel wall, letting his senses drift out into the stone and earth. After about five stops, he finally stood back and pointed to the wall.

"Right there."

That brought even more laughter from the group.

"Boy, if nothing else, you've made us laugh more today than we have in years. There's no gold there," the leader said.

One of the other Dwarves stepped up to the spot and sniffed several times before turning with a shrug. "I smell nothing," he said.

"Well you bought yourself a few more minutes with this deception," the leader said as he started to order his men to attack.

"I am telling you there is gold there," Alex said, before changing tactics.

"I also understand Dwarves like to gamble?"

Several of the Dwarves nodded in agreement.

"I will bet you I can prove there is gold there. Moreover, when I do, you will not only let us go, you will lead us out of here, safely away from Two Thorns. And you will stake us with provisions."

"Is that all?" the leader replied with a laugh, looking around as if Alex were insane.

"No, you will also owe me a favor." Alex added for emphasis, "It's a lot of gold."

At this point Alex could tell even Leander had thought he had lost his mind.

"And if there is no gold?" the leader asked.

"You get to kill us, no resistance," he said to Leander's surprise.

"I can do that now!" he replied.

"Not before we kill a few of you. Who would you miss most?" Alex asked while pointing to the men encircling them.

The Dwarf thought awhile before replying, "Ok, it's a bet!"

Motioning everyone back, Alex handed Leander his bow, quiver, and water skin, then faced the wall and began to concentrate. He had been playing mental games on the entire trip, trying to refine his use of energy in a more efficient manner.

It occurred to him that if he thought more in terms of lasers and less in blasters, he could use less of his own energies in his constructs. Power wasn't his issue, it was control that he struggled with.

As everyone watched, Alex released a narrow bright white beam into the stone. It was no more than a few inches in diameter and tight in its construction. It was far more controlled than his first effort with the Orcs. Around him, he could just make out the whispers of "White Wizard" over the pounding in his head.

Satisfied the beam had reached its goal, Alex redirected the loose energies into the gold itself. It took several minutes, but slowly, a stream of molten gold began to first drip, and then run from the borehole. He could hear the gasps from the Dwarves as it ran like syrup down the tunnel wall.

"Satisfied?" Alex asked finally, while motioning for Leander to hand him the water skin.

None of the Dwarves even looked at him as they all nodded agreement. The Dwarf who had sniffed before stepped up and repeated the process.

"It's a huge find!" he exclaimed, "there was something in-between, blocking my nose before."

Finally turning back from staring at the stream on the wall, the leader stepped up to Alex and said,

"You win. Come, let's eat, rest, and tomorrow we will set you safely on your way."

Slapping Alex on the back and almost knocking him to the ground, he continued, "I am Brokkr, King of the Two Thorns Mountains and leader of this horde." With a flourish, he indicated the Dwarves around them.

Leading them back into the cavern they had started from, Brokkr ordered torches lit for the benefit of the men. With the additional light, Alex and Leander could see the huge mistake they had made. The entire area was set up as the Dwarves' living quarters. There were tables and benches, large wooden chairs and beds set up in singles and bunks. They had wandered right into the middle of the group they were trying to avoid.

"Don't eat or drink anything until I check it," Alex whispered to Leander.

Sitting at a table sized for men a foot shorter than themselves, both men were given food and drink. Alex subtly checked both and found nothing of concern, although deciding the ale might not be good for him at the moment. Even Kinsey got a large leg bone that she found delightful. The Dwarves showed no concerns about having her there and treated her as a favored pet.

When everyone was settled with food and drink, Brokkr asked, "So why the disguises? Hiding from Prince Renfeld's mage round up?"

"What do you know of that?" Alex asked between bites. The use of that much magic had left him hungry and lightheaded.

"Only that he found himself a couple of Red Mages powerful enough to convince the other senior mages to join him or die. A White Wizard like you should have no problems with the likes of them. Never seen such a beautiful borehole in all my days!" he finished, referring to the one spouting gold Alex had created.

While Alex knew he was no wizard, he considered it a poor time to correct the Dwarf. Alex assumed the colors had something to do with the nature of the wizard. Both Ben and Abrianna were blue and green, calming colors. Red was always an angry color to Alex. He wondered what that was all about. Once they got back to Great Vale, he needed to ask Ben.

"You've never worked with mages?" Alex asked.

"Oh, we tried once. We took their labor as a partial payment for some iron stock. None could do what you did alone, and combined, the three of them would have taken all day," he replied in a matter of fact tone.

"You mentioned earlier that the Rangers had approached you? Did they say for what?" Alex asked.

"They wanted us to join them in attacking Great Vale. Said it was Prince Renfeld's destiny to rule all the A'nland lands west of the river. It sounded like a bunch of human politics to us, so we sent them packing."

"You didn't think it was abnormal that the Rangers should be asking?" Leander offered.

"I only thought it odd, as the Elves would know better than to ask us for anything. We figured the humans had finally broken free of their control," Brokkr replied, obviously disinterested in the why.

"We have very little use for any of that down here. Our metals get us the provisions we need regardless of who rules the lands in the west."

With a full stomach and a hard day's effort behind him, Alex was glad to accept one of the offered beds, though his feet hung off the end. With the torches extinguished, he was soon asleep, even with the torrential snoring that surrounded him.

----*----

The following morning, the Dwarves were kind enough to illuminate the area once more. While a good portion of the group went to attack the newly located gold pocket, Brokkr and a few others saw that Alex and Leander were fed, provisioned, and led away as promised.

The Dwarves guided the men into the tunnels for quite a ways. Kinsey seemed unconcerned with them, as the Dwarves had spoiled her with treats and attention, obviously used to such animals. Finally, as they turned a corner, Alex could make out light from more than their torches.

Ahead, he could see the outline of a tunnel opening, showing clear blue sky. As they emerged, he could make out the river T'ybel in a valley below. Looking around, he could see they had come out onto a large flat in the mountains, right next to a torrent of water spouting from the rocks on their right.

The waterfall emptied into a large pool a good distance below, before running off into a stream that was a tributary to the river beyond. Looking around, Alex realized there was no trail leading down.

"As promised," Brokkr stated, his sweeping hand showing the view. "We are far from Two Thorns and safe from the dangers therein."

As Alex looked down over the edge, Brokkr added, "The next closest exit is on the back side of the mountains, far from your intended goal. This is not a trick, Wizard. This is your best choice. Others have survived the jump."

He smiled and nearly knocked Alex over the edge with a pat to his back. "And should you survive as well, I remember that a debt is owed."

With that, the Dwarf King and his men turned and left the three peering over the edge, looking at the pool far below.

While looking over the edge, Alex commented, "Kinsey hates water."

"That should distract her from the fall then," Leander replied flatly.

Handing Leander all the supplies he had been carrying, Alex lifted the two hundred pound wolf in his arms. Turning quickly, he ran for the edge before she could comprehend what he was doing. As he cleared the edge, he caught a glimpse of Leander following suit.

Chapter 16

The two men sat on a rock at the edge of the pool, dripping wet. Kinsey had worked a little higher up the rock, to be as far from the water as possible. The impact on the water from the fall hadn't been as bad as Alex expected. However, Kinsey landing right on top of him a mere moment later was every bit as bad as he thought it would be.

With nothing but their dignity injured, they had collected all their supplies and were planning their next move. Alex noted Brokkr had all their provision wrapped in waterproof materials.

"How thoughtful," he muttered.

Their next challenge was getting to the river below. The waterway they currently occupied continued down a canyon, with no visible footpaths on either side. For them to reach the river, they needed to continue floating downstream. The stream contained a series of smaller waterfalls that were nowhere near the drop distance of the one they had just experienced. For the men, it would be of little consequence to continue on this way.

For Kinsey however, it was going to be the defining moment of her life. Alex was not going to be able to manhandle her down the stream. She would need to do this on her own, without any assistance from him or Leander. For the moment, she was sitting, dripping wet and glaring at Alex.

With no option but to continue downstream, Alex and Leander looked down the canyon, trying to select stopping points, between the waterfalls, where they could pause and regroup. First Leander, and then Alex, entered the stream, each carrying an equal part of their supplies. Not even bothering to try to coax Kinsey in now, Alex intended to try to draw her down at the first stop. However, as he looked back just before the first stop, he watched Kinsey jump into the water, following the two men.

At their first stop, both men praised her as she came ashore with them. After a good shake, she was all tongue and wagging tail. Once everyone had rested, the three repeated the process several times until they finally reached the foothills at the base of the canyon.

Climbing out at the last stop, they took some time to rest and dry out. Alex started a small fire while Leander assembled a midday meal. He made sure to reward Kinsey for her earlier efforts in the water.

"I don't suppose you have another one of those acorn birds on you?" Alex asked between bites.

"No, I was given just the one. As I said before, those are very rare. However, we now understand why the Guild Master was so resistant to the king's request," Leander replied.

Alex nodded. "Do you know where we are?"

"Yes," he responded, "that is the river T'ybel, and this feeder stream is a good distance north of Two Thorns. We need to follow the river south, crossing at some point, to get home."

"How much freedom do the Rangers get inside the castle?" Alex asked, changing the subject, his concern for Cassie and her family evident.

"Far too much, I'm afraid. The Rangers are a much loved and trusted institution. It sickens me to know the depths of the corruption within the Guild."

"Guess that means we need to get moving then," Alex said standing and collecting his half of their load.

With a nod from Leander, the two men and Kinsey doused their fire and continued out of the foothills and into the flats below. The area near the stream they followed was lusher than the landscape they had followed on the way into the mountains. This afforded them a little more cover in their movements. While walking, both men constantly scanned for threats from the south or west across the river.

It was early afternoon by the time they reached the river's banks, and with no visible means of crossing, they followed it south. The trees lining the banks grew in clusters, leaving open areas where the group would sprint from cover to cover. Both knew the farther south they traveled, the more likely they were to run into trouble.

By now, they were sure that both Two Thorns and Windfall had dispatched men with the intent of locating them. Alex suspected their orders were, at best, to capture them, though neither he nor Leander intended on being taken. It was during one of these sprints that they were spotted by riders on the far bank.

"Alex, we've been spotted," Leander shouted, pointing at the two Windfall riders across the river. Far from concerned, the two men on horseback seemed to study the three before agreeing on something. As Alex and Leander watched, one of the men raised a crossbow and took aim at them.

The action caused Alex to string his own bow, though the thought barely registered in his head. The behavior of the Windfall rider seemed foolish, for as he let the bolt fly, both Alex and Leander simply sidestepped the oncoming projectile. It passed them without incident.

However, Alex had let fly a return shaft a mere moment after he saw the bolt approaching. His arrow caught the shooter squarely in the chest, taking him off his horse.

"Apparently Elf bows are much better than crossbows," Alex said as the rider had dropped before the bolt even reached Alex's side of the river. At that, the second rider spun his horse in an attempt to run, but not before Alex sent a second shaft flying. The arrow flew straight, taking him from his saddle as well.

Alex caught a nod of approval from Leander before the captain said, "I wish we were over there, we'd have horses now."

Now it was Alex's turn to nod, and then both men started south again.

"We are good for now, but by tomorrow those two soldiers will be missed. We really need to cross this river before that happens," Leander commented as they walked.

"I'm open to suggestions," Alex replied, not seeing swimming as an option.

Unfortunately, Leander had no ideas either, replying with only a shrug. Alex knew they could attempt a raft, using the river current to help move them along once adrift. However, the time spent building one would put them behind schedule and leave them exposed to more of the roving patrols.

The three walked in silence, Kinsey staying close, as they trekked south. By late afternoon, they had put some distance between themselves and where they had encountered the Windfall riders. In this area, the foothills of the Two Thorns reached closer to the river, creating hills and gullies.

As they crested each hill, both men would scan the countryside looking for riders, before dropping into the gap on the other side. It was in one of these gaps between the hillcrests that they were ambushed. They had no more than dropped into the small crevasse, and then a dozen men sprang from hiding.

Kinsey dropped into a crouch as she growled. With several bowmen mixed in the group, Alex estimated he could only get one before the others shot them both.

"Drop your weapons!" one of the men commanded.

Alex lowered his bow and said, "Look, you are robbing the wrong men. We are Rangers traveling south, we have no valuables."

"Fraud," one of the men said in reply.

"We know who you are. We are not bandits, we are from Two Thorns. Come with us quietly or we bring back your bodies."

With any hope of playing themselves off as corrupted Rangers apparently gone, Alex started to lift his bow again. Unsure of the Elf weaved shirt's ability to protect them, Alex was still preparing to attempt an attack anyway.

Should they be captured, any hope of warning Ben and Cassie in time would be lost. Just before he launched his assault, the man he had been speaking with suddenly sprouted an arrow in his chest, as did the entire Two Thorns force.

Leander turned to Alex with a questioning look on his face, which Alex returned with a shrug. Both men looked up to find archers on both sides of the depression they stood in.

"We have been searching for you Alex Rogers," one said.

Turning to look at Alex, the captain stated, "Elves."

"Are you here to kill us?" Alex asked the nearest of the elf bowmen.

With a confused look, the Elf replied, "No, we are here to rescue you."

"Finally, I meet a mythical creature that isn't trying to kill me!"

----*----

The Elves led the three down to the river's edge, with Kinsey accepting the Elves better than she had the Dwarves. Reaching the riverbank, he saw there were several small boats waiting. There were more elves on the far bank waiting for them to return. More importantly, on the far side of the river there were horses, Alex's black mare in the group.

"How did you find my horse?" Alex asked one of the elves.

"You sent Shadows home, so she came back to us. That was how we knew to come looking for you," the Elf replied as everyone climbed into one of the various boats. Alex was directed to one with room for Kinsey as well, while Leander was placed in an adjacent craft.

Crossing the river, Alex got his first opportunity to look the Elves over more closely. Appearing tall from a distance, Alex realized they were no taller than six foot, some likely just under. However, they were slender, giving them a lanky look and making them appear taller in proportion.

There was a mixture of men and women in this group, the females only slightly shorter than the males. All had fair skin, with the expected pointy ears that the fairy tales described. There was a combination of light and dark hair, with a mixture of long and short hair on both men and women.

Each was dressed impeccably, their woodland attire tailored to fit without the disheveled look of most humans. All had bow and sword, exact duplicates of the ones Alex carried. As a race, they were all very good looking, with the women in Alex's boat simply stunning. One caught him staring and smiled as he quickly looked away.

Once they reached the far bank, most of the party disembarked, leaving one Elf in each boat. As Alex watched, the boats turned and headed upriver, moving against the current with ease. He hadn't realized until now that no one had been rowing the boats across the river.

"Once you master your magic, you will be able to enchant objects as well," one of the Elves commented in passing, noting his stare.

Turning to reply, Alex discovered the Elf had already moved to one of the horses and was preparing to mount. Alex took that as his cue and walked over to his mare, whom he now knew was named Shadows.

"Thanks for fetching help," he whispered to the mare as he rubbed between her ears and stroked her neck.

Mounting, he realized he was pleased to have Shadows back, she being one of the few familiar creatures in his life here. He was also happy to be back in a saddle as opposed to walking. Alex noted Leander had been provided a horse of his own and the group started to head northwest.

"Hey, isn't Great Vale south?" Alex shouted to the lead rider.

"Yes, but we are not going there."

A female riding next to Alex offered, "We were ordered to find you and bring you back to E'anbel. It is in the north wood at the base of the Northern Mountains. Once there, all will be explained."

Alex saw Leander on the other side of the female nod his head in understanding while smiling broadly. Alex assumed E'anbel was a location, maybe a town of some kind, although he didn't remember it on Abrianna's map.

The group picked up its pace, Kinsey trotting easily along nearby and seemingly happy for the exercise.

They continued for the rest of the afternoon at a brisk pace, far harder than Alex would normally push a horse, but none of these seemed effected. Just before dark, they reached the woods that Alex assumed was their goal. The trees were tall and densely packed, giving little room to pass. He could see the mountains in the background, and he assumed they were the Northern Mountains the Elf had mentioned earlier.

During the ride to the forest, they had encountered another fair sized feeder stream. It appeared to be running from the woods and down to the river, and they rode with the stream on their left. They had ridden parallel to its path for quite a distance before he verified that it indeed seemed to originate from the woods.

The lead rider dropped down into the water, using the stream as the path inside the forest. Entering the woods, it became increasingly dark, but the elves seemed not to notice. Finally, when he could barely make out the riders around him, Alex spoke up.

"I can't see where I'm going," he stated.

A voice in the darkness replied, "Give Shadows her head, she will guide you safely."

Loosening the reins, Alex stopped trying to guide the mare and simply prayed there were no low branches. With no idea of the real time that had passed, Alex guessed it was about thirty minutes before he began to see a dull glow up ahead. As they grew closer to the glow, he could now make out the riders around him and saw Kinsey was still safely close by.

The stream was narrower here and the group was forced to form up in single file. The female Elf Alex had been speaking with earlier was in front of him and there were several male elves bringing up the rear. Leander was up ahead somewhere, where Alex couldn't see him. Kinsey was doing her best to stay on the bank and out of the water, while remaining close to Alex.

Alex could now see that the glow was more of a fluorescent shimmering between the trees. The closer he got, the brighter it became, until he could make out everything for several feet in all directions. As he watched, the riders in the lead reached the shimmering wall and seemed to disappear.

Soon enough, the rider in front of him reached the wall and, as she continued forward, she suddenly vanished. Shadows continued right behind, Alex only along for the ride at this point.

Passing through the glowing boundary, Alex emerged into the bright light of a well-lit fair sized city. The forest stream had now become a stone causeway, with buildings all around. Alex looked over to see Leander looking around in wonder.

"This is E'anbel!" Leander declared in excitement.

"Ok?" Alex replied in confusion.

"This is one of the fabled cities of the Woodland Elves. It cannot be found by outsiders, you must be invited in," he exclaimed.

As Leander spoke, Alex looked around at the stone structures, finding them vaguely familiar. He couldn't quite place it, but he had seen these buildings, or something like them, before. The streets were busy, and everyone was Elven. The Elves paid scant attention to the riders or Kinsey as they passed through the streets.

Looking down, he was gratified to see Kinsey following by his side, unfazed by all the changes. The riders continued through the city streets, passing by various vendors and merchants. At one point, Alex looked down a side street to see what looked like the city square. It held a large stone fountain in the center with a statue atop the center pedestal. The image triggered the recognition of where he had seen the buildings before.

The fountain he had just seen was identical to the one at the center of the dead city in the Dark Woods. He now realized that the buildings were of the same design and construction, with the same materials. The fountain here retained the figure at its peak, where the other had been destroyed long ago.

The revelation created a completely new set of question in Alex's head. Was that the dead city of the Dark Elves, or just a result of a battle between the two Elf factions? Abrianna had indicated it was about an abuse of power, so he was dying to learn what had happened.

While all this was going through his head, he failed to realize they had stopped. Moving quickly to catch up, he dismounted, and thanked the Elf holding Shadows for him. They had stopped in front of a large multistory stone building, with a grand set of steps leading up to two very large wooden doors.

Both doors stood open, and as Alex, Kinsey and Leander followed a small group of Elves up, they were greeted by two new Elves. Both females were in fine gauzy attire, similar to sleeveless floor length dresses. The color seemed to shift between shades of light and dark green as the fabric moved.

Looking down at Kinsey with disdain, one of the women said, "Please follow us and we will show you to your quarters. There you can clean up before the meal."

Alex turned to thank his rescuers, only to find them gone without a sound. With that, the three were led into the structure, where he discovered it was apparently hollow in its center. Alex had seen similar Roman construction, where the building was a large square or rectangle with an open central courtyard.

Often there was a pool or fountain in the open central area, creating a private space for rest and relaxation.

Here, the center was a lush green garden with a stone path passing through its center. Turning to their right at the doorway and going around the garden rather than through it, the Elves passed the corner of the square. There they then turned left, stopping about halfway down the open hallway.

One of the two motioned to the open doorway, "You will find everything you need in here. Someone will come for you when the meal is ready."

All three outsiders entered the room, where Alex expected a Spartan prison cell with a door closed behind them. Instead, they entered an open central area, with polished marble floors. There was ample seating and a large central table, similar to a coffee table. The room was well decorated, containing artwork unlike anything Alex had ever seen.

There were open doorways on either side of the main room. Leander headed left, while Alex went right. Peering into the one on the right, Alex found several intricately carved wood framed beds lining the far wall. All contained colorful bedclothes, with overstuffed pillows in quantity. Turning to look across the room, he saw Leander looking into the other doorway.

"We can wash up in here," he replied to the questioning look from Alex.

Crossing the main room, he followed Leander into the anteroom, while Kinsey found herself a comfortable spot away from anything involving baths. Entering, he found a large colorful tiled bathing pool, filled with preheated water. Relieved he wouldn't need to heat the water for the two of them, he began undressing.

Though more barren then the other two rooms, this room was art itself. The walls contained wonderful mosaics depicting scenes of hunts and celebrations. Alex asked Leander if he knew their meaning, but he was as much in the dark as Alex was about the stories they told.

Looking around the room as he undressed, he noticed there was a set of clean Ranger clothes placed there for each of the two men. Inspecting them closely, he concluded that either the Elf made outfits were not as rare as he had been led to believe, or he was definitely hanging out with the right crowd.

A noise behind him brought his attention back to the moment. He found Leander had already entered the water and was scrubbing down. Alex noted a couple of scars on the man's body indicating he had seen more than one fight with a blade. Following his example, Alex entered the water and began cleaning up.

In short order, both men were bathed and dressed in clean clothes, relaxing in the central room. While they bathed, a pitcher of some kind of fruit juice had been left in the main room for their enjoyment. Not too soon after they finished changing, a different Elf came to call them to their meal. As Alex and Leander exited the room, the Elf pointed to Kinsey, "Please ask her to stay, food will be provided separately."

"Kinsey, stay," Alex ordered, not really sure if she would comply. To his surprise, she turned and returned to her resting place. Before becoming a wolf, she had always been a fairly obedient dog, but he was never really sure if she would obey.

"Thank you," the Elf said before turning to lead them away.

They were led farther into the building, and at the rear of the courtyard, they turned into another open doorway. Darker than the courtyard outside, it took a minute for Alex's eyes to adjust to the light in the room. Before him, stretching from left to right was a long wooden table with chairs running down both sides.

Seated from his far left to far right were over one hundred men, all dressed as Rangers.

Chapter 17

Alex and Leander stood facing the room full of Rangers. All were seated at the table and looking at the two of them as they stood in the doorway. From the far left of the table they heard, "Please, come sit here."

Both men approached the far end of the table, where they discovered a small group of Elves seated amongst the Rangers. Alex recognized one of the Elves from the group that had been in the rescue party earlier, however the others were not familiar to him.

The room was far grander than Ben's dining hall, with art, furniture, and decoration of the finest quality.

"Please," the Elf at the end of the table said while indicating with both hands the two open seats on either side of him. He was dressed slightly better than the others, his attire less suited for the outdoors. As with the other Elves he had seen to date, this man was of indeterminate age, though slightly older, Alex guessed, and very handsome. His hair was long, and of a light brownish blonde color.

"So, are you the one we have to thank for saving our hides?" Alex asked a bit sarcastically.

"That and so much more," the Elf replied as the men sat.

Alex's confusion must have been evident, as the Elf continued, "Let's begin at the end, where Captain Leander's questions start. Yes, the men you see here are the lost Rangers, the ones I am sure you presumed dead."

At that declaration, the food began arriving, so the Elf paused to allow the serving staff their moment.

"Forgive me, I am Elion," the Elf continued after they left.

"You saved them?" Leander asked.

"Yes, once we discovered the Ranger's Guild had been compromised, we interceded and brought those condemned to die here. It allowed us to determine the depths of the corruption and provided the ideal mechanism to recover those true to the belief," Elion replied.

"Why not just remove those who had been corrupted?" Alex asked.

"First, we wouldn't be sure we found them all, and second, we don't take direct action. It has had negative consequences," he replied cryptically.

"Is that what happened in the Dark Woods?"

Elion was obviously surprised by the question, and then he smiled, "I see why you were chosen. Yes, that was the last time darkness was openly confronted. It is a constant reminder not to do so again."

"Ok, so that explains why these Rangers are here. Why am I here?" Alex asked.

Elion stared at him for a few moments in a manner that made Alex feel as if he were being judged.

Apparently, Elion found Alex worthy. "You are the ultimate Lost Ranger. We rescued you from more than death. You led a mundane existence, barely scratching the surface of the hidden potential inside you."

Elion paused again as if to give Alex time for reflection. After a moment, he continued, "There are many realities that make up the physical world we all share. Yours is a reality of science and technology. This reality is one of magic, where your mythology comes to life. Personal talents translate differently in each reality, but if you are strong in one, you will be strong in another."

"How do you know about my world?"

Elion laughed, "It is not just your world. I know you have heard the stories that you can never find the cities of the Elves. We move them freely between the realities, never anchoring to one for longer than is necessary. You have legends of Elves back home as well. That's how we know; we once lived there too."

"So why pull people across from one reality to another?" Alex asked, not understanding the motivation.

"My unused potential can't be of great concern to you."

Elion answered with a sigh, "We strive for stability. Frankly, that is why we left your reality. It has spun so far out of control that we gave up trying. Here however, we have been able to maintain a certain balance. Things of nature still live in harmony with man and beast."

"For the most part," said the Elf who Alex remembered from their rescue party.

"Yes, well that brings us to the topic at hand," Elion answered.

"Every so often the dark elements gather forces to upset the balance. When that occurs, we select an individual of sufficient ability elsewhere to counter the threat and return stability to this reality."

"The last time was Ben Griffin?"

Elion paused again, apparently choosing his reply carefully, "Not exactly. Ben Griffin was the last successful major selection. There have been others since then, of more questionable success."

The statement gave Alex a memory flash to his conversation with Ben. The exact phrase he recalled was "…and most never survived past the first few weeks."

"So why me?" Alex asked.

"In your reality, I am told you are a master of technology. You have several advanced degrees in engineering, covering multiple disciplines," Elion stated.

Alex nodded, not entirely happy with the description, but unable to dispute it.

"You are also an accomplished outdoorsman, experienced in blade and bow," Elion added.

"Did you guys pull my resume or something?" Alex blurted.

Elion laughed at the comment, "You might be surprised to learn that is likely. We also use private investigators as well as technological methods. Remember, our magical strengths translate there as well as yours do here."

Alex suddenly got a vision of a room of pointy-eared hackers, stripping the internet of all its relevant content.

Elion continued, "We have sensed the latest buildup for some time now. We tried bringing over lesser talents, in an effort to balance the forces more slowly. However, the individuals were identified and eliminated far quicker than ever before. We suspect the Dark Elves are more directly involved in assisting others, but like us, they too resist any direct action."

The casual nature of the comment around kidnaping people from his world to be pawns here touched a nerve in Alex that was disturbing. Elion must have noticed, because he redirected the conversation.

"As with you, every person selected to come was chosen for the possibly of a great opportunity. Look at Ben Griffin, he became a king," the Elf explained.

"And those family members left behind?" Alex asked skeptically.

"Again, as with you, we do not choose those with close immediate family. For most, this is a fresh start," Elion stated, appearing somewhat offended.

Attempting to placate the Elf, Alex replied, "Ok, so I can see the reasonability of it. I mean, governments draft young men to go to war in a far less considerate fashion. But again, you still haven't explained why you choose me?"

Elion seemed to be again considering his words carefully. "We have determined, as have you, that the Prince of Windfall has gathered several of the most powerful mages in this region for his cause. Those that do not join him, he removes, to prevent them from joining Great Vale. He has not repeated the mistakes of his father in underestimating the strength and intelligence of Ben Griffin. The Windfall army is overwhelming in size, and a single wizard will be no match for the combined power of his mages."

The Elf paused to let Alex consider his words before continuing, "He has corrupted the Rangers and killed off the few transplants we brought over to potentially supplement Ben's magical needs and to balance the engagement."

Alex considered the situation. It looked to be Ben and the Great Vale army against the world…not great odds.

"As things escalated, it was decided to locate and transport a powerful talent of acceptable disposition to restore the balance," Elion finished.

"Acceptable disposition?" Alex asked, as that seemed an odd statement.

Again, Elion hesitated before replying, "It is no secret that great power presents great risk. All cultures hold examples of power mad leaders wreaking havoc. Even in your own reality, example after example exists of this behavior. Your Nymph was so afraid of your potential that she considered killing you. I should affirm, she would not have succeeded, as your magic would have prevented her enchantments from doing you harm."

"Yes," Alex replied, unfazed that Elion knew of Cassie, "you all keep saying I have great power when all I can do is heat things and start fires!"

Elion smiled at that, "You must learn how to use magic, it can't be gifted like a sword or a bow. You may be granted certain enhancements, as you were with language and fighting skills, but the basis of the ability must be there in the first place. Prior to coming here, you had no magical skills whatsoever. Here you must learn how to take those technology concepts of energy, structure, and materials and apply them to their magical equivalents. Only then, will your true abilities be known."

Elion gave a deep sigh before saying, "Ok, enough of this. Let us eat and then discuss your next move later."

Alex hadn't been paying attention to anyone else but those at his end of the table. By now, all of the Rangers were finished eating, and were in separate conversations of their own. He could see Leander's delight at the knowledge that his former comrades had survived the assassination attempts.

For the rest of the meal, the conversation was about anything but war. Alex was far hungrier that he realized, finishing off two plates of some kind of fowl, several fruits, and vegetables. He trusted that Kinsey was being cared for as well as he was.

At the meal's end, Leander excused himself with the rest of the Rangers, while Alex stayed behind with Elion. As he watched them file out, Alex noted that several of the men embraced Leander. He appeared to be quite popular.

"I have something to show you," Elion said, leading Alex away from the path of the Rangers. They had left the way Alex and Leander entered, whereas Elion headed in a different direction.

Passing through an ornate doorway at the far end of the room from where they were sitting, they entered a hallway without windows. Exiting the hallway at the far end, they entered another grand courtyard, with several fountains and exquisite stone statues throughout.

Entering a small room off the courtyard, Elion led Alex inside. Looking about, he saw a plain, square room with a stone pedestal in the center that resembled a birdbath. Standing next to the birdbath was an Elf, peering into the water. Elion beckoned Alex to come stand next to him on the side opposite the room's only other occupant.

Looking down into the water, Alex saw an image of Ben Griffin sitting at the desk in his study. He was studying a map of the area around Great Vale, making notes on a paper as he did so.

"Is this real time?" Alex asked Elion.

Apparently familiar with the term, Elion replied, "It is in the moment, yes. This magic is called scrying, and it allows us to observe those we have an interest in. Unfortunately we cannot hear what we observe."

Alex realized this referred to him as well, "So you've been watching me the whole time?"

"Within the limits of the magic. When you were in the tunnels of the Two Thorns, we were unable to locate you. With the appearance of Shadows, we feared the worst and sent a group to investigate," Elion replied.

Alex was about to ask how Shadows had been able to go from Two Thorns to E'anbel so quickly when something caught his eye.

While he watched the pool, Abrianna and Cassie entered Ben's study. Alex did a double take,

Cassie was wearing a beautiful dress as opposed to her usual more masculine attire. After a moment, Abrianna looked up, as if searching for something on the ceiling. At one point, she looked directly at them while saying something to her father.

Without looking up, Ben said something in return, waving one hand in a gesture of dismissal. They exchanged several words before Ben pointed to the ceiling while saying something to Cassie. At that, Cassie looked up as well, smiling brightly and waving before returning her attention back to her uncle.

"What was that?" Alex asked, "Can they see us?"

"No," Elion replied, "however, once you become more sensitive to magic, you can sense when someone is scrying you. Ben Griffin knows we are watching and chooses not to block it. Someone less accommodating can block the magic, which is why I brought you here. You need to learn how to block this as quickly as possible. We believe this is how the other candidates were located and killed. While you were in the company of Princess Abrianna, you were under her protective block, as you are now under ours here."

"How does he know it's us?" Alex asked.

"You will be able to sense the touch of the scryer. Dark forces will leave a more unpalatable feeling," Elion replied.

With that, Elion led Alex out of that room and into another. Inside were two new Elves, one male, and one female and, as with all Elves, it was impossible to determine their age. Neither of the Elves appeared pleased at Alex's entrance into the room.

"This is Felaern and Alduin," Elion announced, introducing the female first, "they will teach you what you need to know to survive the next few days."

With that, the Elf turned and left Alex with his new tutors.

----*----

Cassie knew they were interrupting her uncle's war planning as she and Abrianna entered his study. Beyond any concerns of impending war, the women had more personal interests to address. Cassie wanted to check on word of Alex; he had been gone far too long in her opinion. Her uncle replied that while there had been no direct word, both he and Abrianna could feel the presence of the Elves watching over them. They both took that as a good sign.

She understood that he may have been trying to allay her fears, but Uncle Ben interpreted it as a sign that Alex was alive and well. He even suggested the possibly of Alex watching them with the Elves at that very moment. While Cassie had been progressing well in her lessons on self-control, the suggestion that Alex might be watching was more than she could resist. She quickly turned and waved before returning to the other subjects of their visit.

While she watched, Abrianna ran through a short list of castle issues, getting her father's decisions in reply. Apparently satisfied with her instructions, Abrianna touched on one final subject she wanted to run past her father.

Both Cassie and Abrianna had been invited to the Ranger Graduation ceremony, which, given recent developments, had been moved from a later date and scheduled to take place in a week. Abrianna felt it would be a great opportunity for Cassie to demonstrate her new self-control and social skills. Distracted, Ben had agreed and then returned to his planning as the women left.

----*----

Sitting alone in the room he shared with Leander, Alex was enjoying a break from his magic education. He had been involved in his concentrated and condensed magic lessons for the last day and a half, working his ass off. Apparently, Elves did not believe in sleep, praise, or positive reinforcement. Between his two instructors, he had been bashed, beaten, and damn near electrocuted without a single apology.

The core content of his lessons so far was learning how to create and use shields, how to mask or block scrying, and the art of invisibility. The success of the last had been a leap of faith, since when you made yourself invisible to others, you cannot see them or yourself either. As part of his instruction, his tutors taught him how to better use his magical senses to replace his eyes. Like he had done in the dwarf tunnels, he could now reach out and better detect objects and people without actually seeing them.

Alex had asked his tutors why some mages used words as part of their magic. Several times in the past, he had heard Abrianna almost chanting as she worked her magic. They explained that some magic wielders used chants or even poems to focus their concentration and assist in the mental formations.

Others only needed mental imagery to perform their magic, as apparently Alex did.

As with everything he had attempted magically so far, it was all about control. His first attempt at shields had cracked the stones in the training room, because he had forgotten to set firm boundaries. Scry blocking was the easiest; he simply imagined himself invisible to observers. That projection disrupted the magic flow and blocked his reflection from view.

He laughed thinking that he had spent his life imagining himself invisible to others; no wonder it was easy. Even when he played football, the quarterback and other players were the ones strutting around the field, not him. He didn't play for the attention, he played to be the best he could be.

Invisibility itself however, was quite complicated, thus more of an art. While the Elves described the magic, Alex interpreted the physics of it. The objective was for him to create shields that blocked all visible light from his body. What people saw was actually the reflection of light off an object. With no reflected light, there was no visible object. While blocking the reflected light was far from easy, he learned that blocking the light without leaving the telltale visual void was the real trick, and even more challenging.

It was the same lack of reflected light that left you blind to your surroundings. As with so many things he was learning about magic, the trick was to enhance your other senses to compensate. He needed to use his magical senses to visualize what was blocked from his eyes. Had he learned this skill earlier, the Dwarves would have stood out in the dark tunnels.

He was very thankful for the new skills he was learning, but he was becoming a bit concerned. Since the first meal on the day they arrived in E'anbel, he had not seen Captain Leander. Alex had asked about the captain's absence several times, but all he got in reply was that the Captain was tending to other issues.

For the last two nights, Alex had returned to the quarters they shared, but only Kinsey was there waiting for him. She was always happy to see him and seemed content to wait for him each day. He suspected the Elves were entertaining her in his absence, something for which he was thankful. As he had only the smallest of downtime each night, he was longing for a good night's sleep.

Besides his concern for Leander, he was also getting antsy about the time away from Great Vale. In addition to the threat of attack any day now, there was the internal danger to Cassie and the other members of the royal family. The fact that the Rangers there were still free to roam the castle unsettled him greatly. The vision of Cassie in her dress was motivation to work harder.

He had asked Elion to send a message the first day they arrived, but the Elf replied they couldn't get directly involved. Alex pushed, but that got him no further.

Returning to his lessons after the small break afforded him by his tutors, he spent the rest of the afternoon in practice. The two Elves seem to back off some after that, spending the rest of the day working on his fine control, apparently satisfied with his overall constructs.

That evening's meal found him alone with Elion and a few new Elves. Leander and the Rangers were nowhere to be found. Another new addition for this evening was the crown on Elion's head. Alex had suspected the Elf was some kind of politician, as he tended to choose his words overly carefully.

"So, are we newly promoted or have you been incognito?" Alex asked as he sat in the offered seat at Elion's right. He suspected he was being overly familiar, but then the Elf was the one who had kept his position a secret from Alex.

Elion smiled, seeming to take no offense.

"No, I only wear the crown on special occasions."

"And tonight is special?" Alex asked, becoming more serious.

"Tomorrow you leave us. Felaern and Alduin tell me you are as astute a student as any human they have ever seen," Elion stated as the food arrived.

Alex was sure Elion was confused. These couldn't be the words of the two tormentors he'd been left with for the last two days. Then another thought occurred to him.

"Leander isn't coming, is he?" Alex asked after the servers had left.

"He will follow you later. You need to return to Great Vale with some haste. Events are transpiring that place the royal family at some risk."

"I can leave now!" Alex stated starting to get up.

"Sit," answered Elion, motioning Alex to take his seat.

"It is not dire as of yet. Tomorrow is soon enough and you will need your rest to complete the journey south. You have been studying for two days straight."

Reseating himself, Alex followed the example of the others seated nearby and served himself a plate.

"What can you tell me of what's going on?" Alex asked between bites.

Elion considered the question before saying, "The Ranger's Guild is holding a graduation event and have asked the royal family to attend as guests of honor."

"Crap," Alex said without thinking. Before he could apologize, Elion agreed.

"Exactly, we believe this is the trigger event for the Windfall offensive. With the royal family as hostages, the king will be distracted."

"When is the graduation?" Alex asked.

"A little more than three days from now," Elion said somberly.

"How am I getting to Great Vale in three days?" Alex asked, surprised that the Elf wasn't in a bigger hurry. He remembered they were close to five days of hard riding away. Moreover, that included a boat ride.

"Through A'asari," Elion replied with a smile.

Chapter 18

The following morning Alex found himself and Kinsey packed and ready to go, standing in front of one of a series of huge stone arches. The arches were actually inside one of the many buildings in the town square. Shadows was there as well, sporting enough supplies to last them for the next few days.

As he stood next to the horse, Alex listened while Elion explained that the stone arches were actually gateways. The one before Alex was one of many gates that linked all the Elf cities, allowing for instantaneous movement between each location.

"This gate is linked to one in A'asari, located in the same location within the city as here in E'anbel. Because of the location you will face your first challenge," Elion explained, indicating their current spot within E'anbel. The gate in E'anbel was in the large building at the North end of the central square, right in the middle of the city.

Alex learned why this presented an issue over dinner last night. Although he didn't realize it, it turned out that he was, in fact, well acquainted with A'asari. He knew it as the dead city in the middle of the Dark Woods. The building he stood in had a counterpart there. Elion was unwilling to elaborate on exactly what had occurred, but it was once a thriving Elf city, now left to ruin and locked in one reality.

Alex remembered seeing the building's twin off to his left as they passed through the city square before the Gorm Orc attack. This one, in E'anbel had fine polished stone floors with ornate statues throughout the great hall. In a way, it reminded Alex of a railroad station he had visited in Los Angeles. Both served the function of a transit point between cities.

The building itself was next to a bustling market on one side, and a crowded community center on the other. The square outside was packed with Elves doing their daily business. With the gate on the other side located in the same place, Alex would appear in the midst of a packed city square, full of creatures supporting the Windfall forces of Prince Renfeld.

However, that was exactly what they hoped to avoid. Alex was informed over dinner that the local population in A'asari had increased significantly since his last visit. Apparently, A'asari was being used as a staging area for the coming offensive.

Although the city was dead, Elion did know the gate still functioned, as they had used it many times over the years. Since only Elves could operate the magic of the gates, it was not a danger to E'anbel. The danger lay in what was waiting on the other side.

"After your last visit, we have seen a great deal of activity inside A'asari. As I said last night, we suspect that a number of creatures have joined the Windfall forces. Regardless, you will find a much more active environment and one not welcoming to your arrival," Elion explained.

"Any suggestions?" Alex asked, remembering his last visit and hoping to avoid a repeat performance.

"Remember what you have learned here. Stealth will serve you well, as the creatures there will care little about a wolf wandering amongst them, but your presence will incite violence. We have booted Shadows in soft leather to mask any sound of her movement on stone."

At that comment, Alex looked to see all four hooves capped in brown leather, making her steps on the stone almost silent. He could see where any scuffing sounds might be attributed to Kinsey, were he and Shadows invisible.

"Good luck, and May the Gods be with you!" Elion said, with a slap on the back.

As he stepped back, he motioned Alex forward with a flourish. With that sendoff, Alex led Shadows and Kinsey into the open archway.

----*----

Alex emerged from the gate in A'asari into a much darker room than the one on the E'anbel side. Thankfully, the room was also devoid of life. Leading Shadows away from the gate and to one side of the room, he could see it was in fact almost identical to the one in E'anbel. He peered out into the square through the open doorway, staying well back in the darkness to avoid being seen by anyone outside.

With Kinsey at his side, he could see far too much movement beyond the walls. He recognized lots of Orcs and a few Gorm Orcs, but the other creatures he saw were foreign to him. He had no idea what they were and wasn't interested in asking anyone. Alex had a fleeting thought, wondering if Ben had an encyclopedia of things that can kill you in that study of his.

Scanning the area, he noted that the various foul creatures had bunched into like groups, leaving irregular open areas throughout the square. He needed to cross the square undetected, and because of the way the groups had gathered, skirting along the edges of the square wasn't going to be possible. Reaching out with his senses, he mapped the groupings in his mind.

Once he had plotted his path through the square, staying well away from any Gorm Orcs who could sense the invisible, he pulled back to prepare himself. Normally he might have waited until dark to see if things settled down, but he was on a tight schedule. If he intended to reach Great Vale in time to intercede in the Ranger's event, he needed to keep moving. Likely, he would be riding in darkness well into each night to ensure a timely arrival.

Felaern and Alduin had taught Alex the key to invisibility wasn't in being invisible, it was making sure the void you created around you looked natural. Invisibility meant that he would prevent the light, in the form of energy, from reflecting off him. It wasn't enough to absorb the energy, he needed to deflect it around him so that it bounced back from things the viewer saw on the other side.

Again, because he was diverting all light from him, he and Shadows would be blind. He hoped the horse would take it well; he didn't relish the thought of trying to calm the mare during the trip across the square.

He planned to lead Shadows, rather than ride her, to better control the situation. Kinsey would be visible to all, with the thought being that any sounds would be attributed to her. As a quick test, he took Shadow's reins and then closed his eyes. Picturing the light rays around her, he gently nudged them until they passed around her body.

Opening his eyes, there was nothing in front of him but empty space. He could see the gate they had emerged from across the room and Kinsey by his side. Looking down, he saw the leather of the reins, terminating in empty space as if they had been cut from the bridle. Using his senses, he could feel Shadows standing patiently.

He watched Kinsey slowly step forward, sniffing the place where she had just seen Shadows moments ago. After a couple of sniffs, she turned to Alex, tail wagging, as she caught the scent of the mare. That reinforced the decision to leave Kinsey unmasked, as a possible explanation of any stray scents as well as sounds.

Satisfied the mare wouldn't bolt, Alex closed his eyes again and this time added himself to the vision of light bending forces. He opened his eyes to complete darkness. He could sense Kinsey, as she approached him and sniffed as she had done earlier.

Alex closed his eyes again, as it helped him concentrate. Then, extending his senses, he led Shadows out the front of the building. He could feel Kinsey at his side, and knew that to those outside, it would appear as if only the lone wolf exited the structure.

Walking slowly to minimize the possibly of stirring up dust and dirt, Alex went down the steps and into the square below. As they proceeded, Alex used his senses to locate and avoid any creatures nearby. It was a constantly moving target though, as none seemed to stay put in one place very long.

As they were passing a group of Orcs, Alex could hear them talking.

"How much longer do we have to wait here anyway?" he heard one ask angrily.

"Not much longer, it's just a few more days and then we get to eat vale farmers," another answered.

"Can't wait to try out these new Two Thorns blades," the first replied.

The Orcs resumed their grumbling as he continued on his way, but the conversation confirmed several things for Alex. First, he needed to get to Great Vale as soon as possible. Second, the dark forces were definitely involved with Windfall in the plot to overrun Ben.

As he considered this, he realized he had stopped walking. Standing right in front of him was the largest creature he had ever encountered in his life. It had to be at least ten feet tall and weigh over six hundred pounds. While he couldn't actually see the thing, it radiated hate and anger. He guessed it was either a troll or an ogre, though he was not sure that he even knew the difference.

It stood facing Alex, sniffing the air, as if it had caught their scent. Alex could detect there were several smaller creatures to its left. Not waiting to be discovered, he directed free energy to the thing's left foot, giving it a hotfoot.

Howling in rage, it swiped at the creatures on its left, while Alex led Shadows to its right. The creatures it pummeled, in turn, attacked the beast for the unprovoked assault. Unfortunately, the commotion caused all the surrounding groups to converge, several bumping into Alex and Shadows. Luckily, there were so many others around that they assumed one of those strays had knocked them down. The fallen simply regained their feet and continued over to see the fight.

With the path now cleared ahead, he picked up his pace, allowing the turmoil to cover any noises they might make in their haste. Within minutes, they were on the far side of the square and headed down the roadway. Alex dropped the invisibility spell as soon as he felt they were out of sight of the square. He then removed the leather booties Shadows wore.

Mounting Shadows, he spurred her into a trot, eager to put as much distance between himself and the packed square as possible. To Alex, the buildings along this path looked to be more industrial than the other parts of the city he had seen on his previous visit. The structures here were larger and plainer in their architecture, with no effort spared to make them attractive.

Curiosity getting the better of him, Alex nudged Shadows to the nearest building and dismounted. Leaving her outside, he peered inside the structure, looking for any signs of life. Using his senses, he scoured the building looking for life. Once he was sure there were no guards about, he entered the room.

His suspicions were confirmed, it was as large a warehouse as any he had ever seen. Inside there were stacks and rows of crates and casks. The markings on the ones nearest to him indicated they contained everything a field army needed to sustain a protracted campaign. Alex had wondered how Windfall expected to supply their army from such a great distance. These pre-staged warehouses would allow them to make short supply runs, thus sustaining a long siege.

Alex recalled the lecture Leander had given him regarding their reconnaissance mission. Unable to pass up the opportunity, Alex closed his eyes and again let his senses roam the area. In a short time, he located exactly what he was looking for. Moving over to one side, he uncovered stacks of barrels, all containing lamp oil. Rolling several into equally spaced spots inside the building, he breached each. As he watched, their contents spilled out all over the stone flooring and spread to the nearby crates.

He mounted Shadows and sent a passing image to the barrel fragments, igniting them and the oil. He then located two more warehouses along his route, packed with the same supplies. Not bothering to repeat the process, as the smoke from the first warehouse was starting to billow; he simply located and ignited the oil in place.

Urging Shadows into a gallop, he looked back to see the entire warehouse area engulfed in flame and smoke. Alex couldn't help but smile as he reached the opening in the southern wall. While this wouldn't prevent the Windfall attack, it removed any doubt that a sustained campaign was now likely.

Exiting the city, he headed directly into the woods. Elion had explained that there was once a road heading south to Great Vale. It looked as if any trace of the road had long been erased; it appeared a solid forest to Alex. Taking Elion's advice, he let Shadows pick her own path through the trees.

With not much more to do than hang on, Alex let his mind wander. He wondered what Elion wanted from Leander and the Rangers they had rescued. He also used the free time to practice the skills the Elf wizards had taught him.

Only stopping long enough to water Shadows and Kinsey, he headed south at as good a pace as could be made through the trees. Twice they had to stop and hide, once as a group of riders passed on a trail they needed to cross. Another time they ran right up to a camp full of soldiers.

Alex noted that these men hadn't even bothered to conceal their identity. All were in full uniform and preparing for battle. He had to fight an overwhelming urge to set the place ablaze, as he had the warehouses. Unfortunately, even a total idiot would be able to associate the two events, so they simply backtracked and gave the camp a wide berth while continuing south.

By nightfall, they still hadn't cleared the woods, but Alex was fairly sure they weren't far from the edge of the forest, so he let Shadows continue until they reached their goal. He had a cold camp that night at the edge of the woods, not wanting to risk a fire. The Elves had supplied dried meat, fruit, and bread as well as some cheese. Kinsey seemed to favor some of the dried fruit, as she had always sported a bit of a sweet tooth.

At one point during the night, he had a passing feeling that someone was watching him, or rather was trying to scry him. As he had put a blocking spell in place, he knew they would not be successful. He could sense it as it passed over him several times, like someone was searching with a flashlight in the darkness, then the feeling left him entirely. He wasn't positive if they were friend or foe, so he just left the block in place. With the fires he had set, it could well be Renfeld's allies.

Then he was up and moving early the next morning; the Ranger event was scheduled for the afternoon two days hence and he had far to go. Feeding Kinsey before saddling Shadows, he prepared to eat a sparse breakfast in the saddle, allowing them to move on quickly.

Stopping to survey the open area beyond the tree line, Alex searched for any sign of life. He scanned the horizon from east to west, looking for movement, but saw none. Moving slowly at first, the three emerged from the woods, and headed across the open fields south.

No sooner had they exited the trees then Kinsey darted off after some small creature hiding in the grass. She chased the critter but lost it when it dove for the safety of a hole in the ground. Continuing south, they started to see farms dotting the landscape. After passing a few, Alex diverted Shadows to one close by.

The house was a small wood and stone structure, probably well over one hundred years old and passed down from generation to generation. When they stopped at a wall made from rock, no more than three feet tall and creating a fenced yard for the family, Alex called out, "Anyone home?"

He sat quietly, listening for any reply, but none came. Dismounting, he left Shadows, and with Kinsey by his side, first knocked, then entered the structure. Inside, he found meager furnishings, but as a whole, the place was well kept. It was however, somewhat disheveled, as if someone had packed in a hurry.

Exiting the house and crossing to the barn, he found no horses or livestock beyond a few loose birds that looked like a cross between a chicken and a peacock. The barn was also missing anything resembling a wagon, the local equivalent of a pickup truck.

It was obvious the farm had been evacuated, likely by order of the King. Having seen firsthand what a northern invasion was like, Alex was sure Ben would not want a repeat under his watch. As Alex emerged from the barn, he found four soldiers in Windfall colors checking Shadows.

"Can I help you?" Alex asked, still in his Ranger colors.

"You shouldn't be here," one of the soldiers stated.

"I have my orders," Alex said, hoping to pull off a bluff.

"We weren't notified anyone would be in this area," the same soldier replied, sounding unsure, while the other three dismounted.

"And Prince Renfeld includes you in all his planning?" Alex asked confidently, as Kinsey appeared by his side, making the soldiers all that more uncomfortable.

"So, you can describe the Prince then?" Asked one of the soldiers, clearly thinking he was clever and going to catch Alex in a lie.

"Yes," Alex replied, realizing he had only seen the prince mounted and at a distance.

"Blonde hair, and currently sports a sling for his right arm, as he recently suffered an arrow wound to his right shoulder."

The disclosure seemed to mollify the four, as their demeanor appeared more relaxed.

"We are sorry, Ranger; we were told all the Rangers of the Vale would attack from within the walls of the city after the ceremony. We didn't expect to see any outside the city," said the soldier still mounted.

"That's because I am a Westland Ranger, on special assignment," replied Alex, reverting to his earlier cover story.

The statement had exactly the opposite effect on the four men than Alex expected. The three on the ground drew their swords, while the fourth announced,

"The Westland Rangers have declared against Windfall and for Great Vale in the upcoming struggle."

With that, the three men charged Alex as he drew his sword. Using the new tricks he learned in E'anbel, Alex slammed a shield into two of the soldiers. The impact sent them flying, while he engaged the third with his sword.

Out of the corner of his eye, he saw Kinsey leap on one of the downed men, his throat in her jaws. He parried the soldier's swing, following with a left-handed roundhouse that took the man off his feet. Carrying the turn, he was in time to confront the third man as he again charged Alex from behind.

Driving out with his sword, he skewered the man before he could recover from his surprise. Alex then turned to find Kinsey dispatching the man he had cold cocked. As he looked up, he found the fourth soldier riding north as if his life depended on it, which it very much did.

Retrieving his bow, Alex lined up on the rider, the open area making the shot easier than those he had attempted before. As he let the shaft fly, he concentrated on the rider, willing the shaft to its target. As he watched, the two converged and the rider fell from the saddle, dead.

Alex turned and searched the three dead soldiers, not finding what he was looking for. Mounting Shadows, he headed back to the fourth man and located the dispatch pouch in his saddlebags. Flipping through the documents, he found the orders sent to the area commands, describing their role in the upcoming battle.

Draping the body over the soldier's saddle, Alex led the mount behind Shadows, returning to the farm where he placed all four bodies in the barn. Covering them with straw, he hid them from casual view. Stripping the horses of their tack and leaving it in the barn with the bodies, he turned the horses loose in the field, where they immediately went to grazing.

By the time he was finished, it was late in the afternoon and he was now behind schedule. Mounting Shadows, he and Kinsey put as much distance as possible between them and the farm as possible before nightfall. Alex debated pushing on through the night in the darkness, but as he approached Great Vale, he was in as much danger from the friendly forces as he was from Windfall.

Finally settling down about midnight in a small stand of trees, he sat quietly in the dark. With Kinsey by his side, he began planning the next day's activities before drifting off to sleep. The following day he was up at sunrise, and rode hard all day to make up for the lost time at the farm.

Again, only taking stops to water Shadows and Kinsey, Alex was determined he would make Great Vale in time to prevent the women from attending the Ranger's graduation. When he finally stopped for the last night of his journey, he was seeing things familiar to him from the trip out with Leander.

Chapter 19

Ben Griffin started his day as if it were any other, with breakfast in his bedroom. However, that only lasted until after breakfast, when he ordered the scouting reports from his commanders. Even though he had delayed in calling up the troops, he had his scouts out in mass on regular patrols.

The morning's reports had the dreaded news he was expecting. They had seen activity in the north woods that was both anticipated and confusing. They had seen an increase in Windfall patrols and a massing of infantry at the forest's edge. They had also seen a huge plume of dark smoke deep in the forest itself.

Ben had no idea what the smoke meant, but he suspected Alex and Leander had something to do with it. He took it as a good indicator, telegraphing that they were still alive and working to upset Renfeld's plans. In that same spirit, he gave orders to start calling up his troops and had any of the outlying farmers still in the north evacuate. Well, any of those that had not already done so. He was not going to allow the slaughter that had taken place the last time Windfall got an urge to expand.

Looking out the window of his bedroom, he saw the tent village created by the troops and refugees.

He had a dreadful feeling that if he didn't see Alex and Leander today, it might be too late. Turning from the window, he headed down stairs to check on Abrianna and Cassandra. He had promised to see them before the Ranger graduation event this afternoon.

----*----

Alex was up before dawn, having spent a fitful night. From all he had gathered, Renfeld had collected a sizable force that included soldiers, Orcs, Ogres, various other dark creatures, mages, and rogue Rangers.

He guessed that the triggering event would be today's Ranger graduation. That was where they planned on taking Ben's family hostage and splitting his attention between the battlefield and his home. With the army of Windfall no more than a day's ride behind him, he had no time to waste.

Alex had to reach Great Vale in time to prevent Cassie and Abrianna from attending the graduation. By the time the sun peeked over the horizon, he had Shadows saddled and was on his way south. Alex set a brisk pace and, by late morning, he started seeing patrols in the distance, crossing the fields and wearing the blue of Great Vale.

When he reached the north-south road leading into the city of Great Vale itself from Portsward, he was able to pick up the pace slightly. Several times, he passed refugees heading south, wagons packed high with their worldly possessions. By noon, he reached a checkpoint stopping all southbound traffic for inspection. As no one was heading north, it was a moot point to check that anyway. When Alex approached, there were several soldiers standing in the shade of a nearby tree.

"State your business, Ranger," Alex heard from the soldier as he approached the checkpoint. The man had stepped up to the road's edge, his hand held high in a halting gesture.

Before Alex even had a chance to answer, another soldier rushed to the first and whispered into his ear.

"Sire, I beg your pardon," the man corrected himself, his manner decidedly more deferential.

"I need to get to the King as soon as possible," Alex replied in haste. "Windfall is coming, and they are bringing dark forces with them."

"Sire, our orders are to man this point until we see opposing forces. The King has ordered all the northern farms evacuated," the soldier replied, alarmed at Alex's declaration.

"Then I would place a man on that rise over there," Alex said pointing to the highest nearby location, "and run like hell when he tells you to. Good luck!"

With that, Alex galloped past the soldiers, now more concerned than ever about getting to Great Vale. Within an hour, Alex dropped into the valley, and reached the outskirts of the city. He could see hundreds of tents, with soldiers everywhere he looked. He noted that it was not enough men. Continuing into the city of Great Vale and barely slowing, Alex headed into town and straight to the castle.

Leaving Shadows with a stable hand just inside the gate, he headed through the courtyard and into the castle keep, the recovered Windfall dispatch case in hand. Getting directions on Ben's location from one of the guards, he hurried inside. Bursting in on Ben's council meeting, Alex found Ben with several of his generals grouped around a table. Noticeably absent was the Ranger Guild Master.

"Ben, where's Cassie and Abrianna?" he blurted out, tossing the dispatch case to the nearest man.

While the generals were appalled at the overly familiar outburst, Ben looked up and replied, "They left early for the Ranger's graduation ceremony. Why, what's wrong?"

"It's a trap. The Rangers are in league with Renfeld," he replied, running a hand through his hair while trying to decide his next move.

"I knew there was something wrong with the Guild Master," one of the generals said.

"I heard rumors he had Rangers looking for dissention among the Palace Guard. When they found none, he petitioned for a place on the King's council."

"When does the ceremony start?" Alex asked.

"Soon," Ben replied. "Where is Leander?"

"He's with the Elves," Alex told him.

"Look, I need to get to the ceremony. Renfeld has over 10,000 troops hiding in the woods, as well as everything you can imagine coming from the ruins in the Dark Forest. He has also recruited every senior mage willing to follow him, killing any who refused. The plan is to grab the women at the ceremony and attack the city after they distract you with the hostages. They had hoped to split your attention and strike from within. I took that case from a Windfall Patrol. It has information on the coming offensive."

"Go," Ben said, pointing at the door.

"You get the girls while I mobilize the army." As he turned to leave, Alex added, "Ben, they are using dark magic. Be ready for anything."

With that, Alex headed out the door. He hoped Ben was better at guessing what lay ahead than he was. So far, all he had been able to do was react. Claiming Shadows in the courtyard, he mounted the horse and headed to the Ranger's Guild as fast as she could carry him.

Kinsey had been keeping pace with him the entire time, treating all the hurrying as a game. Alex led Shadows back out into the city and toward the center of town. The Ranger's Guild was a large stone structure at the east end of the town square. He was thankful Cassie had insisted in pointing it out to him upon their arrival.

Entering the town square, Alex could still see men in Ranger colors outside the building. They were gathering to enter through the two large wooden doors, while others prepared to close them. Thinking quickly, Alex turned himself, Shadows and Kinsey invisible. He hoped Kinsey didn't panic at the change and rode Shadows up to one side of the Guild. Kinsey stopped at first, likely unsure of what had happened, but didn't seem to object to the loss of sight. She eventually just closed in on the horse, and Alex assumed she was just following her nose.

Riding around the corner, he dismounted and released Shadows from the spell of invisibility, but kept himself and Kinsey under its influence. He considered leaving Kinsey outside, as he used his senses to guide them forward, but changed his mind at the last moment.

Guiding Kinsey with a hand on her back, he slipped them both inside the entryway of the Guild building. He navigated them through the outer doors and to one side of the entryway as the assembled group headed through a second set of large double doors and into the Guild main hall.

Alex paused for an opening in the crowd and then led Kinsey inside the hall and to his left. Once inside the main hall with Kinsey, he made himself visible, leaving her hidden to the naked eye. Dressed in his Ranger's tan and green, he was able to blend in as just another member.

Scanning the assembled members, he didn't see a soul he recognized, which was exactly what he wanted to see. With Kinsey still invisible, but at his side, he guided her further inside the main hall and over to the corner on the left side.

Deep in the corner and out of the main traffic flow, he scanned the room looking for the two women. There were benches lining each side of the room, with a raised dais centered on the back wall with chairs and a podium, all empty. Assuming the dais was for dignitaries, he pulled back farther into a shadowed corner and waited for everyone to take their seats.

----*----

Cassie was surprised to find she was actually enjoying herself. She and Abrianna had arrived early, at the invitation of the Guild Master, to partake in a small reception in their honor. They were currently in an anteroom off the main hall where the graduation was about to take place.

Abrianna had helped select the fine gown she was now wearing. It was something she would have never worn a mere month ago. While she felt beautiful, something in her Nymph sense told her things were not right. The men seemed to all be smitten with her, but the feeling was different. It didn't have the same lustful motivation she had known before. Maybe the lessons were working after all.

She had to admit that while the dress was wonderful, the lack of a sword made her feel naked. It was like walking in public in your underwear; she felt exposed. Abrianna assured that her proper ladies didn't sport armament in public.

All this confusion was a result of the lessons her uncle had forced on her. Her lessons had been progressing much better of late, the initial shock wearing off. Magic, etiquette, and social skills had all been on the agenda. The greatest help had come from the two women who were also part Nymph. Their understanding and reflections had given Cassie a real reference in her own inner struggles. This allowed her, for the first time in a very long time, to be pleasant to a group of men without being on guard the entire time.

Her heart did skip a beat from time to time when she saw a man from behind in Ranger colors who looked like Alex. Her mind wandered, wondering where he was, if was he safe, and when would he return to her.

"Ladies, we are preparing to begin the ceremonies. Would you please allow these two men to escort you to the podium?" He gestured toward two Rangers standing nearby.

"Lady Cassandra," the Ranger closest to Cassie said, "may I?" He presented his arm for her.

Taking his lead, the two followed Abrianna and her escort out of the anteroom and out onto the raised dais. Cassie noted that it was located against the back wall of the main hall and centered on two rows of benches facing each other.

As they approached the platform, Cassie could see the lines of Rangers on each side of the room. She wondered which of the rows were graduates and which were journeymen, since they seemed equally numbered.

Her Ranger led her to a seat on the far side of the podium and Abrianna took the nearer seat on the side opposite her. Both the escorting Rangers took places behind the women, a position Cassie found most uncomfortable. She inherently distrusted someone unfamiliar at her back.

While she watched, the Guild Master stepped up to the podium and motioned for the Rangers to sit. Both rows of Rangers took their places on the benches, sitting in unison. The Guild Master motioned for the Rangers at the main entrance doors to drop the bar, locking them all inside. They next closed the inner doors to the hall, barring them as well.

Cassie's discomfort increased as the two took places at the end of both rows. Something was definitely not right.

----*----

Alex watched from the dark corner as the Rangers lined both sides of the room, leaving two men at the main doors. Soon after, a door in the far back corner of the room, diagonal to him, opened. Alex watched Abrianna and Cassie came out, each attended by one of the rogue Rangers. From the women's demeanor, he suspected that they were still unaware of the Guild Master's plans.

Kinsey started a low growl, likely sensing Alex's tension. He quieted the still invisible wolf, both far enough away from the standing Rangers to hide the noise. He watched as the Rangers led each of the ladies to their chairs, and then took their place right behind each one.

Alex knew they were placed there to take control of the women, once the trap was sprung. Scanning the room, Alex counted about forty men, including those at the door and on the podium. The odds were not good, but he had a few things going his way. Thankfully, he also had a few of those throwing knives favored by Cassie, and a two hundred pound wolf on his side.

The Guild Master stepped up to the podium and motioned for everyone to sit and for the doors to be barred. Alex then watched as the only two men behind him moved to the benches between him and the podium. That was good.

As the Guild Master began to speak, Alex loosened two of the throwing knives, taking one in each hand. He also attempted to project a vision in Kinsey's mind for the first time, suggesting a course of action to her.

----*----

The feeling of doom was building in Cassie to a point that it was all she could do to keep her seat. She glanced at Abrianna several times, looking for reassurance that she was overreacting. Abrianna however, had a confused look on her face as well, as if the proceedings made little sense to her.

A movement in the dark corner of the room caught her eye, but as she started to concentrate on it, the Guild Master started to speak.

"Rangers, today is the first day of a new future for us all. After today, we are no longer the minions of those that choose who and what we are. We now are a power of our own!"

Cassie started to get up but she felt a hand on her shoulder and a knife at her throat. Glancing to her left, she saw Abrianna was in an identical state. Looking up, she saw the Guild Master gloating.

"We will help overthrow the tyrant king that lords over our every move," he bellowed. "And with these two in our control, the King will not dare to attack us!"

Suddenly, Cassie saw Alex step out from the corner shadows and say, "Wrong, asshole!"

With that statement, both arms flashed, and knives appeared in the throats of the two Rangers holding them. Cassie spun from her seat, drawing the sword of the man behind her as he fell away to crash on the floor behind the dais. She pivoted in time to see a huge black wolf appear in mid-air, the Guild Master her intended target.

Hitting the Guild Master mid-chest, Kinsey knocked the man to the dais, landing between the two women. As he struggled to free himself by attempting to roll away, she watched as Kinsey seized the man's neck in her jaws. As he clawed to free himself, Kinsey gave a series of violent shakes.

Cassie smiled as she heard the man's neck snap. After a moment, Kinsey released the limp form and looked up at Cassie, her tail wagging in pride at her accomplishment.

----*----

When the two Rangers drew their blades against the women, Alex almost leapt out of the shadows. Recovering in time to stick to the plan, he stepped out just as the Guild Master began gloating over his coup on King Ben.

He released both throwing knives and Kinsey, devastating the dais Rangers threatening the two women. His next move was to set the Rangers closest to him on either side of the room aflame. Backing up, he drew his sword and dagger, while casting a spell at the podium.

There were still over twenty Rangers in fighting form, all up and divided between charging Alex and the dais. Those headed to the women discovered an invisible wall preventing them from reaching their goal. However, initial contact with the shield wall triggered a discharge that stunned them unconscious.

Those headed to Alex found a whirling blender of Elven steel, slicing right through their mail shirts, worn under their tan tunics. Alex noted, thankfully, that their attire wasn't of Elven make.

As he lunged, parried and slashed at the men surrounding him, Alex felt several hits on his arms, legs, and torso. He moved, taking extra care to avoid receiving head blows. His Elven tunic and pants prevented him from being sliced, but the impacts were not without effect. He was going to be battered and bruised, should he survive the encounter.

Stepping clear of a small group pressing him, he stunned them with a quick shield blast, sending them skidding across the floor away from him. Looking across the room, Alex saw Cassie pounding on the invisible wall, attempting to join the fight. Thankfully, the Rangers had triggered his stun trap, preventing her from receiving the same shock.

"Protect Abrianna!" he shouted at her as the remaining Rangers mounted another attack. Momentarily releasing the shield wall to free Kinsey, he restored it before Cassie could follow. As the wall of Rangers approached him, Kinsey attacked from the rear, giving Alex the distraction he needed to weigh into the group. He managed to take out several more before the rest realized what was happening and retreated to a corner near the barred front door.

By now, there were only seven or eight left up and around, and they were a sorry looking group. After sheathing his dagger, he gave a wave of one hand, dropping the shield wall protecting the women.

"Yield or die," Alex declared in a calm, confident voice while pointing his sword at the remaining Rangers. Sensing both women and Kinsey approaching him from behind, he watched as the men slowly, one by one, dropped their weapons.

Looking around the hall, Alex pointed to the door Cassie and Abrianna had emerged from and asked,

"What's in there?"

"It's just a room," Cassie replied. "There is no other way in or out."

"Inside," Alex said to the men, pointing with his sword. The men shuffled along the wall and over to the corner, entering the room beyond.

"You, drag them in as well," Alex ordered, indicating the last men in line and the fallen Rangers, out cold from his stun trap. Once the last man passed through the doorway, Alex closed the door and examined it for a way to lock the group inside.

Sheathing his sword, he placed both hands on the door and envisioned the wood of the door and the frame as a single piece of wood. He opened his eyes and examined his handiwork. The door and frame looked as if they had been carved from a single piece of wood.

"You've come a long way!" Abrianna said, admiring the results of the spell.

Suddenly, Cassie leaped toward Alex, wrapping her arms around his neck and kissing him passionately. Alex returned the embrace, and her passion. The two stood locked in their embrace for several moments.

"Ahem," Abrianna finally quietly exclaimed.

A moment later Cassie broke from the kiss but continued to embrace Alex. With her forehead pressed into his chest and eyes still closed, she asked, "What Brie?"

"We should really be getting back to the castle. I'm sure my father is worried."

"She's right, this is just part one. There is a very large army coming down from the North and Ben is going to need all the help he can get," Alex answered without loosening his grip on her.

Pulling her arms down until both palms rested on his chest, Cassie looked up at him and kissed him again lightly before gently pushing off. Alex released her reluctantly and the three, with Kinsey close behind, unbarred the inner and main doors, and then exited the body strewn main hall of the Ranger's Guild.

Shadows was right where Alex left her. Rather than look for a carriage, both women threw etiquette out the window and mounted Ranger horses, dresses be damned. With that, all four headed to the castle at a run.

Chapter 20

Abrianna led the small group into her father's council room, where they found him and others seated around a large table.

"Father," she announced as they entered, causing everyone to turn. Ben rose, pushing his chair back, allowing him to rush to his daughter. The two met half way, embracing in a hug that only a father and daughter can understand.

"You're unharmed?" Ben asked Abrianna first, holding her out at arm's length, and then looking to Cassie.

"Yes, Father, the Guild Master went crazy. They were planning to revolt and hold us hostage, until Alex intervened," Abrianna replied with a nod in Alex's direction.

"The Ranger uprising is no longer a threat," Cassie announced, her arm entwined with Alex's.

"You dispatched forty armed Rangers, alone?" one of the men at the table asked skeptically.

"There are survivors locked in a room," Alex replied.

"But not many," Cassie added.

Ben motioned for the guards at the door to go deal with the survivors.

"You will need a mage or an axe to free them," Alex mentioned, with an added giggle from Cassie.

"He did have help," Cassie added, patting Kinsey with her free hand.

"And the Guild Master?" Ben asked sternly.

"Alas, he did not survive," replied Cassie in a melodramatic tone.

"Good. Sit" Ben stated, and then turned to return to his place at the head of the table. As he did so, he indicated the open seats for Alex and the women. Abrianna went to the far side to be near her father and Alex led Cassie to a pair of open seats at the other end of the table.

"Before we begin," one of the men at the table announced, "I would like to pass along a message to Alex, Sire. Please accept the thanks of the soldiers operating the checkpoint on the North Road. Thanks to your recommendation, they were able to escape the oncoming forces without incident."

Alex smiled in return, happy to hear the men avoided being overrun. However, the implications of the statement were not lost, either.

"So Renfeld's troops are within a day's march?"

"Yes," replied Ben, "your warning came just in time to get a blocking force in place and halt their advance for now. Thanks to the Guild Master's deception, we are still mustering the majority of our troops."

"They will be ready," one of the men near Ben stated.

Ben nodded in agreement and then smiled. "So now that we have a moment, perhaps you can expand on your initial report. You seemed in a rush when we first saw you today."

The comment brought a few laughs, and smiles throughout the group.

"Yes sir," Alex replied. He then began a detailed recount of his entire trip, working in chronological order. Several times during the next hour, one or another of the men at the table would stop him for a more meticulous explanation.

Ben appeared particularly interested in the parts about the Dwarves and the missing mages of Two Thorns. During the description of their adventures in the tunnels, an idea struck Alex.

"Sire, do you have any more of those acorn message birds?" he asked.

Ben motioned to a bowl sitting on a table against the wall near the windows.

"May I?" Alex asked, receiving a nod of approval from Ben.

While everyone watched, Alex headed to the table and selected a piece of parchment. Located in the same bowl were several of the acorns Leander had used. Alex wrote out a short message and selected one of the acorns. After opening the window, he clasped both hands together as he had seen Leander do and generated the mental image of the message's recipient.

Opening his hands, a bird stood in his palm. Without hesitation, it took off and disappeared out the window, heading north. Returning to his seat, he received several looks questioning his actions. Alex looked at Ben and said, "We'll talk." Ben nodded.

Resuming his tale, he described their plunge over the cliff, looking at Kinsey as he did so. The descriptions of both E'anbel and Elion seemed to entrance the entire room, Cassie included. When he reached the part about his magic lessons, Ben made him repeat it several times. He seemed fixated on the two Elves whom Alex named and Ben recorded on the parchment at his side.

Ben had been taking notes throughout the entire session, as had several of the other men. Each seemed to have his own area of interest. When Alex got to his return to A'asari, he heard Cassie gasp, her memory of the place still fresh.

Here everyone drilled Alex repeatedly, as interest in the magical creatures involved was very high. They asked him to describe types, sizes, and numbers of the various creatures he had observed. He did his best to recount his entire trip across the square, giving estimates of all in residence.

"Invisible?" one of the men asked, clearly disbelieving at Alex's description of his escape from the city. Hearing that, Alex simply disappeared from the table. While feeling Cassie's touch, he was sure she was just checking that he was, in fact, still there.

Reappearing, Alex told them of the warehouses he had set aflame before departing A'asari. That disclosure brought mixed reactions from the assembled group.

"Lack of supplies will preclude the ability of a long siege," one of the men said.

"It does, however, create a sense of urgency in their efforts that may work against us. We are still gathering our forces," another replied.

Alex listened to the men exchange thoughts and ideas, discussing things out of his depth in war planning. Once they had settled on a course of action, Ben excused everyone, except Alex.

"Abrianna, why don't you and Cassie go change," Ben said, motioning them out of the room. With the area cleared, Ben rose and poured both himself and Alex a drink. Alex accepted the offered glass, while Ben seated himself next to him rather than his seat at the head of the table. Taking a sip, Alex guessed it to be some kind of sherry, the sweet taste a welcome treat.

"So I don't suppose King Elion offered any direct support?" Ben asked after taking a sip himself.

With a sigh, Alex replied, "No, in fact I asked him to send one of those message birds while in E'anbel and he refused. He claimed taking direct actions would only escalate things with the Dark Elves."

"And the message bird you just sent?" Ben asked.

"A very long shot I wouldn't include in any plans," Alex said in reply.

"I was hoping I could get the Dwarves to join us. Brokkr said he owed me…it's a long shot."

"You're right," Ben said sadly. "I doubt they'll come. There's nothing in it for them."

"What else did Felaern and Alduin teach you?" Ben asked after another sip.

"Mostly, the three things I mentioned. Invisibility, various shields, and scry blocking. The stun trick worked well against the Rangers, which I learned at the receiving end of several stuns. We did spend a lot of time on control and conservation of energy. I swear Elves must be the laziest creatures on earth, spending as little energy as possible," Alex replied with a laugh.

"You have no idea who they are, do you?"

"No more than anyone else here," Alex answered.

"Frankly the Elves were the first mythical creatures I met that didn't try and kill me."

Ben nodded in understanding and then said, "Felaern and Alduin are a thousand years old. They are the Grand Wizards of the Woodland Elves. To my knowledge, no human has ever been accepted as a pupil. That either speaks very highly of you, or reinforces the level of desperation we are in."

Alex decided to remain mute on the subject, suspecting Ben's interpretation was in error in the first case, and hoping he was wrong in the second. Alex looked up from his drink to see Ben studying him.

"What?"

"Elves never do anything without reason," Ben replied after a second, "those skills were selected for a purpose. We just need to figure out what that purpose is."

The two sat in silence for a bit and then Ben finally asked, "Can you teach me that invisibility trick. I never learned that one."

----*----

Abrianna and Cassie were sitting in a small study near their bedrooms, intended as part of the royal family's private quarters. Cassie was growing impatient, as Alex and her uncle had been locked up in the meeting room downstairs for almost two hours.

Cassie and her cousin had changed into clothes that were far more casual than the dresses they wore earlier. It was the kind of outfit they would go riding in, consisting of pants and a pullover top rather than a blouse. Cassie had returned to wearing her sword, contradicting the lessons of the last few days. Ladylike or not, the events of the day had proven that etiquette took a back seat to survival.

The two women sat talking, mostly speculating on what was taking the men so long. Suddenly, Kinsey came trotting into the room, walked over to one corner, and made herself comfortable on a rug.

Before she could say anything, Cassie felt something brush her cheek. Leaping from her seat, she drew her dagger and spun around.

"It's OK," Alex declared as both he and Ben appeared in front of the two women.

Sheathing the dagger, she stepped forward, first smacking Alex in the chest with her palm and then hugging him.

"That's not funny! You scared me half to death."

"An army at our doorstep and you two are playing jokes!" Abrianna said, shaking her head at the two men.

"My daughter," Ben replied calmly, "you just witnessed the test run for our evening's excursion!"

----*----

Brokkr sat in the great cavern he and his men called home. While the others were still out working, he had stopped for the day and returned to survey the rewards of their latest efforts. The pile of gold before him was the largest find in recent memory. He was anxious to get it back to the main settlement and securely stashed in their vaults.

He had to hand it to the human white wizard, he had delivered on his part of their bargain. The promise of gold the size of a man had been fulfilled threefold. As it was, they were still chasing veins that held the promise of half again as much. He speculated on what he might do to entice the man to locate more undiscovered pockets for them.

Normally, Brokkr held no love for humans, and wizards even less, but this boy was something else. He had an old world honor and bravery about him that he hadn't seen in many years. There was also a slice of naiveté there as well that endeared him to the old Dwarf.

Brokkr had stayed behind, when the three leaped from the cliff, landing in the pool below. He had seen others make the jump and perish, so he was vindicated in his statement of survival, he had just been mum on the percentages.

"You owe the boy more than a favor," said a voice from the darkness that made Brokkr jump. As he turned to the sound, Elion emerged from a side tunnel. How those damn Elves found their way around his tunnels so easily made him furious.

"You are uninvited, and I need no reminders of my obligations," Brokkr said as the Elf approached.

"That may be true, however, Dwarves are not known to rush to anyone's aid unless they are overburdened with gold or jewels," Elion said, stopping next to Brokkr and examining the gleaming metal before them.

"And Elves are not known to venture from their cities unless they are meddling in the affairs of others," Brokkr replied with a snip.

"A debt repaid is an honor upheld." Reaching out, Elion placed a ruby on the top of the pile of gold.

"When the gem glows, have your men gather on the flat, at the falls." Elion turned and headed back the way he had come.

"Not a chance in Hades," Brokkr murmured as he slowly picked up the stone and examined it. As he heard the sounds of his men returning, he quickly tucked it in a pouch in his belt.

----*----

Well after their evening meal, in which Alex and Ben explained their intended activities for the night, the two men slipped quietly out of the castle. Alex laughed to himself as they headed north, recalling the objections of both Cassie and Abrianna. Neither of the women had agreed with their plan. He had to admit that it did not seem to be the best idea, from their point of view.

As it was, he and Ben had argued the same point earlier that day. The risk of losing the king, before the battle had even begun, was a real possibility. Should the two be discovered, it was very unlikely they could fend off the combined efforts of Renfeld's entire army and escape unharmed.

Ben, however, had argued that if the two of them could catch Renfeld and his Red Mages unprepared, their combined strength could put an end to the encounter just as easily. While Alex was not sold on the concept that he had the abilities needed to assist Ben, he at least acknowledged the strategy as sound and the risk well worth the return.

The plan was to head north on horseback under the cover of darkness, getting as close as possible to the Windfall lines. There they would dismount and, just outside the picket line, and become invisible. Once they passed through the lines undetected, they would move into the enemy camp.

The end goal was twofold. The first was to sabotage as much of the Windfall war machine as possible. They cut saddle cinches and harnesses, loosened bracing on catapults, and turned the water and food stores rancid. The men dropped in and out of invisibility when actual vision was required.

The second goal was to gather as much intel as possible regarding the exact nature and number of the Windfall forces. Even invisible, Alex could detect the tents of the various mages throughout the camp. The glow of their power was unmistakable to his senses. He felt yellow, orange and red, but no greens or blues at all. Ben radiated a cool light blue to Alex.

Neither man dared get too close to the red mages, as the closer they got the more likely it was that they would be unmasked. The three powerful Red Mages could sense the two by the same sense of magic, but like Ben and Alex, they would have to be actively searching for it.

For a time, both Ben and Alex hid near Renfeld's tent, waiting for the man to retire for the night. Unfortunately, he had apparently decided to keep the red mages in residence for his personal protection. With the rest of their goal completed, Ben indicated to Alex that it was time for them to leave.

Fighting the temptation to set Renfeld's tent ablaze, Alex followed the king as they retreated from the camp. Slipping out past the sentries was easier, since they were focused on outsiders trying to come in. Eventually the two men reached their horses and were soon riding cautiously back to Great Vale.

"Well that was a good night's work!" Ben stated once they were far enough away.

"I think we could have killed Renfeld."

"Perhaps," Ben answered after a moment, "or the three red mages and the assembled guards would have our heads and the war is over. It wasn't worth the risk."

Alex understood the point, if Ben had been captured or killed, everything would be lost.

Changing the subject, Alex asked, "What's with the colors?"

Apparently, Ben didn't need the question to be explained. "The colors reflect the wielder's disposition, and how the magic affects you. The hotter colors like red, yellow, and orange reflect fire colors, those more inclined to violent magic or destruction. That does not mean violence itself, rather those that wield flame and energy discharge better. The energy mages of Two Thorns were killed by Renfeld because they chose not to join the fight."

Taking a pause, he then continued, "Those like Abrianna and myself are calmer, the blue of the ocean or green of a field. Even the brown of the earth is more in line with our powers. We can manipulate energy, though it's in aid of other efforts. Growing, healing, and creating are our inclination."

"And white?" Alex asked.

"Yes, White is the question now, isn't it?" Ben replied. "But did you know there is also a Black?"

"No one has ever mentioned it, not even the Elves."

"That's because only the Elves have black power. It is what makes the Dark Elves. The interesting thing is only a White Wizard can defeat a Black Wizard. It's the purity of the two that makes them so powerful, all white, or all black. That's why the Dark Elves fear them so, and they are normally only Elf. Human White Wizards are extremely rare and feared by all," Ben finished.

"Why?" Alex asked after a moment's reflection.

"Black is the absence of color. Magic does not influence their disposition. Without that influence, there is nothing that disrupts a calm, calculating nature," Ben said, waiting for Alex to absorb the information.

"White is the combination of all colors in the visible spectrum. They are a blend, and as such, one can never tell what a White Wizard has in their heart."

----*----

They made it back to the castle while it was still quite dark. Alex assumed it was somewhere between 1 and 2am. Bidding Ben a good night, he headed up to his room and discovered an excited Kinsey, her tail flailing as he entered his room. He also discovered the two were not alone.

"Kinsey was worried about you, so I stayed with her," Cassie said from his bed.

"Kinsey was worried..." Alex repeated as he crossed the room and sat on the edge of the bed.

As if she understood all too well that his attention was focused elsewhere, Kinsey found her favorite rug and settled down, watching from across the room.

Cassie rolled from her side, where she was facing the door, onto her back. She had the bed covers folded back so she was exposed from the waist up. Her thin, sleeveless, nightgown clung to her as if it were painted on, an effect Alex assumed was intended.

"Is Uncle back safe?" Cassie asked as she took hold of the hand Alex offered.

"Yes, we both made it back unscathed. We left quite a few surprises for the Windfall army though," Alex added with a laugh.

"Then come to bed," Cassie replied, pulling her nightie over her head and pulling back the covers for Alex to get in beside her.

"Cassie, I can't," Alex replied hesitantly, "your uncle…"

Cassie cut him off, "…has had me in lessons since you and Leander left. I know what you fear and I have learned to control myself."

She paused and sat up to kiss Alex as she lifted his shirt over his head.

"Well, not entirely," she added as she tossed his shirt in the corner and pulled him down on her.

Chapter 21

Alex woke first the following morning, finding Cassie laying with her back pressed into him and his arm around her waist. From her breathing, he could tell she was still sound asleep and resting quietly. He continued to lie there, enjoying the warmth of her body against his.

Knowing all good things must come to an end, Alex was preparing to slip out of bed when a gentle tapping came from the door.

"Sire?" he heard from the other side of the door.

"Yes?" Alex replied, sure the tapping had already woken Cassie.

"His majesty requests you join him in the main dining hall for breakfast, as soon as you are able."

"Let him know I will be right there, please," Alex said with a sigh.

After a moment, he heard, "Excuse me, Sire."

"Yes?"

"His majesty asks that Lady Cassandra please attend as well."

Cassie turned to bury her face in Alex's chest, stifling the giggle that burst forth.

"I'll be sure to let her know," Alex replied as he smiled back at her.

"Thank you, Sire," Alex heard, followed by footsteps fading down the hallway outside. With that, they both jumped out of bed, each looking for their clothes.

"Alex, I didn't bring anything else," Cassie whispered; she stood by the bed, holding up the discarded nightgown that had spent the night on the floor. It took Alex a moment to shake the vision of her standing there before he acted.

Rifling through the clothing in his wardrobe, Alex produced a Ranger pullover and belt. While she slipped the shirt on, he found something resembling black stretchy leggings and tossed them at her as well.

"What are those?" Alex asked as she caught them in midair.

"These are to be worn under pants as armor. They are of the same origin as the Elven shirts and will guard against sword and arrow. Those pants you wear make these unnecessary," she said pointing at his trousers.

He dressed quickly as she slipped the leggings on, but held up the belt, with the unspoken question across her face. Stepping up to her, he took the belt and placed it around her waist, over the shirt. The length of the man's shirt made the tunic appear more of a dress, stopping about mid-thigh. In addition, with the sleeves rolled up neatly, to the correct length, it appeared almost stylish. With the leggings, the local modesty standards were almost accommodated.

He then slipped his dagger and sheath in the belt and led her to the mirror.

"Not bad, if I do say so myself," Alex stated, watching Cassie admire the look. She had a Peter Pan thing going that Alex found incredibly sexy.

"Feminine, yet functional," she replied with a smile, while drawing and sheathing the dagger in a mock fighting stance.

Pointing to her bare feet, Alex received a shrug in return.

With Cassie satisfied that she was presentable, they left with Kinsey close behind. Apparently, Kinsey had enough of being left in the room, and Alex was not going to argue with her. They headed down the main stairway, with Cassie drawing stares from the staff and guards, though all held their tongues.

As they entered the dining room, all conversation ceased with Cassie's entrance. They walked straight to the table that held Ben, Abrianna and several of the men Alex had met the day before.

"Cousin, what have you done?" Abrianna said after a moment.

"You like it?" Cassie asked, unfazed by the comment.

"Alex helped me pick it out."

Then she kissed her cousin's cheek first and then her uncle before finding a seat next to Alex.

Alex couldn't quite interpret the looks Abrianna gave him, figuring them to range somewhere between irritation and admiration.

Ben, however, had only one expression, and Alex translated that to "Call me uncle."

"I wanted to speak to you this morning, before all hell breaks loose," Ben began.

"Cassie, your attire is more appropriate than you know. I need you to watch over Abrianna as she tends to the wounded. Should things go badly, you two are to retreat to the Rangers of Westland. They have pledged loyalty and will take you in."

"Yes Uncle," Cassie replied, taking Alex's hand.

"Alex, as you might imagine, I have need of your talents. The morning's scouting reports indicate activity across the entire front line. I am afraid today is the day, my boy." Alex felt Cassie squeeze his hand as Ben completed his statement.

"Yes sir," Alex answered without looking at Cassie, but squeezing her hand in reply.

"Let's eat," Ben said, and with a flourish of his hand, the serving platters were delivered, covering the center of the table.

Alex noted that nobody appeared overly hungry, most taking small portions. He forced himself to eat a normal amount, putting on a good show for Cassie, and displaying that he was not concerned. Once everyone had an opportunity to eat, Ben sent them all on their way, leaving only Alex and a few select men.

As Cassie and Abrianna rose to leave, Alex stood as well, only to be engulfed by Cassie's embrace. After a long moment, she finally drew back, reluctantly releasing her grip. She and Abrianna headed to the open doorway, before pausing. Seemingly oblivious to anyone else in the room, Alex followed and stepped forward to give her another kiss before saying, "Keep Abrianna safe." Then in a louder voice he said, "Kinsey, you go with Cassie. You take care of Cassie."

Kinsey got up and trotted up to the two women, her tail wagging in anticipation of a trip outside.

With that, Cassie turned and followed her cousin out of the chamber, Kinsey close behind. With her exit, Alex turned back to the table, only to find everyone staring at him.

"My girlfriend is a Nymph, what more can I say?"

"The less, the better!" Ben replied while indicating Alex should take his seat at the table once more.

From there Ben began ticking off the duties and responsibilities of those in attendance. It was here that Alex finally learned the identities of the men around him. These where Ben's generals, the men leading his army, cavalry and archers. It was also at that moment that Alex noted Ben had no royal wizard.

Alex also realized Ben had made no mention of their night's activities to the group. He had simply instructed his generals to be vigilant of opportunities, where bad luck may befall the opposing forces. It made Alex wonder if Ben still suspected turncoats in his ranks.

It also explained Cassie's orders, watching her cousin's back. Alex suspected it secretly delighted the redhead, placing a sword squarely back in her hands again. It did comfort Alex knowing Kinsey was close by the two women.

----*----

Cassie was waiting on Abrianna in the courtyard, one hand on the hilt of her sword, Kinsey at her side. Cassie's sword belt hung just below the dagger Alex had given her. Abrianna said she needed to change from the dress she had on at breakfast to clothes better suited for a field hospital.

As she waited, Cassie stifled the urge to break out in a happy dance. Her first night with Alex was everything she had hoped it would be, her inner Nymph overjoyed. Yet here she stood, sword on hip, preparing to fight for her life, and Brie's, if necessary. She had reached the balance she had always dreamed of but thought impossible.

While Cassie was marveling over all the changes to her life, Abrianna appeared at the top of the stone steps. She was now attired almost exactly like her cousin, in a Ranger's tunic, belted over the same black elven leggings, with tall leather boots. The major difference between the two was the lack of a sword, but she did sport a dagger tucked neatly to one side of her belt.

"Brie?" Cassie asked, certain she was seeing things.

"After careful consideration, I see the value of this outfit. It's lightweight, yet provides exceptional security in its material characteristics," she replied.

Cassie stared at her for a moment before saying, "Besides, it's so damn cute!"

"Yes!" Abrianna shouted as they both broke out laughing.

Moments later, they mounted waiting horses and headed to the field hospital set up just outside the city, Kinsey trotting along next to Cassie's horse.

----*----

Ben had dismissed his generals, each with their orders, but asked Alex to stay.

"What do you think?" Ben said after the last of the men left the room.

"I think you don't trust someone."

"Is it that obvious?" Ben asked with a sigh.

"No, but I know things they don't, and you have chosen not to share," Alex replied.

Ben sighed again before answering, "I have no reason to believe they are not loyal. However, after the Guild Master, I am suspicious of everyone."

"Everyone?" Alex asked with a wry smile.

"Boy, whether or not you realize it, you are family now!" Ben replied with a laugh.

Alex watched as Ben got up and walked over to the window that overlooked the northern approaches. Following him to the window, Alex could see the tents of the soldiers strewn across the countryside. He got a pang as he realized Cassie was out there somewhere, closer to danger than he was.

"How can you do this all so calmly?" Alex asked. Turning, Ben gave him a confused look.

"Here we stand, bantering, when a violent horde is just on the other side of the northern rise. People we love are in serious danger," Alex explained.

He saw the understanding in Ben's face as he replied, "I forget this is your first experience with war. I received my first taste of battle as a young cavalry officer. It's something I will never forget as long as I live. We were on patrol when we wandered too far north and into a Yankee ambush. I lost half my men that day, barely escaped with my life. Got this for my trouble."

Alex watched and Ben pulled his shirt away, displaying a scar from a bullet in his shoulder.

"From that day on, I swore I would never again go to battle unprepared."

Alex recalled all the memories he had of Ben, studying or conferring. The man had been preparing for this day since he met him.

"And where do I fit in all your preparations?" Alex asked bluntly.

Ben smiled broadly before replying, "You, my boy, are my ace in the hole!"

----*----

Alex was struggling to understand how sitting in this watchtower on the outer wall of the city was making him an ace in the hole. Ben had explained that he had the only Elven Bow available, so he was their designated sniper. From this vantage point, he would have complete visibility over the entire battlefield.

His orders were to take down targets of interest and protect those he could. It seemed a small task, but all Ben would say when questioned was, "Tell that to Jack Hinson."

Ben explained Hinson was a devoted family man and a successful farmer near the Tennessee/Kentucky border during the war. After the Yankees murdered his sons, he took his custom rifle and began a mission to exact a terrible vengeance on those that had done him wrong. During the course of the war, he was credited with over 100 kills. Some of his shots were achieved at over half a mile in distance, which Alex understood to be unheard of in those days. Alex could hear the sadness in Ben's voice as he described the man's anguish over the loss of his sons. Ben's explanation of this became all too clear though, with his parting statement. Pointing to a group of tents near the main road by the city's edge, he said, "Abrianna and Cassie are over there."

Ben left two archers in Alex's company, designated as his spotters. They were to act as his eyes, scanning the battlefield, while Alex took the shot. From their vantage point in the tower, Alex and his spotters could see the expanse of valley floor before them. It was a clear day, so Alex had little fear of the weather affecting his shots. There was very little wind.

In the distance and well out of bow range for the moment, he could see the banners of the approaching army. Alex watched in fascination as the Windfall formations maneuvered across the open field. The front units stretched from one side of the northern end of the valley to the other.

Behind the front ranks, he could see various other nonhuman formations spread throughout the lines. The large creatures, like the one Alex had hotfooted in A'asari, stood out as they towered over the others around them. While they made tempting targets, Alex suspected it would take more than his bow to bring them down.

Alex noted that Ben had placed men in the towers on either side of his. As Alex watched, a man next to Ben would wave a particular flag and the men in the towers would repeat the action. With each flag, the Vale troops would perform a maneuver, compensating for changes in the Windfall deployment. Using his enhanced sense, he focused on locating the magical members of the units before him. He spotted several less powerful auras, and they were far fewer in numbers than he had expected. As he continued to search, he was suddenly awash with a blast of red. It didn't come from a single person, rather it was the collective radiance of the three red mages. Alex located them right where he expected, in the middle of Redfield's banners and at the rear of the army.

By now, the entire force was visible as they came down the far slopes, entering the valley proper, while following the gentle slopping curves of the northern approaches. They were still quite a distance away, and were moving at a walk. As they progressed, he could see Renfeld's banners slowly making their way forward. Alex wasn't sure of the protocol for such things, but he suspected they were going to exchange words in some fashion before all hell broke loose.

Sure enough, when the Windfall troops halted no more than a few hundred yards from the Vale forces, Ben and a select few others came forward. Alex instinctively nocked an arrow at Ben's appearance, the action sparking both of his spotters into vigilance.

While the three in the tower watched, Ben led his small group out to meet a similarly assembled collection from Windfall. Alex could see Renfeld in the group, surrounded by the red glow of the three mages accompanying him. The party worked their way forward through the Windfall lines until they were at the head, facing Ben and his entourage.

Without warning, a red bolt of fire streamed at Ben from one of the three mages. At that same instant, Alex raised his bow and fired, his instincts taking over once more. As the red fire splashed harmlessly against Ben's shields, it stopped as suddenly as it started. While everyone watched, the mage dropped from his saddle, Alex's arrow embedded solidly in his chest.

Renfeld's remaining mages scanned the area; Alex assumed they were looking for the telltale bloom of magic that they expected accompanied the arrow. However, Alex had used the magic of the bow and not his own, so he had left no magical remnants to give his position away.

Ben, however, turned in his saddle and while not looking Alex's way, gave an approving nod of appreciation. Alex watched as the two groups exchanged words, with Ben indicating the dead mage on more than one occasion. Finally, in what appeared to be an act of frustration, Renfeld waved his group back and everyone returned to their lines.

----*----

Ben had ridden out to parlay with Renfeld before the fighting would begin. It was customary for both heads of state to meet in one last effort to negotiate a means to avoid bloodshed. He had never seen it work, but he thought the idea was nice.

As he and a few of his bodyguard rode forth, he could see Renfeld mirroring his actions. The red glow of the three mages with him was unmistakable. With each step they took, bringing the two parties closer, Ben noticed one of the three glowed with a greater intensity.

When the red bolt shot forward, it splashed harmlessly against the shields Ben had already created before them. Taking the lessons he had learned from Alex the day before, he marveled at the ease with which the elven technique absorbed the attack, strengthening his own defenses. He was sure the red mage was surprised to discover the undetected shield, another technique imparted to Alex from the Elven masters.

Ben was pleasantly surprised to notice that the offending mage had sprouted an arrow, courtesy of Alex and his bow. Ben knew that Alex was confused at his decision to leave him behind and in the tower. Ben feared Alex's inexperience on the battlefield would get him killed uselessly, his value wasted. He knew Alex's value was far greater than he understood.

Turning to nod in no specific direction, he acknowledged Alex's shot and mentally ticked off one of the three major powers he was to confront this day. He watched them scan his lines for the telltale signs of magic that he knew wasn't there. Unlike the snipers of his day, there would be no smoke or flash giving sign of where the Elf bowman lay hidden.

"That was a poor decision Renfeld, and a violation of parlay," Ben said across the open space between the two parties.

"Are you going to tell my father?" Renfeld replied, in a sarcastic quip.

"No, you stupid boy," Ben replied, "it means you forgo the right of yield. Should you fall today, no quarter will be given and you shall die where you lay. I would chastise you further, but you have already paid for your mistake." Ben pointed to the fallen mage.

"It is not I who will fall today, old man," Renfeld said, "he was but one of many magic wielders I have here today."

Ben laughed. "So, they all mean so little to you then."

Taken off-guard at the comment, Renfeld paused before replying, "They all know the dangers and the rewards. We are done here." With that he spun his horse and returned to his lines, the others following close behind.

"Well, that wasn't a total waste of time. One mage down and an army to go," Ben said aloud to no one in particular as he and his escort turned and rode off.

Chapter 22

Abrianna and Cassie were in the field hospital, preparing for the expected flood of wounded. An invention her father had implemented before becoming king, these hospitals had saved many lives over the years. By placing them close to the fighting, it allowed the healers to treat the wounded as quickly as possible. She didn't know where her father had gotten the idea, but it was a huge morale booster for the troops. The hospitals were also a way to reassure the families that their men would be immediately cared for in case of injury.

The thought of her father gave Abrianna a pure sense of panic, knowing he was again at the head of the army. Unlike other kings that led from the rear, her father was a military man at heart and led his forces from the front. Neither she nor Cassie knew where Alex was at the moment, but she was sure Cassie was just as concerned for him as she was for her dad.

With the thought of Cassie, she turned and watched as her cousin commanded the staff in their preparations. Currently acting as the Cassie of old, Abrianna could also see the changes in her, as she no longer avoided interacting with men. Addressing men and women alike, she pushed, poked, and prodded all into action with authority. She was sure it was all a mask to hide the concern for Alex.

Abrianna noted Kinsey had managed to find a spot under one of the cots, where she could keep an eye on everyone without being stepped on.

----*----

Watching Renfeld and the surviving mages retreat, Alex had to suppress the urge to fire off another shaft. Though he might get lucky, it was not worth the risk of exposing his position. He was sure Renfeld now had spotters of his own searching for him.

The return of the leaders to their respective camps seemed to ignite both sides. From his vantage point, Alex could see archers forming up behind the Windfall front lines. Within seconds, a flight of arrows sprang from their bows, headed directly into the Great Vale forces.

The sky filled with the deadly missiles and Alex watched as the Vale forces simply awaited their arrival. At the last moment, they raised their shields, interlocking the edges and creating a continuous barrier. It was then he noticed the shields had a strong resemblance to Roman infantry shields.

Remembering Ben was a graduate of the The Citadel, The Military College of South Carolina, Alex recognized the value of that education here on the battlefield. It seemed the Elves had placed great thought in bringing him over, unlike Alex's selection; he was just a regular guy and had no real training. As the Vale archers released a return volley, Alex took advantage of the distraction, locating a strong yellow magical bloom.

Waiting until the Windfall troops raised shields, he let fly a shaft, driving it through the man under the raised shields and skewering the soldier behind him as well. The exchange of arrows continued for several cycles, giving Alex the impression that each side was attempting to provoke the other into action.

Each time the Vale forces fired, Alex chose a target in various parts of the field, reducing the number of mages with each shot. Unfortunately, Renfeld had retreated to the rear of his formation, placing him out of Alex's range and negating the possibility of a quick solution.

After impaling an orange-bloomed mage, Alex noticed a distinct change in the Windfall formations. In multiple spots throughout the lines, large tension catapults and trebuchets were being moved forward. While the men next to him expressed concern at this turn of events, it was all Alex could do to suppress a laugh.

----*----

Ben had been watching the exchange of arrows between the two lines, his version of a light artillery exchange. While they had taken a few casualties, he had noted Alex's successes in each round, removing high value targets with each and every volley. He had to admit, the boy was a wizard with that bow; there was far more than Elven magic at play. He had seen few Elves that could make shots like his.

As expected, the Windfall archers weren't able to provoke Ben into the charge Renfeld was hoping for. The Prince was positioning his version of heavy artillery forward, so that he might press Ben into rash action. Ben was, in fact, preparing his troops for action, but not because of any concern from the latest developments. His next thought was of Alex, hoping the boy remembered his part to play in the coming Windfall assault.

Grabbing a man next to him, Ben whispered instructions in the man's ear. Nodding in response, the man smiled, and then ran off into the tents behind the Vale lines.

----*----

Cassie was standing to one side of the tent with her hand on the hilt of her sword, watching as the latest wounded arrived. She noted they were mostly minor leg and foot wounds, extremities exposed to incoming arrow flights she was told. She watched as Abrianna and the other healers treated each quickly and efficiently. From everything the wounded shared as they were being treated, the Vale forces were delivering more than they got.

Considering the imbalance in numbers, she hoped that was true and not just soldier's bravado. She still had no idea where her Uncle had placed Alex on the battlefield. Knowing he wouldn't expose him recklessly, she also understood he had a kingdom to defend.

As it was, she was on edge. Every time the tent flap moved, she expected to see Windfall soldiers, or worse, Alex with the wounded. She moved over to where Kinsey lay, stroking the wolf to help calm her own nerves.

----*----

Alex quietly watched the battlefield, his spotters pointing out the various war machines as they were pushed into position. While he was unaware if the Vale forces possessed more than a few of their own to return fire, he didn't see much activity on this side of the battlefield.

As the order was given along the Windfall line, Alex could see the tension catapults being prepared. Consisting of a twisted rope forming a torsion bundle, it had several lengths of rope with the throwing arm inserted in between them. When the rope was twisted, using the smaller levers at both sides of the frame, the torsion bundle would rotate the arm forward at high speed. As the arm flew forward, it launched the missile, in this case flaming pitch balls.

Alex knew that those balls were intended to land in the middle of the Vale forces, the burning pitch sticking to whatever it touched. While their shields would be of some protection, the reality was there would be massive casualties.

Intermingled between the catapults were trebuchets, using counterbalances instead of torsion ropes. While the torsion catapults would fling missiles into the front lines, the trebuchets launched their loads in a high angle. This allowed them to reach deeper into the Vale lines, placing Cassie and the rear support in danger.

Alex felt the eyes of his spotters on him as he stood watching the impending onslaught. As he watched, the Windfall artillery set their payloads ablaze. With a smile, he sent the slightest of images to one and then another of the catapults.

Suddenly, one after another of the torsion catapults exploded in flame, shooting splinters and fire in all directions. Chaos erupted along the entire Windfall front as soldiers and creatures of every kind ran burning or lay dying.

Next, the trebuchets attempted to launch, only to lose their counterweights in mid swing. This caused their flaming projectiles to go straight up and land in the midst of the Windfall lines. With mayhem reigning, Alex watched as Ben ordered his archers to begin firing into the Windfall forces anew. Satisfied with their previous night's work, Alex smiled broadly at the imperfections they had introduced into the various weapons of war. Ben had drilled him repeatedly on when to introduce the last imperfection, allowing for the greatest impact.

It was then that Alex saw Ben's flagman wave a signal flag he hadn't seen before. With the towers repeating the communication, tents along the entire Vale front dropped away, revealing catapults of their own. Immediately set aflame, each launched its payload over the Vale lines and directly into the Windfall front. As he watched, Alex saw soldiers and creatures set aflame, running blindly into others nearby.

Within moments, a second, and then third wave of flaming death rained on the Windfall troops. Alex couldn't imagine standing with the men there. He realized that he was so distracted, he had forgotten to fire his bow.

It was then, with all the mayhem, that Renfeld ordered his forces to attack. As the Windfall lines surged forward, Alex began firing at anything wielding magic or directing troops. Both spotters continuously directed Alex to targets, as all could see the magic users by now.

As the two forces clashed, Alex watched the Windfall cavalry emerge on the right flank, attempting an end run in the Vale lines. He laughed aloud as most fell from their horses, their saddles falling from their mounts as the cinch gave way under the pounding load. With their numbers reduced by half, the Vale cavalry rode them down, decimating the force and continuing on to press the Windfall lines at the edges.

It was then that Alex noted several extremely large troll like creatures pressing the troops on the left.

Should they breach the lines there, they would have a straight run into the Vale rear, and right into Cassie.

He fired several arrows into the beasts with little effect.

Throwing caution to the wind, he set the bow aside. Concentrating, he directed the free energy around him onto a vision of a laser. Extending his arm and pointing at the beasts, a white line of energy emerged, slicing the creatures into pieces. As they fell, the Vale forces pressed forward, closing the gap.

That, however, allowed every other magic wielder on the battlefield to locate Alex. Besides the few remaining minor mages mixed in amongst the troops, both red mages now assaulted Alex's position in the tower. While Ben had been dealing with the few magical attacks on the battlefield, Renfeld had held the red mages in reserve.

Now Alex was facing attacks from both mages as well as the more traditional efforts from the soldiers below. Any archer who thought himself close enough fired arrows at the tower. While his lessons had prepared him for the power of the attacks, they were less than helpful in addressing how one defended and attacked at the same time.

Thankfully, both his spotters had retrieved their own bows, and were countering the attacks from below as best they could.

----*----

Ben was not overly pleased about their current situation. While every one of their previous efforts in the enemy camp had borne fruit, Alex's magic had been brought into the fight far too early. He had no idea why the boy felt the need to expose himself so soon. He had to rely on the belief that he had used good judgment in doing so.

While Ben's cavalry was pressing on the Windfall right flank, the rest of the Windfall line was slowly pushing his forces back in the middle. He himself had taken to sword, his ever-present bodyguard at his back as he drove forward. His main goal had been to close in on the few remaining mages embedded in the Windfall line.

In between dispatching adversaries, he could see the splashes of energy above him as Alex fended off wave after wave of red energy bolts. He only hoped the boy had the smarts to deal with the pair, as he was currently occupied with his own set of troubles.

----*----

The serious casualties had started arriving, filling the beds and open floor spaces. Cassie watched in frustration as Abrianna moved from patient to patient, doing what she could for each before going on to the next. With no magical ability outside of the water, Cassie did whatever mundane tasks were required of her. Fetching bandages or ointments, she was constantly on guard should a Windfall breakthrough put them all at risk.

----*----

Alex had managed to fry a few stray mages while containing the red mage attacks. For the moment, they seemed content to keep him occupied as they fired bolt after bolt in his direction. He began to suspect they were attempting a war of attrition as the Windfall lines continued to press the Vale forces back.

Every so often, he would feel something slam into the base of the stone tower they occupied. Splitting his focus for the briefest of moments, he used his senses to check the structure below. There, he discovered the reason for the delaying tactics. The stones below them were close to failing; soon the entire tower would collapse under them. Placing a small shield to protect the area, he shouted at his spotters.

"Get ready to move, this tower is about to collapse," he said.

While continuing to absorb the red assault, he formed a blast of his own, focused at the base of the mound the two wizard occupied with Renfeld. Slipping it under his shield, it hit with enough force to knock everyone there off their feet, disrupting the attack and allowing him to relocate.

"Now, move!" Alex shouted as he sprinted to the stairwell with bow and quiver in hand.

Running down the stairs at breakneck speed, the three men exited the tower as another blast rocked the stones, causing it to collapse behind them as they cleared the area around it.

Finding Shadows waiting for him, Alex mounted, leaving his bow behind, while ordering his spotters to find a new spot on the walls to cover the infantry with their bows. With the Windfall forces so close, the need for a long-range bowman was gone. Riding hard, he cleared the city gates and headed to the north road. Passing the last of the town structures, he entered the tent city where Abrianna and Cassie would be treating the wounded.

He found the front lines uncomfortably close to the tents, with red and blue clad men engaged in battle. Riding into the foray, he began frying anything resembling a Windfall supporter. Alex barely heard the cheer around him as the Vale troops acclaimed his intervention.

Pushing Shadows forward, he fired off bolt after bolt, clearing the sections before him and rallying the Vale forces there. Working discreetly at first to avoid friendly fire incidents, he pushed into areas of only Windfall troops and creatures.

Unfortunately, there were so many that they closed in behind him.

----*----

Cassie was moving a patient near the opening when the tent flaps moved, indicating more patients were arriving in the already filled tent.

"There's no more room," she announced before looking up.

"We can make room for you," the orc replied as he swung his sword at Cassie.

Fortunately, a soldier near the orc had retained his sword, blocking the down stroke and giving Cassie time to draw her own weapon. Leaping from the floor, Kinsey struck the orc from behind, taking it down. Cassie thrust forward into the orc, only to have two more take its place. The soldier at the doorway took one's leg off as it entered, causing it to fall and die in Kinsey's jaws. The last orc lunged at Cassie, only to be tripped by another patient. The fall took the orc straight into Cassie's blade and off to whatever hell it deserved.

Gathering the loose weapons from dead orcs, Cassie armed the more mobile patients while they prepared for more attacks. She looked at Kinsey with a smile, thankful Alex had insisted she go along with the women.

----*----

Using his senses to scan the battlefield, Ben could see his cavalry pressing the Windfall right flank, but they were just too few in numbers to roll it up. From the white flashes on his left, he assumed Alex had survived the tower collapse and was pressing the enemy there. Ben had retreated to a point in the center of his lines where he could better rally his forces against the pressure of the Windfall advance.

Unfortunately, it was becoming very clear that he didn't have enough forces to rally. It wasn't that Great Vale had taken huge losses, it was the overwhelming numbers that Windfall brought to bear.

The lion's share of their forces were, in fact, not Windfall soldiers at all. Renfeld's army was made up of large groups of Orc, Gorm Orc and other nasty creatures; their numbers seemed limitless. Fortunately, Alex had apparently dispatched the trolls Ben had seen earlier, but the lesser creatures would be their downfall if he didn't come up with something, and soon.

----*----

Alex backtracked to the Great Vale lines in an effort to give relief to the battling soldiers there. He had abandoned Shadows for fear of losing the horse to a Windfall sword or spear. To those around him, he seemed impervious to sword, spear, and arrow. Only he knew that he had constructed a shield around him, similar to the way he became invisible.

Leaving only the sword and spellcasting hands exposed, he was able to cut swaths through the Windfall forces with near impunity. He mentally cautioned himself not to get too cocky though, as several times he had nearly tumbled to the ground, buried under the onslaught. Massed attacks could push him beyond his limits, and he was continually pressed by the sheer weight of numbers.

Once he was back at the front line, he turned, and with all the force he could muster, slammed an invisible wall against his pursuers. To the amazement of the Vale soldiers around him, the Windfall forces flew in all directions, creating a gap for them to exploit.

Turning to the rear, Alex noticed several small groups of orcs darting between the tents. In a panic, he sprinted to the tents where he had seen them lurking, catching several of the roving orcs by surprise before dispatching them. A motion to his right drew his attention, as he saw the last of several orcs entering a tent.

----*----

Cassie had organized a defensive perimeter inside the tent that allowed Abrianna to continue treating the more critical patients. The less injured soldiers took up arms in defense of their comrades. Kinsey was never far from her side during the entire effort.

As they finished moving the last critical patient, four orcs entered at one end of the tent. The first orc sprang at one of the downed soldiers, but the man next to him slashed at the orc's legs with his blade; and the orc was quickly dispatched. Cassie leaped to face the other three, her sword held out in front of her with the Elven dagger in her other hand. Kinsey moved between Cassie and the orcs, her snarl alone a threat of impending death.

The three remaining orcs spread out in front of Cassie and Kinsey, shoulder to shoulder. She could see them grinning at what they perceived as an easy kill. As everyone watched, all three orcs lost their heads, their bodies dropping in place. Standing over the three, sword bloodied, stood Alex.

"Alex!" Cassie screamed as she rushed to embrace him, only to bounce off him at the last moment, landing on her butt.

"Sorry," Alex said as he dropped his shields, and reached out to help Cassie to her feet. Kissing him first, she finally asked, "What was that?"

"Shields," he replied with a grin. "Which gives me an idea. Get all the wounded you can find in here now."

Following his instructions, Cassie, Abrianna, and the other staff moved everyone they could find into the tent while Alex continued to dispatch any wayward orcs he could locate, an ecstatic Kinsey at his side.

"OK, we are good. Now what?" Cassie asked from the tent flap.

After he directed Kinsey inside, Alex said, "Hang tight until I return." Then he set a shield over the entire tent.

"Alex, no!" Cassie shouted, when she realized he had locked her in again, away from the fighting.

"Sorry babe," he replied as he re-shielded himself and headed off to find Ben. Turning back, he saw several orcs pounding against the shield, as Cassie shouted unladylike phrases at his back. Stopping, he fried the orcs before continuing on his way.

Chapter 23

Alex found Ben by his aura, the flashing blue bolts flying in all directions. As he climbed the mound Ben had chosen for his last stand, he cast a few white bolts of his own against the forces pressing their center. From this location, it appeared that the Windfall forces had withdrawn a bit, until Alex realized they had just stopped and the Vale troops were retreating.

"You've looked better," Alex commented as he stood next to Ben.

Ben glanced sideways, doing a double take when Alex dropped his body shield.

"Nice touch," Ben replied. "You need to teach me that one, if we survive this."

They could both see Renfeld and the two red mages who had moved forward and off the edge of the valley. They were farther down the slope, moving with their advancing front lines, but keeping a safe distance from all but magic.

"We had some trouble on the left flank. I had to step in and set things right," Alex commented as they surveyed the pause in the fighting below.

"The girls?" Ben asked without turning to look at him, the concern evident in his tone.

"Safely tucked under a bubble until I release them or I die, I suspect."

"Cassie spitting mad?" Ben asked with a laugh.

"Oh yeah," Alex replied with a laugh of his own.

Doing a quick survey, Alex could see that they were still woefully outnumbered, although the only magic blooms he could find were the two red mages on the hillside by Renfeld.

"What is he waiting for?" Alex asked Ben.

"He's repositioning his forces to push up the middle and crush me. I insulted him earlier, so he plans on making this personal."

"So what's our plan then?" Alex asked hesitantly.

"I'm open to suggestions."

"I was afraid of that," Alex replied as the two men watched the Windfall troops reorganize.

"Well, I lead from the front," Ben said as he slapped Alex on the back and headed down the mound and into the massed Vale troops.

After a moment, Alex followed, catching him in a few strides. Alex noticed the questioning look from Ben.

"Hey, it's my understanding that after last night, we are family now. And southern families stick together," Alex said with a grin.

"That we do, my boy. That we do," Ben replied with a laugh.

As they reached the front lines, Alex leaned over and whispered in Ben's ear. The king nodded and after a few try's, created the body shield he had seen Alex using earlier. Alex could see the shimmering light blue armor encasing his body.

Completing his own magical armor, he watched as Ben turned to his bodyguard.

"Stay here!" he ordered.

Alex knew the soldiers could not see the magic encasing them. For what they were about to do, it would be suicide for the Royal Guard to follow.

With that, the two men stepped forward and challenged Renfeld's men.

"Come forward, cowards!" Ben shouted, while Alex slammed a white bolt at Renfeld and the red mages behind the Windfall lines. The force of the impact sent the three flying again, though the shields of the mages prevented any real injuries.

The insult was more than the prince could tolerate, however, as he screamed obscenities from his position on the ground.

"One thousand golds to the man that brings me their heads!" Renfeld shouted at his troops.

The troops immediately charged, expecting little resistance at over 100 to 1 odds. After the first few steps, Ben turned and signaled his own lines. Suddenly a flurry of arrows devastated the men in the front lines, with a second flight right behind the first.

The Windfall forces continued the charge however, with the lead soldiers converging on Alex and Ben. Alex used his laser-like bolt to cut swathes in the oncoming masses. Ben in turn sent balls of energy bursting into men and orcs alike. The overpowering smell of burnt flesh was almost beyond tolerance. As the two men engaged the converging masses, a sudden cheer arose from the Vale lines. Everyone seemed to pause as the Vale forces gestured behind the Windfall lines.

Lining the rim of the valley stood the one hundred missing Rangers, all mounted with Leander at their head. Mixed in with the Rangers were over one hundred Dwarves, mounted and afoot, with Brokkr standing next to Leander.

As Alex watched, they slowly started down the slope. Suddenly the Vale troops moved forward as well, passing Ben and Alex, placing the remaining Windfall forces squarely in between the two converging groups. As the two Vale forces closed on the hapless Windfall troops, confusion reigned at the center. Alex watched as the Rangers and Dwarves took out entire sections of the Windfall lines, while the Vale troops engaged them from the near side.

Alex turned to the place he last saw Renfeld, only to see the Prince and his remaining mages riding like the wind to the northwest. Alex cast one last bolt in their direction, giving a greater sense of urgency to their flight as it splashed across their shields.

With their leaders gone and caught between the two forces, the Windfall troops yielded in waves. Several of those same Windfall troops turned on the foul creatures in their midst when the orcs refused to quit the fight. It wasn't long before the battlefield was only filled with those recovering the wounded of both sides.

Windfall prisoners were disarmed and sequestered to one area, a select few chosen to assist with the wounded. Ben had ordered that all wounded Windfall troops be gathered for medical treatment. The order did not extend to any of the dark forces, however, and any found alive were quickly dispatched by both sides.

While Ben supervised the troops at the surrender, Alex made a hasty retreat to release the shield he had placed over Cassie, Abrianna, Kinsey, and the wounded.

"By all the gods, Alex Rogers, if you ever lock me away again!" Cassie proclaimed as she strode defiantly over to the man and kissed him passionately.

Alex held her tightly, assuring himself he would absolutely lock her away again if it ensured her safety.

"Father?" Abrianna asked as she rushed up to them.

"He's safe as well," Alex replied. "He's overseeing the Windfall surrender."

"And Renfeld?" Cassie asked, still in Alex's arms.

"He and two of the red mages escaped after Leander appeared with the missing Rangers," Alex answered.

"Leander is back?" Abrianna asked, her intense interest in the man a surprise to both him and Cassie.

"Yes, he and King Brokkr broke Windfall's back," Alex stated without going into detail. It was probably better the two never knew how close they had come to death.

"Abrianna, there are a lot of wounded," someone said as they passed the group. Hearing that, Abrianna headed off to continue her work.

"You better follow her and keep her safe, there are still orcs about," Alex said, giving Cassie a quick kiss before sending her and Kinsey off in Abrianna's wake.

----*----

After the battle, all efforts had gone into recovering and treating the wounded. Between the returned Rangers and the Dwarves, all the surrendering Windfall troops were collected and disarmed, then settled safely under guard with food and water. Under Ben's orders, those Windfall soldiers with injuries were treated with the same care as the soldiers of the Great Vale. The healers were dispersed throughout the battlefield.

Alex however, spent a significant portion of the afternoon disposing of the bodies of the foul creatures left to rot. With the aid of the surviving Vale mages, they vaporized the remains, turning them to ash where they lay. By the latter part of the day, Alex had to instruct all the mages in the energy saving techniques he had been taught by the Elves.

Once the situation outside was stabilized, Ben opened the city and the castle to all, providing food and drink in celebration of their victory. The revelry was only tempered by exhaustion, most combatants choosing to find a comfortable spot and settling in, their families around them.

Busy overseeing the accommodations for King Brokkr and his men, Alex noticed Ben was nowhere to be found. He finally located him in his small council room, fretting over documents, drawings, and maps spread across the table.

"Hell of a celebration you have going on in here," Alex said as he walked in.

Ben looked up before replying, "I'm beginning to see you have a total lack of respect for authority."

He pulled a chair out, indicating Alex should sit.

"Renfeld is still at large, and unless I can get a pledge of loyalty from his troops, I can't release them," Ben stated, pointing to Windfall on the map.

"If he returns home, we would have to lay siege to the city to root him out, and that would be difficult with the city open to the sea at his back."

Pulling one of the maps to him, Alex studied it for a moment before asking, "Do you have any more detailed maps of the city and drawings of the castle? Oh, and one of the coastline above and below the city as well."

Ben nodded, shuffling through the piles until he found what he was looking for. Alex reviewed each then nodded, smiling. As a student of history himself, Alex remembered reading about a small US Marine unit, in the late 1800's breaching a castle through a very creative access point.

"Ben, you can let them go whenever you like. They can't stop us," Alex replied with a grin.

"You know a way in?" Ben asked while reviewing the castle drawings Alex had been studying.

"Oh yeah. However, you may not like the route," Alex replied with a laugh. He pointed to one of the drawings depicting the seaward approach to Windfall Castle.

Ben didn't see the access referred to at first, until Alex put his finger on a specific detail in the drawing. Alex could see the recognition on Ben's face as he realized the significance.

With a smile, Ben replied, "Not me, my boy, you are leading this raid!"

In a short time, they conceived a plan that would have Alex take a small group of Rangers to breach the castle, while Ben led a force to the gates of the city as a distraction. Alex was unhappy with a particular part of the plan requiring Cassie's assistance, but neither man could see how it could be avoided.

----*----

Returning to the revelry downstairs, Ben and Alex entered the main dining hall, where they expected to find most of their honored guests. Sure enough, as they entered the room, Alex was engulfed in the embrace of King Brokkr. As the Dwarf was only about five foot tall, it was like a hug from a young nephew, only bone crushing.

"There you are!" the Dwarf bellowed, the smell of beer strong on his breath.

Recovering from the vise-like embrace, Alex replied with a wheeze, "King Brokkr of Two Thorns, may I introduce King Ben of Great Vale."

With a nod toward the Dwarf, Ben said, "In greatness and glory, I rejoice at your arrival, most Nobel King of the Two Thorns."

Brokkr took a second, and then replied, "And I am humbled in the presence of your wisdom and graciousness, King of the Great Vale."

Alex watched as the two kings faced one another solemnly…and then both burst out in laughter.

"Now that that crap is over, let's drink!" Brokkr bellowed.

The two embraced each other and Alex followed them to the king's table at the end of the hall. That was the same table where Alex had dined the night before leaving with Leander on their scouting trip north.

"Brokkr, I hate looking a gift horse in the mouth, but how in the world did you make it here in time?" Alex asked; he'd been sure that his request for assistance was unrealistic, debt or not.

"Ah," Brokkr replied with a smile, "a more accurate description has not been said!" After another strong pull from his beer stein, Brokkr continued, "My debt is paid, but you now bear the burden of a new one. I enlisted the assistance of King Elion of the Woodland Elves, gaining the loan of his prize horses."

Ben must have seen the confusion on Alex's face because he added, "Pegasus, my boy. Elion has a stable of flying horses."

Alex searched his memory, but couldn't recall any winged mounts.

"Don't strain yourself, lad," Brokkr said, laughing at Alex's confusion.

"The wings are only visible when they are flying, all other times they are identical to any other horse."

Alex was suddenly curious about Shadows ability to make it to E'anbel from Two Thorns in so short a time.

"Do you think Shadows is one, too?" Alex asked, suddenly suspicious of his mount.

"It's likely," Brokkr replied with a nod from Ben.

"And he had me riding like the wind to get here in time?" Alex asked with an irritated look on his face.

Both Ben and Brokkr laughed at the question, "Welcome to the ways of Elves!" Brokkr replied.

They all turned to find places at the table. For this occasion, Brokkr sat to Ben's right, instead of Alex, a circumstance that bothered him not at all. Instead, Alex searched for Cassie; he was sure she would be at the king's table or among the crowd of celebrators nearby. Searching the entire room, he couldn't see the tall redhead anywhere among the occupants.

What he did find was Abrianna and Leander, huddled together in quiet conversation off to one side of the hall.

Abrianna was still dressed in her Ranger's colors, making the pair look like a young couple in matching outfits. Alex was never overly intuitive of others feelings, but from the look of things, those two had a very distinct interest in one another. Good for Leander, he thought.

Approaching them, Alex was greeted with beaming smiles, though he doubted Abrianna's was at his arrival. Leander on the other hand, embraced Alex as a brother.

Grabbing him by the shoulders, he said, "It is so good to see you again. King Elion sends his regards and wished me to express his admiration for your achievements since leaving E'anbel."

Alex was sure the Elves had been following his every move since leaving their city, watching in the scrying pool. It was probably them he had felt on his trip to Great Vale.

"I can't tell you how happy I was to see you on the hill today," Alex replied.

"I was happy to be there in time. We rode hard from the gate in A'asari to ensure we would arrive before it was too late."

Alex chuckled. "It almost was too late."

Then he asked, "Have either of you seen Cassie?"

"She left just before you arrived, with Kinsey at her side. She mentioned something about a bath, you know how that girl feels about water," Abrianna said with a wink.

Nymph or not, a bath actually sounded great to Alex. Making his excuses, he left the couple to continue the conversation he had interrupted, and he headed upstairs. He entered his room, lifting his shirt over his head as he did so. Expecting Cassie to be in her own suite, he was startled to find her in his bath, Kinsey curled up nearby.

"Your uncle is not going to be pleased to learn you've taken up residence in my room," he stated before kissing her.

"My uncle is delighted that I am not currently living naked in the woods, in a spring, and enticing wayward travelers," she replied after the kiss.

"Now finish undressing and get in before I decide that I prefer the woods!"

With that, Alex finished removing his clothes and slipped in the tub behind Cassie, so that she rested back against him. She pulled both his arms around her so that he literally wrapped entirely around her.

The two sat quietly, Alex enjoying the warmth of the water and her body next to his.

"I think Abrianna and Leander have a thing for each other," Alex finally said, breaking the silence.

Cassie laughed and said without turning, "You are just figuring that out? He has mooned over her since coming to the castle, though she showed little interest in him. I think it's his time with you that opened her eyes and finally gave him the courage to act."

Laughing at her assessment, he replied, "So you are saying that I'm a bad influence."

"Only when it comes to women," she said, squeezing his arms so he wrapped her tighter.

After a moment, Cassie asked hesitantly, "So what were you and uncle discussing? I saw you enter the small council room."

"Renfeld escaped the battlefield," replied Alex, "Ben and I were discussing how to deal with that."

"Do you think he returned to Windfall? Will there be more fighting?" Cassie asked, concern evident in her tone.

"Ben is sending out scouts to find him, but if he does go back to Windfall, we have a plan."

"What are you going to do?" Cassie turned at the waist to face him.

"How do you feel about saltwater?" Alex asked with a smile.

Chapter 24

For the next several days, everyone in the kingdom of Great Vale was absorbed in the cleanup efforts. As part of those efforts, the Windfall prisoners were released periodically, after being organized into small groups. They were sent home to be with their families, and were instructed not to return to the castle in Windfall. Each group of prisoners were provisioned and allowed sufficient arms to make the return trip home safely.

The Dwarves of Two Thorns were given a grand send off after all the prisoners were released. Ben and Alex saw the king to his horse, Alex examining it closely for any indications of wings. At their parting, Alex again acknowledged the debt paid by Brokkr, and his new obligation to Elion. That concerned him little, as an argument could be made the Elion still owed him plenty.

Ben had given the Dwarf King his personal guard as a royal escort out of the city and up the north road, insuring a safe trip out of the valley before they took flight home. While there was little concern for the Dwarves safety, it was a sign of respect and appreciation.

With most of the major distractions gone, Ben had the community focused on rebuilding the damaged parts of the city, leaving work on the castle and keep itself for last. While the others worked on the rest of the city, Alex had taken to scaling the exterior walls of the city and the castle. When asked what in the world he was doing, he simply explained he was doing a survey, locating weaknesses in the stone structures caused by the fighting. With the collapsed tower as an example, none questioned his motives.

The walls of the city were about thirty feet in height, with the forty-foot towers interspaced for interlocking fields of fire. Alex could see Ben's military experience at work here, as the placement of the towers ensured every approach was covered. In addition, at no point along the wall could an attacker find cover from fire.

Inside the city walls, the castle walls were of equal height and configuration, defining the smaller plot of land for royal residency. The keep within towered to a full one hundred feet, permitting a grand view of the surrounding city and beyond. It also functioned as the focal point for those entering the valley from beyond its rim.

At first, everyone would stop to watch Alex as he climbed, most shaking their heads in disbelief. They would stare as he started at the base of one of the walls, and then locating hand and foot holds, work his way up to staggering heights. On several occasions, he would sink a metal spike into the gap between the stones to provide a foot or handhold. Soon it became commonplace, and of no concern to the community.

What was of particular concern to the community was the tent city still in use just outside the city's North gates. Due to the significant number of wounded being treated there, it was decided to let the field hospitals stay, rather than try to transport the injured.

Families from both sides of the conflict made the trek across the open countryside to visit, and eventually return home with their loved ones. In complete command, Abrianna made sure no one was allowed to leave until they were sufficiently returned to health and out of danger. With Abrianna so busy amongst the tents, Leander had placed several of the returned Rangers there for protection. While no threats remained, his actions did not go unnoticed by Abrianna. While not officially designated their leader, the orphaned Rangers looked to Leander for direction and leadership.

As it turned out, Leander had been provided a sealed message from King Elion of E'anbel for Ben's eyes only. In the missive, Elion requested that Ben recognize Leander as the new Master of the Ranger's Guild in Great Vale. To assume the position, he requested Ben release Leander from any obligations to the King's Guard.

Ben was only too happy oblige the Elven King's request, holding a gathering and releasing a proclamation after everything had settled down. Leander, completely unaware of the message's contents, was speechless at the announcement. Abrianna provided a congratulatory kiss, something not unnoticed by her father.

Alex was first in line to congratulate the man, Cassie by his side.

"So I guess it's up to you to clean up the mess I made in the Guild building?" Alex commented as he gave the man a pat on the back.

"Yes," Leander answered with a smile, "Elion mentioned you may have wrecked a few things, and it was for the next Guild Master to clean up. He simply failed to mention that it was me!"

"Well, Abrianna and I can speak first hand that the blood was spilled by us all, but the burnt furniture was all Alex!" Cassie said with a grin.

"It is my disappointment that I wasn't there to help undo the corruption," Leander replied solemnly.

"You are going to get your chance," Alex replied, receiving a confused look from Leander and

Abrianna in response. Before either could ask, Ben called all four to the small council room. Entering the room, Alex found a few of Ben's generals, men he had met before but never seemed to remember their names.

Once everyone was seated, Ben made an announcement.

"Well, we have confirmation that Renfeld did return to Windfall. The scouts report that only a small number of his troops returned as well, most taking our advice and returning to their homes."

"That means he cannot act until he can raise sufficient forces to support him," said one of the men at the table.

"We know that he has sent emissaries across the Western Sea, looking for support," another of the men at the table added.

"If we act quickly, we can prevent him from continuing this campaign," a third offered.

"Yes, that was my thought as well. However, even without a standing army, Windfall can hold out against a sustained siege," Ben replied, looking directly at Alex.

"I'm ready," Alex said.

"Ready for what?" Cassie asked, not looking overly pleased at the exchange.

"Alex and I have a plan for preventing a siege. However it does require a sizable force at the city gates," Ben replied, interrupting any answer Alex had for Cassie.

"I will also require a small number of men, preferably Rangers," Alex said.

"Why Rangers?" one of the generals asked, appearing somewhat put out that his soldiers were to be left out.

"These men won't be wearing armor or mail, and need to be experienced at climbing. Rangers are accustomed to such conditions," Ben again answered for Alex, effectively cutting off any debate.

"The Rangers will commit whatever resources you require, Sire" Leander replied to Ben while looking at Alex.

Taking the hint, Alex asked, "If you are available, I would prefer you lead the Rangers. That should prevent any judgments pronouncing the Rangers are returning to politics."

"I would be delighted to assist," Leander answered, his smile offset by Abrianna's frown.

"You require nothing else?" one of the generals asked Alex, apparently unconvinced of the mission's ability to succeed.

"Just one more thing. Does anyone know of a Water Nymph available for such a dangerous mission?"

"I get to wear my Ranger outfit, right?" Cassie replied, now with a grin.

----*----

The following morning, Alex met with Ben privately in his study while Cassie and Leander went to select the five Rangers that were to accompany them. Alex had provided them with just enough information to select likely candidates, but Ben had sworn him to secrecy on the details of the mission.

As Alex entered the study, Ben opened the conversation, "Before we get started, how is my niece handling things?"

Alex understood that this was Ben's polite way of acknowledging the fact that Cassie had moved into his room and his life. Within days after the battle, Alex had discovered most of his drawers and wardrobes now contained Cassie's things. Kinsey was also minding Cassie better than she did Alex. He wasn't sure if it was the females ganging up on him or the fact that Cassie spoiled Kinsey rotten.

The difficult part was that while the arrangement was quite common in his old world, Alex was positive it was scandalous behavior at this time and place. Even for Ben, who was a man from his reality, the 19th century concept of cohabitation was not readily embraced.

Apparently, Ben could see Alex was struggling with a reply, so he added, "Look, boy, I know you love the girl or I would have stopped this before it started. While the rest may think it improper, I just want to know what's in her head."

"Oh," Alex replied, relieved that he was not at the receiving end of a morality lecture, "she assures me that she has no thoughts of running off into the woods. She tells me the lessons you provided were a godsend."

Appearing relieved at the information, Ben followed up in a fatherly tone, "And what's in your head?"

Alex stopped in mid reply, thinking on the question. While he knew he was in love with Cassie, he couldn't really say why. Was it her magic? She had assured him that couldn't be the case as it faded when she left the water. Was it her beauty? He had known stunningly beautiful women before and had never felt this way. Was it really love or just an infatuation? He honestly had no idea, but he knew he couldn't live without her. He wanted her in his life.

He had not really been able to make plans past whatever battle they were fighting. What future did he see for himself here in this reality? What future did he see back home without her? Finally, looking at the sword returned to the wall where Ben kept it ready, the answer became apparent. Ben was a man of old southern tradition, a man of honor.

"Sir, with your permission, it would be my honor to take your niece's hand in marriage," he replied.

"Right answer," Ben returned with a smile, "I will dance at your wedding, but right now we have a villain to deal with."

Alex laughed, "Where did you hear that!"

Now it was Ben's turn to laugh, "I don't remember. I think it was some damn kid transported here years ago. He didn't last, but the phrase stuck in my head."

Taking the chair opposite Ben, the two began plotting the routes each force would take to reach the castle at Windfall. While each part of the plan was straight forward, the timing of the event was critical. Each needed to converge on the castle at just the right moment to ensure success.

While Ben's group would be taking the more direct route via the main road, his force was considerably larger. Moving an army of any size was not something done in haste. Alex's smaller group needed to travel farther west arriving at the sea, south of Windfall. Once there, they would follow the coastline until they reached the bay at Windfall.

Once the route plan was finalized, Ben assessed that both groups needed to leave the following morning. Estimating the traveling rates, he determined they would arrive simultaneously at their designated attack points four days later. That presumed they could extend the normal daily travel time to beyond the ten or so hours in the saddle. His troops would be starting and ending in darkness to make the schedule.

As they completed listing their logistical needs, there came a tap at the study door.

"Come in," Ben replied while turning his papers over to cover their work.

As both men turned to watch, first Abrianna and then Cassie entered the room, followed by Leander and five nervous looking Rangers.

"Ah, the volunteers," Alex proclaimed in a cheery voice, as he walked over to greet Cassie in a more personal manner.

"Enough of that," Ben said.

"Yes uncle," Cassie replied, still clinging to Alex's arm.

"Sire, these are the men you requested. All can swim and are proficient climbers, though most scale trees, not stone," Leander announced.

"Excellent," Ben said. "You men understand that the mission you volunteered for is quite dangerous?"

"Sire, they understand. They also understand that this mission is to avenge the Rangers not fortunate enough to be rescued by the Elves," Leander replied, with nods for the assembled men.

"That it is," Ben acknowledged.

"It will also remove the instigator responsible for the deaths of hundreds on the battlefield."

Turning, Ben shuffled through a chest on one side of his study. He removed a stack of Ranger tunics, all of Elven make and collectively worth a fortune to the men. Alex recalled that Abrianna had said her father's weapon suppliers did not include Two Thorns. She had said that he had other sources. He suspected that Elion was more active in supporting Great Vale then he let on.

"Please accept these as a gift from a grateful King," Ben told them, handing the stack to Leander for distribution. Alex couldn't help but smile at the looks on the Rangers' faces, he suspected that these men came from poor families and had never possessed such valuable, yet necessary, attire. Should things go badly, they would need every advantage to survive this mission.

His only satisfaction was Cassie would not be involved in the most dangerous part of the attack.

----*----

That evening, Alex was pleased to see Ben had invited the Rangers to share dinner with the royal family and select others. Alex had left Ben's study earlier that day with the Rangers, directing their preparations for the morning's departure. He knew Ben had delegated his portion of the preparations to his designated officers.

While the officers prepared the troops for movement, Alex heard that Ben worked with those he intended to leave behind, insuring he was leaving nothing unguarded in his absence. Apparently, while not of great concern, there was still the remote possibility that a sizable band of rogue Windfall soldiers could appear. Ben was not about to leave Abrianna and Great Vale behind unprotected.

As expected, Alex selected the seat next to Cassie. Both were pleased to see Abrianna ushering Leander into the chair by her. It was an act acknowledged by her father, who appeared to be suppressing a grin. Alex suspected Ben felt as good about the potential union as he and Cassie.

Their dinner was spent in stories and laughter, discussing anything but the military excursions planned for the following day. Alex sat in silence as he watched the others enjoying the evening. Leander was in top form as he charmed his love interest and her father.

Abrianna seemed to glow as she laughed and joked, frequently touching Leander's arm in an affectionate manner. Ben and Cassie appeared to be continuously surprised at Abrianna's flirtatious manner, though neither seemed even slightly inclined to put a stop to it.

As the evening drew to a close, the Rangers excused themselves, retreating to the special quarters Ben had provided. Following only moments after Leander and Abrianna, Alex and Cassie came upon the couple secreted in the shadows of a passageway. From their silhouette, it could only be interpreted that the man had finally gathered the courage to kiss the woman properly.

Cassie led Alex back the way they had come, and selected an alternate route to their room, one that would not interrupt the couple. Finding Kinsey waiting in their room, excited to see them both, Alex was happy to enjoy one more night of comfort before heading again into the countryside.

----*----

The following morning, all rose early and after a quick meal, Alex's team assembled in the courtyard. Ben had greeted them at breakfast, and then he was off to his troops, who were assembled just outside the city gates.

Alex watched as first Abrianna and Cassie, and then Abrianna and Leander said their goodbyes. Alex had asked Abrianna earlier to watch over Kinsey. Alex was happy to see Shadows was still his to ride, wondering when the Elves would recall her, knowing her value. As they were preparing to mount their horses, with Abrianna and Kinsey at the top of the stone steps watching, Alex leaned in on Leander.

"So when are you going to ask for her hand?" Alex asked the new Ranger Guild Master.

Leander looked up in surprise, "You know?"

Alex laughed aloud, "You are kidding, right? Even her father knows."

"The King?" Leander replied with a horrified look on his face.

Alex could only nod; he knew he would laugh again if he opened his mouth.

"I doubt his majesty would approve of a low born soldier vying for his daughter's hand," Leander said as they both mounted. That comment did bring a laugh from Alex.

"Leander my friend, I can absolutely assure you that being a lowly soldier will not in the least prevent the king from approving," Alex replied.

Before he was able to continue, Cassie pulled up next to the two men, bringing the conversation on the subject to a halt.

"Are we ready?" she asked, as she halted her horse next to the two men.

With a nod from Leander, one of the Rangers led the party through the streets of the city and out the west gate. Outside the city walls, there were still several structures, where the city had grown beyond its limits. It again reminded Alex of how prosperous and popular Great Vale was.

They had barely cleared the last building when they emerged onto a stone bridge that crossed the small river that ran North-South through the valley. Looking at Cassie who was riding next to him on his left, Alex nodded at the river.

"Is this the one?" He asked with a bit of a smile.

Cassie looked as if she didn't understand the question at first. Then, blushing, she seemed to be debating her answer before simply smiling.

"Yes, we were right over there," she answered, pointing over her left shoulder. Alex could see a gently sloping bank between the buildings and the water, a perfect place for picnicking or wading in the river.

"It was mid-summer and we had come down to cool off, as we had done many times before. Mother had packed a lunch and we were planning to spend the afternoon," Cassie began, "Abrianna had jumped in first while I helped mother, then I quickly followed. The bank was very crowded, covered with families from all over Great Vale.

"I had barely entered the water when I felt a sensation I had never experienced before. I was suddenly extremely aware of my body and felt entirely overdressed," she finished with a deeper blush.

Alex had noticed the Ranger escort, Leander included, had given the couple some privacy, putting distance in front and behind them as they rode. He leaned over to give her a quick kiss before she renewed her tale.

"It was then that I turned to find all the boys who had been playing nearby were standing on the bank and staring at me. Mother parted the crowd and rushed us back to the castle. That was the last time I was allowed in the water with anyone, until you," she finished.

Alex reached over and took her hand as he nudged Shadows closer to Cassie's horse.

"Then you are about to make a screaming comeback," Alex replied with a grin. Cassie gave him a confused look as she squeezed him back.

"Cassie, why haven't I met your mother?" Alex asked, suddenly surprised at the thought.

"Oh, I had completely forgotten with everything that has happened. Uncle sent her to visit the ports across the Western Sea as his emissary. Abrianna and I were to go to Windfall to discuss shipping agreements, and she across the sea to negotiate the trade pacts." Cassie replied, shaking her head. "Thank the gods, uncle sent her from a ship in Westland rather than through Windfall. She would have likely perished at Renfeld's hands,"

"Well, if all goes well, we may have that trade deal soon enough," Alex said with a smile.

The eight rode for the entire day, the west road to Windfall taking them in the general direction they required. By nightfall, they reached the first traveler's inn along the road. Cassie had visited here recently during her trip with Abrianna, so they had decided to go straight to their rooms for the night rather than risk anyone recognizing her. All assumed Renfeld had spies everywhere, suspecting he was concerned about a Great Vale retaliation.

With the roads so empty of travelers, each had a room to themselves, though Cassie and Alex still doubled up. Not staying for breakfast, the eight were back on the road at sunrise, Leander secured fresh traveling rations to split among the riders as they continued their trek.

Chapter 25

The Ranger Leander had chosen to guide the group west was originally from Westland. This was important because by midday they left the roadway, as it took a more northerly turn and away from their necessary route. From there, the road headed north and into the Great Forest. Alex was sure the road north was the route Abrianna and Cassie had taken the day he met them. Although it had been barely weeks ago, it seemed an eternity.

Alex was also aware that Ben and the army were not far behind them, and would continue on this road. Ben's group was to remain on the road, continuing into the forest and eventually go directly to Windfall. Both groups would be pushing hard to make the trip in four days.

Outlined by Ben, the route the Rangers were taking would lead Alex's group cross-country for miles. It led deep into Westland before they eventually reached the coastline just south of Windfall. From conversations between Ben and Leander, Alex was under the impression that they would pass several small villages along the way, as Westland was devoid of a large city.

Because Westland was a supporter of Great Vale and a holdout on Renfeld's plans, Alex expected no opposition to their passing. The eight riders rode at a steady pace, not pausing beyond the need to water the horses. Alex could see the changes in the terrain as the valley gave way to rockier rolling hills.

Proceeding deeper into Westland, he saw the strong resemblance to the Scottish Highlands he had been told to expect. He had visited there on a trip to the British Isles, taken by its beauty. The weather was similar, though not as wet.

At one point, Alex paused to look back at the valley behind them. In the distance, he could see Ben's army on the road and heading into the Great Forest. It gave him a surreal feeling; once more, he was heading off into a fight.

Never an overly competitive man beyond sports, Alex had always avoided things like bar fights or skirmishes on the football field. While he played with emotion, he never let his feelings get the better of him. In reflection, he wondered if it was just that he had never had anything he felt strong enough about to get in a fight over.

Watching Cassie as she rode next to him, he realized he had killed in her defense and was preparing to do so again. All this while placing her in harm's way at the same time. The plan called for her to assist in the assault on the castle, but she was to remain safely behind. Still, Alex knew no plan was perfect and she was going to be far too close to the fighting for his liking. His preference would have been for her to remain safely behind with Abrianna.

Cassie noticed his gaze and smiled in return.

"What?" she asked curiously.

Before Alex could reply, the lead Ranger halted and announced, "We are coming to a village."

The riders all came abreast, allowing them to survey the small valley ahead. Really more of a depression among the rolling hills, there were several small structures clustered in a haphazard grouping. He could make out a stable with an adjoining inn. The other buildings were nondescript and he could only guess at their function.

Alex could see people moving about, tending to whatever business they had before them. Checking the sun in the sky, he could see they still had several hours riding ahead, so stopping for the night was not an option.

"Do we go around?" Alex asked Leander as the two scanned the surrounding countryside.

"Can't say there are no Windfall spies about. Even though the battle is over, they will still be reporting back to Renfeld. Better to stick to the plan," Leander replied after considering the question, knowing they had already been seen by those below.

Before leaving, they had decided on a cover story, should anyone ask. They would say they were on a Ranger training mission, orienting replacement Rangers to the surrounding areas near Great Vale.

Nodding in agreement, Alex made a sweeping gesture, indicating that Leander should lead the way into the village. Smiling, Leander nodded back in acknowledgment and then spurred his horse on ahead of the others.

As the riders entered the village, the only one attracting any attention was Cassie. Dressed in the Ranger colors, she was a novelty in both appearance and in position. The Rangers didn't allow women in their ranks, so the implication given by her attire brought questioning stares. She also looked damn good.

Alex could tell Cassie was enjoying both the attention as well as the implication that she was as good as any of the men. Truth be told, for this mission she was better. While the riders were temporarily the center of attention, no one challenged the group as they passed through.

Leander continued through the village and out the far side, leading the riders farther west. They continued this way for several more hours until they reached a small depression just before sunset.

"Shall we stop here for the night?" Leander asked Alex as he came abreast of where the Guild Master had halted.

"Looks good to me," Alex replied as the others started to dismount and begin preparations for spending the night.

Alex had to fight the urge to rush over and assist Cassie as they prepared camp. Remembering her attending to Abrianna on the trip through A'asari and on to Great Vale, he knew her to be quite competent.

As he watched her, he had to suppress a laugh, for her movements were slightly exaggerated. This was the Cassie he remembered from their first encounter, daring you to question her ability in carrying her own weight. He could see the Rangers continually glancing her way as she tended to her horse and prepared a bedroll next to Alex's chosen spot.

Alex was only too happy to start the fire since the men had barely located enough scrub and other firewood to have one at all. The landscape was devoid of any sizable trees, containing mostly small bushes and grassy hillsides. The depression they occupied provided a reasonable windbreak as well as hid their firelight from view.

Once everyone settled down by the fire, one of the Rangers passed out skewers of meat strips ready for roasting. With bread and some dried fruit, Alex was more than satisfied by the meal's end. He had asked for the water skins, and chilled the contents for the group to pass around as a luxury. The day hadn't been overly hot, but a warm ride, nonetheless.

The evening meal completed, Leander set a watch, split among the Rangers. While Alex and Cassie offered to participate, the men would not hear of it. All agreed that a rested magician was much more valuable, and royalty simply did not stand watch, period. As they all settled in for the night, Alex was a bit sad that Kinsey wasn't there as well. Besides a great companion, her ability to detect intruders in the night was a welcome trait, sorely missed on this trip.

The following morning, the party was up at sunrise and on the trail, such as it was, within half an hour. Breakfast in the saddle consisted of dried fruits and a honey-sweetened bread, specifically packed for Alex. His preference for pastries was now well known by the entire kitchen staff.

The Ranger from Westland had the group headed almost due north by this point, the Great Forest still occasionally visible in the distance to the east. While the goal was to circle around to the west coming at Windfall from the far side, they didn't want to stray too far west and create an excessive gap to reach the bay where the city lay.

As they rode north, Alex noticed Cassie moving between each of Leander's men. She would ride with one man for a ways, engaging him in conversation. Several times he heard her giggle or laugh at some comment, always friendly, but never too familiar.

Alex never really thought of himself as a jealous man, so the slight pangs of discomfort came as a bit of a surprise. He had to chide himself that any man involved with a Nymph, even part Nymph, would be well served to control his jealousy. Eventually he chalked the whole thing up to her exercising the new learned self-control.

By midday, they had located a freshwater source, thanks to Cassie, and both watered the horses and refilled their skins. Alex purified each as they were filled to ensure no potential issues would arise later. As everyone began to mount up, Cassie moved over to where Alex stood.

"Uncle says a good leader ensures his or her men know they care," she stated with a knowing smile. "And they will know if you are insincere."

The last comment spoke volumes. Alex knew now that Cassie wanted the men to understand she was not just a member of the royal family, she was one of them. In truth, she was certainly sharing their trials and tribulations. Every member of the party was as much at risk of losing life and limb as another.

Sharing a quick kiss, both mounted and the rest of the party did their best to pretend they never saw the event. Alex waved to Leander as the Westland man led the group north. Alex noted in passing that two of their team dropped behind, always insuring Alex and Cassie were protected front and rear.

Riding through the afternoon, Alex watched as Cassie continued her rounds. At one point, she was riding with Leander, the two appearing as if they had been friends for ages. Watching as they chatted, Alex suddenly burst out in laughter.

"What so funny?" Cassie asked as she turned in the saddle.

"Sorry," Alex replied. "I was just watching you two talking so nicely, and then I remembered the first night I met Leander. I thought you wanted to gut the man right then and there!"

At the memory, Cassie blushed ever so slightly, while Leander nodded with a grin. Cassie graced Alex with a snub, sticking her tongue out and then returned to her conversation as if she were never interrupted.

It was late in the afternoon when the group found themselves in another village. Similar to the first one, it was placed in a small valley, running east and west and containing a dozen buildings. The inn and stables were readily identifiable, with a dry goods and sundries store beyond.

"Do we stay here tonight?" Leander asked Alex as he caught up with the leaders, who had stopped and were looking over the valley.

Checking the sky, Alex suspected they had no more than an hour's light left as it was.

"Are we on schedule?" Alex asked the Ranger tasked with getting them to their destination on time.

"Ahead, actually. We will make the coast tomorrow afternoon," the man replied with confidence.

Alex had put a stop to the practice of calling him sire. Neither royalty nor a military officer, he'd had enough of faking his station in life here. It was only Leander's insistence that he was, in fact, a Ranger by Elven decree, that he stopped objecting to that title.

However, should he marry Cassie, his station would be decided once and for all. He had received Ben's permission, so he needed to complete that proposal before too long. He was quite positive that now was not the time, though.

"Let's do it then. Might as well get a good night's rest, tomorrow night will be long and won't be so pleasant." He waved the men on into the valley.

The group entered the village at its east end, the inn, and stables being central to the cluster of buildings. Again, it was Cassie that drew the stares as the eight riders arrived in town. Alex paid the grooms for the care and feeding of the horses, insuring that all received grain as well as feed.

The stable was a large wooden structure, as one might expect of what was essentially a big barn. Alex could see several other horses in attendance already, and he presumed they belonged to occupants at the inn.

With their mounts tended to, Leander led the party into the inn, pausing to scan the room's occupants as they entered. Alex got the impression that all inns in this realm had the same architect. The only distinguishing feature of this place was its two story stone walls. Most inns he had seen to date tended to be stone on the first floor with wood above. He presumed the lack of local wood had driven the choice here.

As before, the bar was again on the right with kitchens behind, a stone fire pit central to the room, and windows on the open three walls. There were several men at the bar, Alex thinking it not so unusual for being late in the day.

A couple of the Rangers went to the back of the room and began sliding tables together to accommodate the eight of them. Again, Alex found himself checking for Kinsey, the habit ingrained in him by now.

Everyone grabbed a chair as a serving girl, no more than 18 years old, came up to the table. When she realized the number of Rangers present, she turned and hurried off into the kitchens behind the bar. Soon an older man came out, the look of resignation clear on his face.

"Rangers eat free," he declared, speaking with less enthusiasm than a man at the gallows would.

"We pay our way, but thank you for the offer," Alex replied.

With that news, the man's disposition brightened measurably.

"And how may I help the noble Rangers this evening?" the man responded with a smile.

"Room and board for eight please," Alex answered.

The man's brow furrowed as he did the mental math before he replied, "Only got four open rooms, you are going to have to double up, I'm afraid."

"Not a problem." Cassie declared, startling the man, who hadn't detected a woman in the mix.

"Ah, yeah, ok, so what would you like?" the man replied, recovering his composure and too polite to inquire about a woman in Ranger colors.

Unfortunately, two men at the bar weren't as well mannered. Now, why two men would mouth off in front of seven armed men and one armed woman, Alex wasn't sure. The possibility that they were Windfall spies did pop into Alex's head as he watched the exchange, but he suspected they were just deserters; perhaps they were drunk and smarting from their defeat, or just stupid.

"What's with the bitch in Ranger colors?" one of the men said to the other in a loud voice. Leaning back against the post behind him, he took a drink from his stein.

"Don't know, since Windfall lost to the Vale, things have gone downhill badly," the other replied before taking another drink himself.

"Windfall killed too many. They ran out of real men and had to recruit maids and whores," the first said, drinking and then laughing, still leaning on the post behind him.

It was Alex's opinion that the men weren't worth bothering about. Cassie however, didn't seem to agree; she pushed back from the table and calmly walked over to the two.

Alex waved the others back into their seats when they all began to rise. He did draw two of the throwing knives from his belt. Still sitting, he slid to one side and made sure he had a clear opening between himself and the two instigators.

With her hand grasping the hilt of her sword still in its scabbard, Cassie stepped up so she was between the two men, staring both down with her icy green eyes.

"I think you owe me an apology."

"I think you owe me a kiss," the man on her right said, leaning in while grabbing for the back of her head.

With that, Cassie violently slid her sword straight up, driving the pommel of her sword under the man's chin and snapping his head back. She drew her dagger with her free left hand, placing it against the man's throat.

As she did so, the man on her left drew his hand back to strike her across the face. Alex's hand flashed, and the knife flew across the room, pinning the man's hand to the post behind him. There was a scream of pain, and then cursing as he tried to pull the blade free. The second knife pinned the other hand next to the first.

Alex calmly walked over and disarmed both men, then frisked them. Not finding anything interesting, he gave Cassie a peck on the cheek and sent her back to her seat. Hesitant at first, she finally conceded her prize and returned to her place at the table.

With both hands pinned to the post, the one man could only whimper while the other lay partially unconscious on the floor. It was then that two Westland Rangers appeared at the doorway, scanning the room and surprised to see so many in Ranger colors.

"What is going on here?" one of the two men asked.

"Do you know these two men?" Leander asked.

"No," one of the two replied, "they showed up a few days ago and have been making a general nuisance of themselves, harassing travelers from the east."

"I am the new Guild Master from Great Vale," Leander declared, "we are on a training mission and these two challenged one of my members."

"Apologies Guild Master, we were informed of your appointment. Westland stands ready to assist Great Vale," the first Ranger replied with pride.

"We will deal with these two so you are free to continue your mission unburdened," the other replied.

The two Westland Rangers stood silent for a moment, before one finally got the courage to ask the question on both their minds.

"Is it true you were appointed by King Elion himself?"

----*----

After the local Rangers removed the two Windfall deserters, the evening became very pleasant. The eight received royal treatment from the innkeeper, both for removing the troublemakers and Leander's notoriety with the local Rangers. As the evening wore down, everyone found a roommate and headed upstairs, with Cassie and Alex a foregone conclusion.

Once in their room, both stripped down to wash out their clothes and clean up. Alex watched, struggling with the thought of when to propose, as Cassie prepared for bed. While a bath was impossible, each washed up as best as they could. They both climbed into one of the two beds, with their clothes laid out to dry all over the room. Alex waited until they settled into comfortable spots before extinguishing the light.

In the darkness of their room, he had just decided to pop the question when he recognized the slow regular breathing of Cassie, sound asleep.

Chapter 26

The following morning, everyone was dressed and ready before sunrise. Eating a fair meal, Alex tipped the innkeeper well, apologizing for the disruption the night before. He wanted to confirm he was leaving the man with a better than average opinion of those from Great Vale. Cassie nodded and smiled recognizing the effort Alex was making on her uncle's behalf.

The eight riders collected their mounts and were off by the time the sun started to appear on the horizon. Alex could see it was going to be a clear day; there wasn't a cloud in the sky. The land was starting to change, resembling the Scottish Highlands less and less. The craggy rocky outcrops were being replaced with gentle rolling hills of grass and brush.

Cassie was apparently done with her socializing and stayed close to Alex. The two again rode in the middle of the Ranger formation, though not by a choice of their own. As they rode, Alex evaluated asking Cassie for her hand then and there.

Eventually, he decided to wait, trusting that the right moment would present itself, and left it at that.

----*----

After four days of hard riding, the group huddled on the beach at sunset, looking out onto the harbor at Windfall. From their location, they could see several ships tied up at the wharves, with even more at anchor out in the bay. Centered between the wharves was the castle itself, a huge stone structure that ran right out into the water for several feet.

The castle and its keep within was a stone walled monolith, centered in the midst of smaller wooden buildings. The city surrounded it on three sides with the bay acting as its limit on the west. The walls were of similar height to Great Vale, but the keep was no more than sixty feet in height at it's tallest.

On either side of the castle, they could see the city as it spread out for quite a distance in both directions. Most of the buildings close to the water's edge had the look of warehouses, used for shipping and receiving of goods from the vessels in the bay. All one and two story wooden buildings, they were in remarkably good condition, giving Alex the impression that Renfeld's father, at least, cared for his city.

Unlike Great Vale, this was not a walled city, so Alex could see far into the city itself. Unfortunately, from this location, they had no visibility to the far side of the city where Alex expected Ben and his troops to announce themselves at any moment.

As darkness approached, they were still several hours from the designated zero hour. Ben and Alex had agreed they wanted it very dark before Alex attempted his seaside assault. As they waited, it had finally come to the point where Alex needed to explain the plan in detail to all involved. Gathering everyone close, he relayed the instructions.

"Ok, so I guess it's time to tell you why we are all here," he started with a bit of sarcasm.

After a few laughs, he continued, "The plan is for me to scale the side of the keep there," he said, pointing to the stone wall emerging from the harbor waters that acted as the west wall for the keep itself. The castle walls sprang from either side of the keep, creating the boundaries for the courtyard and smaller buildings within the walls.

"Once I'm at the top, I will lower this rope," he added while holding up the coil in his hand, "and then you six will scale the wall and join me."

"How are you going to get inside?" Leander asked.

"There are guards along the top of the walls, they will see you," another added.

"I have that covered, don't worry," Alex replied with a smile.

"Not me?" Cassie questioned, the indignation apparent in her voice. "Then why am I here?"

"I'm glad you asked," he said, his smile even broader.

"My lovely fiancée here will take us to the base of the keep wall underwater."

One of the many things that Alex had learned from Cassie about Water Nymphs was their ability to displace water. It was the reason a nymph could emerge from a pool of water completely dry. As they entered or exited a body of water, they simply pushed it back in all directions, leaving a pocket of dry air around them.

Cassie had demonstrated it one evening in her bath. She sat in the bathtub, and pushed the water away in all directions, leaving her high and dry in the center. In her haste, she had almost flooded their room as the displaced water started spilling over the rim of the tub. Alex cherished the vision of her naked in the tub.

As Alex explained the magic to the Rangers, he received nods of understanding, but he noticed Cassie looked confused. The briefing completed, the others prepared for their parts of the coming assault, and Alex moved over to Cassie.

"What's wrong?" he asked as she stood before him looking into his eyes.

"You called me your fiancée," she replied in a soft, unsure voice.

"Oh my god, you're right," he said in mock surprise.

Dropping to a knee, Alex took Cassie's hand in his, and looking up into her teary eyes, asked, "Cassandra, would you please do me the honor of becoming my wife?"

She did not even pause as she replied, "Yes! Oh, by the gods, yes! But Alex, my uncle..."

"Has already given his blessing," Alex said as he stood.

She jumped into his arms and, after a lengthy kiss, Cassie asked, "Alex, this is a funny place to propose."

With a laugh, he replied, "If anything happens to me in the next few hours, I didn't want the question to go unasked."

After another kiss, the couple separated to accept congratulations from Leander and his men. Leander gave Alex a knowing smile, acknowledging now how Alex might know of the King's feelings around his marrying Abrianna. Alex had already traveled that road.

While Alex was talking to the others, he heard Leander promise Cassie they would safeguard her fiancée's safe return. The group spent the next few hours waiting for some indication that Ben had successfully completed his part of step 1 of their plan.

Suddenly, out of the darkness, a small bird appeared and landed in Alex's lap. Looking down, Alex watched as the bird exploded in a puff of smoke, leaving a parchment in its place.

Alex lifted the paper, reading it before passing it around. The strip of paper only contained one word.

"Ready?"

Turning it over, Alex produced a pencil and acorn of his own. Writing a one-word reply, he passed it around before closing both hands around the paper and acorn. Generating a mental vision of Ben on his horse, he opened his hands and received a fleeting glimpse of the bird as it launched itself from his palm, disappearing into the darkness.

----*----

Ben sat astride his mount, the troops around him patiently waiting for his next order. They had staged the march into Windfall so that their arrival, just outside the city, was no more than a few hours effort. Ben knew that should things go poorly, he would need fresh men and not ones that were exhausted after an extended march into the city.

As the city was without walls, he could see the lights throughout, a thriving community about to be turned upside down. If things went well, the people would be spared the devastation of a siege.

On the far side of the city, he could see the castle walls, the east gate well marked by its flanking guard towers. Behind that, the keep rose high above, various windows alit as well. He presumed Renfeld was hidden in one of then, waiting on their next move.

While there was no delusion that Renfeld was unaware of their approach, he was confident the man had no idea of their real intent. Once Ben had arrived at the agreed upon staging point, he had sent a message bird and was waiting for Alex's acknowledgement.

Suddenly a bird arrived out of the darkness, landing in Ben's outstretched hand. As the smoke cleared, the small parchment lay open across his palm, one word clearly written across its length.

"GO!"

----*----

Alex gathered everyone at the waterline as he again explained their next steps. Placing Cassie in the center of the group of Rangers, he addressed the rest. "OK, when we enter the water, everyone needs to be touching Cassie. She will push back the water and keep it back until we reach the base of the castle wall. While in contact with her, the magic acts as an extension of her on you."

At the mention of all the men touching her, Cassie suppressed a giggle. Alex caught it, smiling in return. He reaffirmed, then and there, that you couldn't be a jealous man with a Nymph in your life.

When everyone reached out to touch Cassie, Alex noted everyone selecting arms and shoulders, a clear demonstration of proper behavior on their part. Alex reached out, touching her tummy, causing her to giggle once more.

Backing into the water, Alex led the group in. Reaching head height in the seawater, he looked up as the water closed in above them; it became completely black.

"Ok, here we go," Alex declared and continued to move forward, his fist full of the front of her tunic to help guide her.

Now it was Alex's turn to contribute, as he reached out with his senses to guide the group along the bottom of the bay. Avoiding the occasional anchor line from the ships above, they slowly moved their way to the base of the keep wall. He found the sea floor to be solid for the most part, not the soft sand or mud he expected.

Everyone was armed with sword and dagger, Cassie included, and Alex also retained a large coil of rope. It was strung diagonally across his body, opposite the direction he carried his sword across his back. He also had a leather pouch on his belt. Inside, he had the climbing pitons he had been using on the walls of Great Vale.

While practicing after the battle, Alex had discovered that there were portions of the castle walls where the stones left no hand or foothold. In those places, he would take a piton and, using the magic of shielding force, drive them in the cracks without the need for pounding. There was only the slightest of sounds when the stone and metal scraped, but not nearly enough to draw undo attention.

Once they reached the base of the keep wall, Alex announced their arrival to the group. As he did so, he created a small illumination, allowing everyone to see. He made sure it was not bright enough to be seen from above on the castle walls where the guards patrolled. Fear of discovery had been the reason Alex had not provided illumination any sooner.

Looking down, he could see they were touching the seafloor. Everyone's boots were covered in sand and mud. That was all about to change.

"Ok, we are here, but there is about twenty feet of water above us," he declared. "I can try and float us up?" Cassie offered but she seemed unsure.

"I have another idea, but we are all going to get wet," Alex said to the group.

They watched Alex form a shield in the open airspace, like an upside down bowl. He knew only he and Cassie could see the shimmering shield, she because she was now magical in the water.

"Ok Cassie, you can let go," Alex stated.

With that, small bits of water inside the shield fell to the seafloor and more rushed under the lower edges of the shield bowl. Everyone was now standing ankle deep in seawater on the seafloor. Dirty boot problem solved.

"Now, as I raise the shield, the water will flow under and we will float up with it. As it gets close to the surface, I will need to kill the light so we aren't spotted."

Waiting for everyone to acknowledge him, Alex began raising the shield bowl until everyone was soon treading water. Pausing to take stock, he again started raising the shield until they were no more than a few feet from the surface.

Here he dropped the illumination, returning them to darkness, and then he continued to raise the shield. As he did, the group followed until everyone was bobbing on the surface in the calm bay waters, the moonlight verifying they were now next to the stone keep wall.

"Don't go anywhere," Alex whispered as he winked at Cassie.

Turning, he began to scale the stone face slowly. At its base, the wall was covered with encrustation, allowing for a multitude of holds for hand and foot. Eventually he reached the bare stone, well above the waterline, and had to search for secure hand and foot placements.

Reaching a point without options, he pulled a piton from the pouch and nudged it into the seam between the stone blocks. Forming a small shield in the palm of his hand, he slammed it forward, shoving the piton into the gap. He required several more pitons in a row before he reached the point in the climb he had been dreading.

Above him and to his left was the stone feature Alex had pointed out to Ben in the drawings. The stone had been laid in channels, sloping inward, away from Alex, and providing a groove about four feet wide. Once he was able to get up into the groove, he would be able to wedge between the sides and work his way up to the wooden cover at the top.

Moving cautiously, he found the way fouled by debris sticking to the stone walls. He had expected such and practiced using the smallest amounts of magic to clear a path. His biggest fear at this stage was there might be someone with magical abilities who would spot his glow with every usage of magic.

With his path mostly clear of debris now, Alex moved into the stone channel itself, wedging himself between its walls. Working himself up the channel by pushing his back against one side and feet opposite, he reached the top. There he found the wooden lid he expected, consisting of planks laid long ways across the channel and blocking his passage. Listening for the slightest sound and using his senses, he satisfied himself that no one was above.

With a magical shove, he forced the wooden planks loose and then finished his climb. Once he was over the edge, Alex found himself in a small room, no more than six feet squared. There was a single wooden door on the far wall. Barring the already closed door, he located a large metal ring anchored into the stone. Tying off one end of the rope, he dropped the other through the opening and into the water below.

He immediately felt it go tight, as someone below had started the climb to join him. Within minutes,

Leander's head appeared in the opening created by the removed planks.

"Really Alex, the garderobe?" Leander declared, with a distasteful look on his face.

"Hey, we are in, right?" Alex replied as he helped the man inside. He remembered Ben had used that name as well for the castle latrine.

Years ago, Alex had heard a story about the US Marines held to a stalemate in a battle where the defenders held a stone castle. A small detachment had breached the walls by climbing through the latrine and opened the gates. It was that event that had given him the inspiration for this assault.

Here in Windfall, they had located the latrines on the waterside of the castle. This allowed the waste to drop down the wall and into the sea, to wash away with the tide. This also allowed Alex to approach unseen and breach the perimeter of the castle as the Marines had done in his world.

While Alex watched the door, Leander assisted the others, until all six Rangers had safely made the climb. With the last man inside, Alex opened the door to peer outside and into the hallway. He had been cautiously using his magical senses to search the nearby rooms for their target. He tread lightly as he did so, not wanting to alert any magical personnel of their presence.

Looking both ways from the doorway, he could see a stone lined hall with wooden plank flooring running the length. The hall ran a good distance each way, with the occasional wood and ironbound door unevenly spaced on either side of the hallway. There were tapestries and wall hangings throughout, but none of the suits of armor so prominent in the movies Alex had seen containing castles.

Pulling himself back inside, he was just in time to see Leander assisting Cassie from the opening.

"You are not supposed to be here!" Alex grumbled.

"I am not about to let my newly betrothed risk life and limb alone, nor wander about without my protection," Cassie whispered back defiantly.

Before Alex could reply, Leander held a finger to his lips, and then pointed to the door. As they all listened and watched, someone walked up and opened the door Alex had closed but failed to bar. Without looking up, the guard stepped into the middle of the group of Rangers.

In one swift motion, Cassie drew her dagger and drove it into the man's throat before he could sound the alarm.

"See," she declared defiantly, while removing the dagger from the man's throat. Two of the Rangers caught the falling man and quietly set him in the corner of the room.

Alex sighed in resignation, not at all liking the precedent this set in their relationship. Turning to the rest of the group, he pointed to the door, and then led them out in single file. Looking back, Alex could see Leander falling in behind Cassie, who was sporting a broad grin.

----*----

Ben led his forces into the streets of Windfall with strict orders not to harm a soul. His scouts had verified there were no hostile forces in the city itself, as Renfeld had withdrawn with what remained of his troops to the protection of the castle walls. Under normal circumstances, Ben might have labeled it a cowardly act, leaving the undefended people to face the approaching army, but he was sure Renfeld knew he would never harm an unarmed populace.

The streets were deserted, most of the buildings shuttered tight. Had they not scoured them earlier, he would have been paranoid, fearing an attack from any direction. As it was, he suspected Renfeld couldn't field the numbers needed for such an attempt. The reports Ben had received on his approach confirmed that most of the troops from the last engagement did not return to the city.

So now, with the go message from Alex, it was Ben's job to make as big an entrance as possible. His goal was to draw Renfeld's people to the east side of the castle near the gate, reducing the number of eyes on the west end.

As the Great Vale force neared the castle and keep within, Ben made sure to keep his men as far out of bow and magic range as possible. If Alex's plan worked, this would be a near bloodless coup. If not... well his best hope was to drive Renfeld overseas and away from Windfall. That option was not at all appealing to him. It simply meant he was delaying the inevitable, creating a rematch at some future date.

Ben's real concern, though, was not Renfeld. It was the two red mages he still had in his employ. At near wizard level in power, the two could prove a real challenge to Alex, should he be caught unprepared.

----*----

Alex was using his magical abilities to scan the areas in front of his small force. He allowed his senses to travel throughout the hallways and chambers, looking for any signs of life. So far, he hadn't been able to detect either Renfeld or the two red mages he kept in his company for protection.

He was also trying not to leave a trail of dead bodies in their wake, so Alex avoided any wandering staff. Besides a distaste for killing noncombatants, bodies were a nuisance; eventually someone would discover one. At one point, he had considered trying to make everyone invisible, but discarded the idea as unmanageable. Only he would actually be able to navigate in that mode.

Moving from the far west end of the keep to the east, Alex started finding a substantial number of individuals with his senses, clustered in groups. He imagined they were all observing Ben's entrance into the city. That's when he touched two strong red waves. The feeling was almost like a hot wind blowing across him as he pulled his senses back for fear they would detect his touch.

The mages were still several levels above them and farther east, meaning Alex needed to locate a stairway to take them up. Pulling everyone together, he passed along the intel in whispered tones, and then started forward again.

Chapter 27

Ben could see significant movement along the top of the castle walls as well as in the upper structures of the keep itself. He continued to scan for any sign of magical blooms, indications of where the two mages might be held up with Renfeld. Any assault on the castle at this point would be pointless; the troops on the walls could more than defend against ten times their number.

Even with his own abilities, a magical attack by Ben would be dealt with by the red mages as effectively as the troops on the walls. He would have to expose himself, and then protect himself, while trying to breach the castle gates; not a great option.

Though the distance was great, he attempted to use his senses to search the castle himself, roaming high into the keep above. Closing his eyes, he projected his mind into the upper areas of the keep. As he wandered the upper rooms of the fortress, he touched something that told him Renfeld's father, the king, lay dead in his chambers. Whether by natural causes or his son's hand, he could not tell, but the sensation was one of a noble passing.

Continuing to scan, he sensed a power surge in the upper keep, one only explained by the presence of the two red mages. Opening his eyes, he identified the balcony and windows where Renfeld sat hidden.

Unfortunately, he had no way of notifying Alex.

----*----

Alex was able to locate the stairs leading up into the upper areas of the keep. The same stairwell also went down to the lower levels and parapet overlooking the main gates. Turning to Leander, a plan formed in his head. "Take some men and head down to the gates," Alex whispered. His thinking was that with Ben inside the walls, the rest of Renfeld's forces would have to surrender to the overwhelming numbers.

"You go too," Alex said to Cassie, thinking that once the gates opened, she would be safely enveloped by Ben's men.

"No!" was her forceful reply.

In no position to fight about it, he shook his head, and then pointed to Leander and two other Rangers.

"Ok, take these two and get the gates open, the others can stay with us."

Nodding, Leander leaned in on the three remaining Rangers. Alex caught the whispered instructions just before Leander turned to head down the stairwell.

"Watch her!" he said, and then smiled at Alex before leaving.

Ignoring the instructions, Cassie moved up behind Alex as he started up the stairs. Moving slowly and sticking to one side of the stairwell, Alex continued up while scanning ahead. He was positive that the mages were above them and to the east. He had no doubt that Renfeld hid with them.

Exiting the stairwell on the next level of the keep, Alex peered around the corner and felt Cassie come up behind him. Sliding into the hallway, he motioned the others to follow. As a precaution, Alex formed a shield in front of his group, setting the boundaries just inside the walls and allowing it to move in advance of them.

Stepping out into the center of the hall, he pushed the shield in front of them, progressing down the hallway slowly. Stopping at the first door, he had one of the Rangers check, though he felt no life inside. The man moved forward cautiously, opening the door and then slipping inside. He returned shortly, waving everyone inside.

Alex was the last to enter, dropping the shield as he did so. From the size and decor on the room, Alex was positive they were in the royal bedchamber. There on the far wall, was a bed framed between two open windows. On the bed before them was a body of a man, Alex guessed him to be well into his 70s or 80s.

"The King?" he asked no one in particular as the group approached the bed from both sides.

Everyone nodded at the question, accepting it as more of a statement. Evidently, Renfeld got his wish granted; he was now King of Windfall. However, Alex intended to ensure it was a short-lived reign. He motioned everyone back from the open windows, resisting the urge to look out since someone below might see them.

Turning away from the body, Alex went back to the door and paused as he used his senses to search the adjoining rooms. His senses roamed to the far end of the hall where he received an energy backlash as he touched both the red mages nearby. Their magical reaction suggested they were ready for him. Suddenly from the open window behind them, he heard a commotion that sounded remarkably like fighting in the courtyard below.

----*----

Ben had pushed a small portion of his forces forward, keeping them hidden among the buildings and out of the view of those in the keep. Unsure of Alex's progress in breaching the keep, he wanted them ready for a quick response should an opportunity present itself.

The plan was nonspecific at this point, since neither Ben nor Alex was sure of what he would find once inside the castle and keep. The lack of troops on the walls was a positive sign, as was the quiet from within the walls.

Now, Ben was with a group that sat in an alleyway, on foot and across from the east gate, the one he hoped to breach. He had left the major portion of the troops farther to the rear, with orders to make themselves as visible and menacing as possible without risking their lives in the process.

Suddenly, Ben heard a scuffling on the parapet over the gate. He watched as a body dropped off the edge, trimmed in Windfall red. Then he saw two Rangers running above the gate. Within seconds, the gates opened and Leander stuck his head out.

"Come on!" He whispered urgently.

At that, Ben lunged forward, with his personal guard on his heels. Passing through the gates, he and his men were met by Windfall guards rushing from the keep, swords drawn and ready for a fight.

As Ben entered, his shields splashed with red attacks from above.

----*----

Waving for everyone to come to him at the door, Alex again peered out into the vacant hallway. His senses indicated the two mages were waiting farther down the hallway. Placing his shield out in front as before, he stepped out into the hall, followed by the Rangers and then Cassie. Moving cautiously forward, Alex could sense the magical heat radiating from the two mages as they were engaged with the attack on the castle. Alex assumed Leander must have reached the gate, allowing Ben to attack, and gain entrance to the castle grounds. Any other assault would have been foolish; even with its diminished forces, the castle was easily defended.

Moving to the far end of the hallway and passing several doors along the way, Alex was abruptly confronted by both red mages as they made a hasty retreat from the room they had been in. Slamming into his shield, both quickly recovered and immediately attacked his magical barrier with their own combined energies. Alex worked to absorb, rather than deflect their onslaught, a trick learned from the Elves.

A commotion behind him caused Alex to risk a look over his shoulder. In a glance, he saw Cassie in Renfeld's grasp, a knife at her throat, rendering the Ranger tunic useless as protection. With him were several armed men, all engaging the three Rangers as they defended Alex's back. He could see Renfeld backing away as his men kept the Rangers from retrieving Cassie from his grasp.

Alex had been so focused on the two mages, assuming Renfeld would stick with them for protection, that he had forgotten to check the other rooms as they passed by. Clearly, Renfeld had been hiding elsewhere as he let the mages lead the castle defense. Now Cassie was the victim of his error in judgment.

Unable to withdraw from the magical attack in front of him, he had to set the risk to Cassie aside and deal with the biggest threat to them all in front of him. Sparing the slightest distraction, he turned for a second and slammed several of the swordsman in Renfeld's guard with a shield, sending them skidding down the hall and leaving Renfeld almost alone, Cassie still under his blade.

Unfortunately, the two mages took advantage of the distraction behind him, pressing Alex harder from the front. While the tricks he had learned from the Elves helped him absorb the energy attack, the mages seemed to be pushing him with shields of their own. Since they were pushing and firing at the same time, Alex assumed they were incomplete shield constructs, targeting small points against his own broad shield wall.

With the sounds of battle behind him fading, he risked another glance, catching the Rangers in pursuit of a retreating Renfeld. His last glimpse of Cassie was as Renfeld pulled her into the stairwell, her face a picture of rage and frustration.

He was caught in a stalemate against the red mages; Alex could continue to fend them off, but was making no progress in resolving the confrontation. Whenever he tried to push them one way or another, the two combined their strength to nullify the attempt. With every moment he wasted, Cassie was being dragged farther away from him by Renfeld. If the man managed to escape to a ship, Alex doubted Cassie would survive the voyage.

Looking about him in desperation, he developed an idea to end the conflict. He began to back down the hallway slowly, as if the mages were gaining ground on him. As he retreated, he carefully drew in the edges of his shield. This allowed for a slight gap on either side between stone and shield edge, one not detectable to the two mages who were hammering its center.

Waiting for one of the minute pauses in their assault, Alex sent two bolts crashing into the stone on either side of his shield. Stone fragments of various sizes erupted from the walls, taking both mages off their feet.

Dropping his shield entirely, Alex followed up with a blast to the wooden flooring under his opponents, as part of the bolt splashed across their shields. He watched as they dropped through the flooring and out of his view. Rushing to the opening in the floor, Alex could see both men, laying in twisted heaps a good fifty feet below him. Evidently, this part of the keep extended over the great hall below, creating a greater drop than Alex expected. Smiling, he was happy for the fortuitous turn of events. Below, he could see several of Ben's men standing around the bodies, looking up at him in surprise.

Turning, Alex rushed into one of the rooms on the west side of the keep, searching for a window overlooking the harbor. Entering a large study, he found the window he was searching for and could see that Renfeld still held Cassie at knifepoint as they rushed along the wharf. Farther out, he could see two men ahead of the pair, readying a small boat that would take them to a ship waiting at anchor. He debated using magic against them, but the risk to Cassie was far too great.

He decided to wait and see which ship they boarded and then he would try to fire a bolt and disable it, preventing it from departing with his fiancée. He dared not leave the window for fear of missing his opportunity. Alex watched as the four entered the little boat, Renfeld holding Cassie close with the knife still at her throat. He was taking no chances, insuring he prevented her from escaping in the transition from wharf to boat.

A movement behind him caused Alex to spin in place, almost firing off an energy charge as Ben entered the room with several of his guards close behind. Alex turned back to the window as Ben joined him at his side. They stood in silence watching the small boat start out into the harbor.

With one man in the bow of the boat and the other in the middle, rowing, Cassie and Renfeld were forced to sit at the rear. Even though this presented a great target, Alex was not willing to endanger Cassie in the attempt. The fact that Ben was here meant Leander had been successful in his assignment, he realized. At that moment, Alex caught sight of him and the two Rangers running out onto the wharf below, joining the others already there, and all too late to stop Renfeld.

"Is that Renfeld?" Ben asked, as Alex felt the energy buildup around Ben.

"With Cassie as hostage," he replied hastily, preventing Ben from completing what was on his mind.

"What happened?" Ben asked without turning to look at Alex.

"We got separated in the fight and while I was dealing with the mages, Renfeld caught Cassie from behind. I'm waiting to see which ship they try for and go for that instead of risking Cassie."

Ben simply nodded at the explanation, as both men continued to watch from the window. By now, the sun had just started to rise, going from half-light into the soft glow of early morning. It was then that Alex noted what Cassie had done.

Sitting far to one side of the boat, with Renfeld still holding a knife to her throat, she was able to stick her hand into the water without slouching or bending. As Alex watched, the boat ever so slightly began to slide sideways. The man at the oars was doing his best to compensate for the turn, but he was soon unable to prevent the boat from slowly spinning.

From their viewpoint, both Alex and Ben could see the confusion in the boat, as it started to spin faster and faster. When Renfeld dropped the knife from Cassie's throat in an attempt to hold on or be tossed from the boat, Cassie leaped over the side. Diving deep under the water, she disappeared from view, leaving the three men alone in the boat. Alex could see Cassie's head pop up several feet from the spinning boat as she increased its speed.

"Now," Alex said to Ben, when he saw Cassie was safely enough away from their target.

If as one, two bolts of energy, one light blue and one as white as snow, burst forth through the open window, catching the spinning boat and igniting it into a huge ball of burning flame and smoke. When the smoke cleared, they could see Cassie as she made her way back to the wharf, where Leander and several of Ben's troop stood waiting for her. The little boat was nothing more than floating ash on the surface of the bay.

"Well boy, that settles that!" Ben said with a grin, slapping Alex on the back with the palm of his hand.

"The King is dead in the room across the hall," Alex informed Ben.

"Yes, I sensed it earlier. With Renfeld gone, his ashes in the bay, the royal line of Windfall is dead," Ben replied. They both stood quietly, watching the activities on the wharf below.

"Cassie said yes," Alex blurted out, not sure what else to say.

There was a moment's confusion on Ben's face before the recognition hit and he smiled broadly.

"A royal wedding, that's wonderful!" he replied. Then with a funny look on his face, he added, "Have you thought about where you want to live?"

Thinking the question odd, Alex replied, "Not at all, why?"

"How do you feel about the title, Lord Protector?" Ben asked.

"It seems I am now the monarch of two great cities. As I am already established in Great Vale, I am in need of someone to represent my interests here in Windfall. You would need to run the city and protect its people. Besides, the living accommodations aren't bad here by the sea."

He gestured at the castle around them with one hand.

Alex stood there in shock, overwhelmed by both the honor Ben was bestowing on him and because he realized he didn't have the slightest idea of how to run a city.

"Understand Alex, this is not over. Renfeld had allies, and I believe they will not consider his death the final say on who rules these lands. Add to that the influence of the Dark Elves and I suspect we are still in the thick of it. I need someone here I can trust."

Speechless, Alex searched for a reply, as Cassie burst into the room and rushed to him, still dripping wet from her swim in the bay. Ignoring her uncle, she kissed Alex passionately, before parting and acknowledging Ben without separating from Alex's embrace.

"Hello Uncle," she said with a smile, "we are getting married."

"So I hear," Ben replied with a laugh.

"We need to get your mother home. There will be no wedding without her!"

"It's funny we haven't heard from her," Cassie said absently.

"Yes, well think on it Alex and let me know," Ben stated, and then walked out with his men, leaving the two alone.

"Think on what?" Cassie asked, still clinging to Alex's arm.

"Our future, where we might live," Alex replied without explaining Ben's entire offer or the fear of continued fighting.

"Oh good!" Cassie replied, apparently delighted that plans were in motion for their life together.

Turning, the two started to leave the room when Cassie suddenly stopped and turned back to Alex.

"Do you think we could get a place near the water?"

Made in the USA
Monee, IL
04 October 2022